THE BUTTON MAKER

CONVENIENT WOMEN COLLECTION BOOK THREE

DELPHINE WOODS

PEPPER POT PUBLISHING

Copyright © 2019 by Delphine Woods

All rights reserved.

No part of this book may be reproduced in any form or by any electronic or mechanical means, including information storage and retrieval systems, without written permission from the author, except for the use of brief quotations in a book review.

❦ Created with Vellum

INSPIRED BY

Ding dong bell
Pussy's in the well
Who put her in?
Little Johnny Flynn
Who pulled her out?
Little Tommy Stout
What a naughty boy was that
Try to drown poor Pussycat,
Who ne'er did any harm
But killed all the mice
In the Farmer's barn!

PROLOGUE

*H*e rallied himself from the last blow. His pride had been stung. The poison was lacing through his veins. He balled his fists, curled back his lip in a snarl, and lunged.

Somewhere at the back of his mind, behind the blood flow and the rage, he heard something shatter. High pitched, sharp – glass. He recognised the sound too late – he was moving too fast. He slammed into the jagged bottle edge, unable to stop himself.

The glass thrust into his neck. He did not feel the pain, just the sense of an action cut short, his goal deprived. He lashed out, stumbled back. His throat was held tight by the bottle, gripping him like an enemy's hand.

Warmth spread slowly over his chest, uncontrollable, like the shameful sensation of pissing oneself. The ground met his backside as he slumped to the floor, the pain now penetrating his mind.

There was a commotion above him. He tried to look, but as he struggled to see, agony blinded him.

Then, the vice was gone, his neck was freed, and his chin

slammed into his chest. Blood gushed from his artery, hot and fierce, and drenched his abdomen. He gasped for air, and salty bubbles burst in his throat. His mouth filled. He spewed and dribbled as the world around him shrank, darkened, until there was nothing but black.

CHAPTER 1

October 1853. Wallingham Hall.

Osborne ducked under a low branch, squeezing his thighs tight around his stallion and digging in his heels. Dead leaves flicked up under the beast's hooves and tumbled over the sheer edge of the woodland. His hounds gained speed beside him, their tails pricked high, their teeth and tongues showing.

He would ride like this all day, with the sun streaking through the thinning canopy and stroking his back, trying to soothe him, trying to make him slow down. But he could not slow. He needed to feel the hardness of the ground stomping into his animal's legs, he needed the wind to slap and bite at his skin, he needed the cold sweat to run down his spine as sharp as nails; he needed the pain that would allow him to stop thinking. Only then would the image of his father, smiling and waving from his carriage, vanish. Only then would his guilt fade.

The dogs dived out of sight and into the undergrowth. Squirrels and pheasants shot from their hiding places as the hounds tormented them. The stallion swerved one low flying pheasant, losing its footing and sliding off the edge. Its rear hooves slipped on fallen leaves as it struggled for firm ground.

Osborne leaned forward, holding onto the horse's mane, urging it onwards. He kicked and thrust forward, and in a moment, the horse's rump was in line once more, and Osborne could sit back in the saddle. He did not let the horse slow – he smacked it on the backside so it would hasten.

The gallop made his flesh wobble and his eyesight blur. He blinked, and his father returned in the darkness … The tight smile, the carriage rolling away, the fog of Osborne's breath on the windowpane …

He opened his eyes, shook the sight out of his mind. He reached for his necktie and unfastened it, feeling the chill of the air waft over his wet skin, and heard his dogs barking.

It was an unusual sound; not one of exaltation from the chase. His dogs were alert, and growling fiercely. He followed the noise, gently tugging on the reins so his stallion slowed to a trot. His dogs met him halfway into a dip in the hillside, their hackles raised, and led him on.

He heard water splashing as he emerged near a natural pool. The sink of the land had only just started to fill in again after the hot summer, and the water was black and dank, with orange leaves and green spots lying on its surface. It took him some moments to see the two dark, moving figures at the other end of the lake, and to detect where the noise was coming from.

A woman was submerged under the water, and her arms were flailing wildly, like swan's wings when they try to take flight. A man crouched above her, his arms straight and powerful, his hands about the woman's neck, grimacing as he held her down.

Osborne was off his horse and sprinting towards them before he knew what he was doing. Like in dreams, it seemed to take too long for him to reach them. The woman's arms were slowing. Her legs, which had struck out at the man's groin, had gone limp.

She would die, and Osborne would not have saved her.

He pushed on harder, his muscles screaming at him, his leather soles sliding on the loose ground and tripping over tree roots.

The woman's arms were now still. He could make out the rise and fall of the man's chest, exhausted from his kill, but still, he held her head under.

Osborne sprinted harder, crying out in rage, and the man raised his head to meet Osborne's gaze just as Osborne crashed into him, bowling him several feet away from the woman and knocking the air from his lungs.

Osborne turned to the woman and dragged her out of the pool. Her skin was whiter than last night's full moon, and the red crescents around her eyes and the cut on her pale lips were striking. Her short, wet hair splayed across her cheeks. Her bodice had darkened where it had soaked up the stagnant water. She was not breathing.

Osborne wiped her hair out of her face and rolled her onto her side. Water spilled out of her mouth. He hit her on the back.

'Come on,' he whispered and hit her again between her shoulder blades. Still, she did not stir.

'Come on!' She would live. She had to live.

He rolled her onto her front and slammed his palm against her spine. Water trickled onto the fallen leaves, but she remained limp in his grip.

'Please,' he breathed to anyone who might be listening. He hoped God would hear him.

He shook her, then slapped her again, over and over, fear and rage making him feverish. She had to live! Today of all days, she had to live. Osborne could not let her die.

Suddenly, a torrent of brown water flooded out of her mouth. Her body convulsed against him, shuddering as the water continued to slide out of her, as she struggled for air.

He collapsed into the earth, weakened by relief, as she fell back onto her side. Her blue eyes found his as she clutched her throat and wheezed, and then they rose to look beyond him and widened in fear.

Just in time, he saw the woman's attacker stagger to his feet and attempt to run. Osborne pounced on him at once. He grabbed the man's greasy coat and spun him around, and landed a brutal blow on his face. The man fell backwards as blood seeped into his eye.

'Who are you?' Osborne said, his fists raised and ready to deliver another blow, his voice rough with exhaustion and adrenaline.

The man cradled his face, and his gaze dropped to the woman behind Osborne. She had pulled herself to the nearest tree and was resting against its trunk, one hand still clutching her scarlet throat, the other holding onto a small leather case. To Osborne, she mouthed two words:

'Help me.'

The man clattered to his feet and charged at the girl. Osborne heard her yelp and caught the man by the throat before he could reach her.

In Osborne's grip, the man seemed oddly small. A scattering of ginger whiskers shadowed his cheeks, and his eyes were a pale, mean blue. His cap had been knocked off in the scramble to reveal a closely cropped head of red hair. He was the type of man who would dissolve in a crowd.

'Your name,' Osborne hissed, and the man flinched.

'She was trying to kill me!'

Osborne would have laughed at such a ridiculous notion if he had not been chilled by the unmistakable lilt of the man's accent. Osborne cast him away and wiped his hand on his trouser leg. Filthy vermin – he shuddered at the thought of his skin against such a man.

The man crashed onto the ground but recovered quickly. 'She got my knife there.' He pointed to somewhere near the water, but Osborne did not bother to look. 'She got my knife, and she was going to kill me. I swear it.'

'What is your name?' Osborne said.

'Jim.'

'Jim what?'

The man licked his lips and searched the ground by his knees.

'Jim what?'

'Wilde. Jim Wilde.'

Osborne sniffed and wiped the wet tip of his nose on the back of his hand. His cheeks burned, and he knew they would be as pink as a whore's. He took a long, slow breath, and willed himself to stop shaking.

'You are on private property, Jim Wilde.'

'I was lost.'

'What were you doing here?'

'I was heading for Liverpool, for the docks. I got lost.'

'Were you poaching?'

'No!' The man struggled to his feet, and his head shook violently from side to side.

'I don't care for poachers.' Osborne had dealt with the likes of him before, the kind that lie as easy as breathing, the kind who shoot you when your back is turned.

'I was not poaching!'

'Who is this woman to you?'

'A stranger. I don't know. She ambushed me.'

Osborne glanced at the girl. She was weeping, her clothes quivering. She looked little more than a child.

'Please, let me go. I am innocent.'

'Innocent?' Osborne's laughter bubbled up his throat. He laughed harder when he saw the terror in the man's eyes. He dipped his hand inside his coat and felt the cool, wooden handle throbbing to be held. He had waited a long time for this moment.

He pulled the revolver out of its holder and pointed it at the man's chest.

The man balked, stumbled backwards. 'Please …'

He liked to see the fear. He wanted to hear the man beg for his life. He stepped closer, cocked the hammer. The man shook his head, his eyes flicked to the left as if searching for an escape.

'Oh no,' Osborne said, 'you are not going anywhere.'

He pulled the trigger before the man had time to flinch. Through the smoke, he saw the man drop.

The woman shrieked and, when he turned, he found she had fainted against the tree.

His breath shuddered out his lungs, and shivers washed over his body. He stepped towards the man – who had fallen onto his face – and kicked him onto his back. The life was slowly draining from him, the blood sliding down the slope towards the water's edge. His dead eyes gazed vacantly up at the sky.

Osborne cocked his gun once more and aimed it at the man's heart. The shot echoed through the woodland.

'Scum.'

CHAPTER 2

 ctober 1853. Wallingham Hall.

CAT FELT THE WARMTH FIRST. Heat spread from the tips of her toes all the way to her shoulders. A moment of lucidity; the unusual softness against her skin, the nearby sound of someone breathing deeply, the paleness against her closed eyelids. She rolled her head to one side, letting her warm cheek rest on crisp cotton and her dreams flash in her vision. She was being pulled into the darkness again when her empty stomach churned. She would have slept, but with each grumble in her gut, the more the light beckoned. She peeled her eyes open and squinted against the brightness.

She was alive.

She was reborn.

Above her, a canopy of dark, chiselled wood showed images of woodland creatures frolicking amongst themselves, and dense green curtains were pulled back and fastened to the thick bedposts. Opposite where she lay, a vast window let in the white light from a cloudy, autumnal day. She blinked the murkiness of sleep from her eyes and looked to her left to see the fire at the end of the room, the burning logs sizzling and cracking and spitting out shards of amber light. Sat beside it, with a guard to shield the flames from her skirt, was a girl, perhaps no more than sixteen years of age, darning old stockings.

Cat pushed herself up onto her elbows. She lay in the middle of a large bed with embroidered sheets, and she could make out the lump of a bedpan under the covers near her feet, which accounted for the warmth.

'You're awake.' The girl hopped up from her seat by the fire and went to Cat's side.

'Where am I?' It hurt to speak, and her voice came out as rough as gravel. The girl offered her a glass of water before she answered.

'Wallingham Hall.'

Cat sipped the water and felt it slide soothingly down her throat. 'I don't know it.'

The girl rested her backside on the foot of the bed. 'Do you know your name?' She spoke as if Cat was a child or an imbecile.

'Cat … Catherine.'

'Catherine,' the girl whispered as if trying to imprint the name onto her mind. 'Can you remember what happened to you?'

Cat looked to the window. There had been blue skies that day, a low sun which had made her eyes water, a pale moon still in the other half of the sky.

'Well, I suppose it'll come back to you soon enough.'

'How long have I been here?'

'Over a week.'

'I've been sleeping?'

'You had a fever. Didn't know whether you'd pull

through, tell the truth. But you woke up a couple of days ago, long enough for me to give you some broth. Seems you're a strong one.' It did not sound like a compliment.

Cat's stomach moaned again. She pushed her arms into it, hoping she would make it be quiet. The girl stood and clasped her hands onto her hips.

'I need to tell Master you're awake. I'll bring back some food.'

Cat tried to smile. She wanted the girl to warm to her – she needed to see a kind face right now – but she feared her smile came out more like a grimace. She was so tired! Her body had never felt so heavy. She rested her head against the pillow, her eyelids already wilting as the girl plodded towards the chamber door, when she realised she was wearing nothing but a nightgown. Fear made her sit up straight, and her head throbbed from the sudden motion.

'Who put me in this?'

The girl stopped. 'I did. I fixed you up under Master Tomkins's orders. He saw to it that you were well cared for.' Her lips twisted as she stared back at Cat, her gaze both blank and hostile at the same time.

'Who is Master Tomkins?'

'The man who saved your life.'

Cat swallowed and shied away from the girl's irritation. 'Where are my things?'

'Your clothes have been washed and are drying. You know, it was a very brave thing that Master Tomkins–'

'My case? I had a case with me.'

The girl pursed her lips, then said, begrudgingly, 'Under the bed.'

'Have you been in it?'

The girl held Cat's gaze, jutted her chin into the air. 'Master Tomkins would not allow it. Said we should treat you like a lady until we know who you really are.'

Cat shivered. *Who you really are …* She could not afford to make enemies here, so it seemed. Already, she had offended the maid. What was she thinking? She inhaled and forced the worry from her mind and a smile to her lips. 'Your master is a kind man.'

'He is. The kindest.'

'I am sorry.' She brushed her forehead with her fingertips. 'You have taken such good care of me. I have had a shock, as you said. Please forgive my rudeness.' Bracing herself, she looked up at the girl.

The maid dropped her chin, sniffed, fiddled with her apron. 'Yes, well. It's to be expected, I suppose.'

'Would you mind telling me your name?'

The girl hesitated. 'Nelly.'

'Thank you, Nelly.'

'Right.' Nelly cleared her throat, turned to the door, and after a moment's thought, left.

In an instant, Cat had thrown back the bed covers and had dived to the floor. Her case was where Nelly had said it would be, and Cat dragged it out, scraping it across the woollen rug. She unfastened the buckles and lifted the lid. The familiar smell of town – tobacco, coal, and foul oil – filtered into the air and made her insides swirl.

She grabbed the wig of dark hair and searched the room. She would have liked to have burned it, but the smell would be too suspicious. She considered throwing it out of the window, but of course, someone would find it – it wasn't like town here, where anything worth anything would be stolen in a second. She could do nothing but stuff it under her mattress and hope no one would find it before she had time to destroy it.

Next, she brought out the bottle of brown liquid. She held it close to her chest, unable to part with it. She should have tipped it out of the window, but the thought of losing it was too much. She shoved it between the mattress and the headboard, hoping the glass would not break.

From the bag's snagged lining, she retrieved a bent, gold ring. She pressed it to her lips, felt a momentary rush of comfort, then reluctantly placed it back beside some shillings. She closed the bag and slid it under the bed. Once back between the sheets, she smoothed down her hair and the covers, closed her eyes, and waited for Nelly's return.

SHE DID NOT OPEN her eyes when she heard the door click, but when the silence continued, she stopped pretending to be asleep. At the doorway, a man loomed. His thick chestnut hair was parted on one side, and coarse sideburns stretched from his ears to his mouth. He glared at her as he wrung his hands.

'Catherine. Catherine what?'

Cat pulled the cover up to her chin, and the man lowered his gaze for a second. 'Davies, sir.'

'Catherine Davies from where?'

'Birmingham. Master Tomkins, is it?' She sat up a little higher in the bed, and he had to crane his neck so he could maintain eye contact. 'I must thank you for saving my life. You are a brave man, sir.'

'Nelly said you could not remember anything.'

She felt herself flush. The bed-pan by her feet was making her sweat. 'Not all of it yet, but I remember you.'

His lips twitched upwards, then he shrugged. 'It is what anyone would have done.'

'No. Not anyone.' In town, no one even saved a baby from the rubbish piles. Honestly, she was grateful. She would be with Mother now if it hadn't been for him.

'You are not ... Irish?'

She frowned at the odd question, and he watched his toes twisting into the rug under his feet.

'No, sir.'

His feet stilled. When his eyes returned to hers, they were less guarded – handsome eyes, she could not help but think.

'I would prefer it if you called me Osborne.'

'Osborne.' She tested the sound of it – it came out between her lips like a long sigh.

'Did you know the man who … hurt you? He said you were attacking him.'

A flash of steel, the taste of the water, a pale face rippling before her … she shook her head. 'I can't say if I was or wasn't, sir. I can't remember, but I don't think myself capable of such a thing.'

'Neither do I.' He laughed suddenly, and it was so loud that it startled Cat. He did not seem to notice her nervousness. 'People like him will say anything.'

'Would you like to come in?' She did not want to talk about the man who had tried to drown her – her chest was still too sore from the pain of it all. And really, it was silly for Osborne to stand there, half in and half out, allowing neither of them to get a good look at the other.

'Are you …' Osborne scratched his temple. 'Are you well now? I believe you were very sick.'

'I am well, thanks to your generous care.' She nodded towards the chair, and for a moment it appeared that Osborne was considering it, but then he straightened up and rolled his shoulders back.

'Birmingham, you said? It is a fair way from here. What were you doing at Wallingham?'

She opened her mouth, but she had not yet thought of the excuse she would give.

'Forgive me,' Osborne said, 'you cannot remember. Do

you know if you have family in town, someone I should inform as to your whereabouts?'

'No, sir.'

'You have no family, or you cannot remember?'

'I have no family in town, sir.'

'Right.' He considered this, his thumb picking at the latch on the doorframe. 'Then I should like you to stay here until you are fully recovered.' He cleared his throat. 'It would be my pleasure to have you as my guest.'

'You're very kind, sir.'

He nodded and pulled his gaze off her and towards the flames as Nelly returned carrying a tray. Osborne stepped aside to let her through, and she curtseyed as she passed her Master, then smirked once her back was turned to him and her eyes were trained on Cat. She set a tray containing a shallow bowl of steaming beef broth and a slice of white bread on Cat's lap. The saliva in Cat's mouth ran thin as the scent of meat wafted up to her in sheaths of steam.

'Anything else you'd like?' Nelly said.

The girl bit her lips to hide her grin before she walked back towards Osborne. Cat picked up her spoon and hoped Osborne had not noticed.

'Nelly and I shall leave you to your lunch, Miss Davies.' His formality had returned. He gestured for Nelly to exit and was about to close the door when Cat stopped him.

'Master Tomkins, would you tell me what happened to the man?'

'You have nothing to worry about.' He smiled softly, and his brown eyes met hers earnestly. 'He cannot hurt you now. He is dead.'

Numbly, she nodded, and Osborne shut the door behind him. Then, the spoon fell from her hand and crashed into the broth. She pushed the tray away from her as a tear fell onto her cheek.

CHAPTER 3

November 1846. Birmingham.

THE NOISE of the cutting machines jabbed into her skull. Relentless. An ocean of sound, of banging and clattering, of metal stomping into metal, of jaws gnashing, of small feet scurrying along the dusty floor. A pair of those little feet belonged to her. Hour after hour, she ran around scooping up linen circles and taking them to the table to be sorted. Her feet had long grown hard and calloused on the soles so that they didn't feel the odd bits of stray metal clippings that pointed skywards, ready to impale.

By this time in the day, her eyes were sore and prickling, filled with strands of linen that floated in the air. Below her hips, the feeling had gone, and she scampered along without realising her legs were moving at all. There was an ache in her lower back that never left her, even in sleep, and her stomach had long stopped its moaning for food, knowing it would get none for a good while.

She rested her eyes on the blackness through the windowpanes. A yawn escaped her small mouth, and she wiped the itch from her eyelids.

As she stared, she felt something pressing on her ... Mother's gaze pierced through Cat's semi-conscious state, and Cat jumped back to work, the fatigue pushed to the furthest corner of her mind. There was no time for resting. When she looked at her mother again, she received a smile.

After time was called for the day, and the machines were put to sleep, there came a rush of feet – a stampede of women and children jostling through the narrow alleyways of tables, eager to breathe in the night air. Her mother grabbed her by her sleeve and dragged her along, for it was the only way she would keep up and not get crushed in the waves of working women who needed to get home and get the tea on. They tumbled out of the factory, squashed together like the circles of metal and linen and pasteboard they had been cutting. Hemmed in either side by the brick walls of the factory, there was no time to slow, no time to stop to catch a breath, no time to slip on the slick cobblestones.

And then the crowd spilled into the streets. Cat no longer felt strange arms digging into her sides, no longer saw the dark wiggle of someone's skirt an inch from her face. She was out in the open, and she was safe.

Her mother pulled her under a streetlamp, lowered her cap, and tightened her shawl. Mother did this every night, making sure Cat's pale and pretty face was hidden, her slender body, which was shifting from a child's towards a woman's by the minute, was covered from prying, unwanted eyes. Then she took Cat's hand and led her homewards.

Sometimes, Cat wondered what she would do if she didn't have her mother to guide her. She still had not learnt the pattern of the back streets in the gloom, when nothing looked the same, when buildings all blended into one, when people were nothing more than shadows. She imagined roaming in the darkness for all eternity, shrinking from rats that ran out from the gutters, sliding on indistinguishable waste, avoiding clusters of dark clothes that lingered on street corners.

It always took longer to get home than she thought it would, but when they crashed through the door to find the familiar sight of the fire burning in the kitchen, her little sisters happily mending clothes, her brother watching over them with umbrage, she couldn't help but smile. Lottie and Helen ran to her for an embrace, twisting their skinny arms around her legs in a fierce grip for such small children.

Mother set about fixing the tea. She cut seven slices of hard bread while Helen got the dripping from the cupboard and Cat poured each of them a cup of small beer.

That night there was one slice of bacon left, and Mother carefully laid it in a pan over the fire to cook in time for Father's return home. Each of them took their place around the table and stared at their slice of bread, mouths watering, and waited.

Time passed slowly, but without a clock, the wait could have been anywhere from seconds to hours. They cradled their cups of beer, holding it to their lips and sipping so that it would last longer. Mother rested her elbows on the table and put her chin on her steepled fingers, fixing her gaze on the far wall. Lottie laid her cheek on the table and closed her eyes and was asleep before Mother could tell her to sit up straight. Michael scowled at Mother and his meal, kicking his feet into the floor until Mother finally allowed them to eat.

The meal was over in a few seconds. Cat's beer washed down the lump of stale bread that had stuck in her throat, and as she ran her tongue over the roof of her mouth, she felt the gritty greasiness of beef dripping and longed, in vain, for more. Their next meal would not be until the sun was just about to rise.

Their eyelids drooped. Mother's chin fell onto her chest, startling her awake until she did it again. The muffled noises from the houses all around them acted as lullabies until Michael started sniffing.

'What's wrong?' Cat said, her voice thick with sleep.

'I can smell burning.'

There was a moment of stillness as everyone breathed in, then panic.

Mother's chair screeched along the floor as she flung herself towards the fire and gripped the panhandle. She screamed as the metal burnt her skin, then chucked the pan onto the table. It skidded across the surface. Michael lifted his arms just in time and jumped out of his seat. The pan came to a halt at the edge of the table, and all of them stared at the black, shrivelled thing that sizzled inside it.

Mother's face was white. Lottie began to cry. Michael scowled again. Helen ran to Cat and buried her face in her skirt.

Then the door opened.

None of them moved as their drunken father clattered into the house. He was a big man. Too big. He had to bend his neck to avoid hitting his head on the ceiling. He clattered into the furniture, ruining the place which Michael and the girls had tidied earlier.

His eyes were half-closed as he made his way towards them and sank into his seat at the head of the table. Cat handed him a cup of beer before he could shout for it, and Mother scraped the last of the dripping onto his two slices of bread and placed it in front of him.

'What's that?' Father pointed at the pan, frowning.

Mother picked it up by the handle as if she was going to

do something with it, but stopped. Would she tell him the truth? The silence stretched as Father tried to identify the sight in his blurred mind.

'Ma burnt your bacon,' Michael said.

Cat glared at him, but he didn't blush. He stepped behind Father, so he would avoid any blows that might now occur.

'Sorry,' Mother whispered, her lower lip trembling. She turned to hide her face, and the sound of her snivelling filled the silence.

Father stood up, pressing his fists into the table to steady himself. 'Christ, woman!' He wiped his wet mouth on his sleeve, then stumbled towards her.

The children scuttled away from him. Cat grabbed Helen and Lottie's hands and dragged them towards the stairs, telling them to be quiet and to cover their ears and to get into bed quickly. Michael lingered on the stairs listening.

'Michael! Come on.'

Michael stayed where he was, his face blank as Father erupted.

Cat was grateful that she could not see. Her father spat a barrage of abuse at her mother, the words just as painful as the final blow that landed on Mother's cheek. The sound of the crack echoed through the house.

Silence.

A moment later, Father was stumbling towards the door. He didn't see Cat and Michael on the stairs, their faces pressed through the gaps of the banister, or at least, he didn't acknowledge them. He tugged the door open and disappeared into the darkness, retreating to his favourite beer house.

Cat tiptoed down the stairs to shut the door and shut the cold outside. She wished she could have locked it so that he would not be able to return later, but that was a silly and unchristian desire.

She lingered, wondering if she should go to her mother who she could hear sobbing in the kitchen, but decided against it. Mother was too proud to take sympathy from her daughter.

'Bed,' she said to Michael and shoved him when he refused to move.

'Don't touch me.'

She leaned into his face, an exact replica of their father's. 'You want Pa to find you here when he comes back?'

A flinch in the muscles around Michael's eye told her she had won. He turned away from her and stomped up the last few steps. She followed behind him and slid into the bed beside Lottie who was crying. Cat stroked her sister's blonde hair, the same shade and softness as her own, until they both fell asleep.

THE FACTORY FLOOR was pounding as usual, though the thought of Sunday tomorrow made the workers lazier, dreaming of a day of rest and a roasted dinner if they were lucky enough. Cat did not run to collect the linen circles, but walked with haste, all the while flicking her eyes between the dark windows and the dark mark on her mother's face. As she scooped up the circles, she felt the penetrative stares of the women as they cut their metal, their prying eyes searching for a clue as to why her mother had yet another bruise on her face, and if there was any sign of harm on Cat. It would be another topic to gossip about; now the husband's started on the children and all.

Cat did not meet their gaze. She set her mouth straight and tight and kept her cheek turned on them until the day was over.

Outside, a thin mist of rain clung to the air. Mother fixed Cat's cap and shawl, took her hand, and guided her home.

They were soaked through by the time they got inside. Cat hung their cloaks before the fire and watched as the steam began to rise and swirl in the room.

There was no bacon tonight. The bread was cut as thin as possible. Again, they waited. Helen's stomach growled. Lottie sighed. Michael picked his fingernails.

'Eat,' Mother said, picking up her bread reluctantly.

'We should wait for Father,' Michael said.

The bread hovered before Mother's mouth.

'You can if you want.' Cat bit into her food.

Lottie and Helen copied her with a grin. Mother nibbled on the hard crust. Michael folded his arms and watched them from under his stitched eyebrows until hunger got the better of him. He snatched up his bread and bit into it as if he was biting into Cat herself.

It was over sooner than everybody would have liked, and still, Father had not returned.

'Go to bed.' Mother heaved herself onto her feet and gathered the plates to wash.

Cat herded Helen and Lottie upstairs and into their nightclothes, rolling old stockings over their feet as the girls giggled from her cold hands. She tucked them into bed and kissed their foreheads as they yawned. Michael dived under the covers and rolled away from them.

'Aren't you coming in?' Helen said to Cat, rubbing her chubby fist into her eye socket.

'Soon.' Cat took the bible from the bed stand and crept downstairs.

Mother sat at the table, staring at Father's plate and the two slices of bread upon it. She didn't notice Cat, and Cat thought she might have been sleeping with her eyes open.

'Ma?'

Mother inhaled and smiled. It seemed to take all her energy. 'You should get to sleep, Cat.'

'I wanted to keep you company.'

Cat sat next to her mother. They listened to the noises around them: the family in the house behind them, lively with chatter and laughter; Mrs Smith next door with her son and his family, banging about, all bundled in there unhappily; the patter of feet outside and the whispers of fleeting conversations.

'He's late tonight,' Mother said.

'He's forgotten the time.'

A ghost of a smile lifted her mother's lips. She rested her chin on her hands.

'I thought time might pass quicker if we read.' Cat put the bible on the table.

'You know I can't.'

'I could teach you. I could teach you the way they do at Sunday school.'

Mother reached for Cat's chin and stroked it. 'My clever little girl.'

Cat opened the bible to Genesis. She cleared her throat. '"In the beginning God created the heaven and the earth."' She pushed the book towards her mother. 'Now you try.'

Mother laughed and looked at the page below her, biting her lip. 'I like it when you read to me.'

'"And the earth was without form, and void, and darkness was upon the face of the deep–'

'Smart girl, you are, Cat.' Mother reached for her hand and held it tight. The bible lay discarded. 'Too smart for your own good.'

'What do you mean?'

Her mother's eyes glistened in the firelight. 'This is all there is for us, Cat. This is our lot.' She gestured to the cramped kitchen around them, and her chin wobbled.

Cat wrapped her arms around her mother's neck. Ma smelt of the factory, and of grime and grease and copper and soot. Her hair was coarse against Cat's cheek as her forehead rested heavily on Cat's shoulder. They did not move for minutes.

'I wish there was something better for you out there,' Mother whispered, and her hot breath tickled Cat's collarbone before she pulled herself upright and wiped the tears off her face.

'I'm happy here, Ma, with you.'

Mother kissed Cat's cheek. 'I won't be here forever.'

It was an absurd notion. Always, Mother had been with Cat. Why would she leave? The thought was both ridiculous and terrifying, and when Mother rose to pour water into the kettle, Cat almost lunged after her and grabbed her hand.

'Let's have us some tea.'

Cat watched Mother set the kettle over the heat. The skin on Mother's hands was cracked, the knuckles were bulbous and swollen, her back was too hunched, and her feet shuffled as if she was half-sleeping. The firelight made the bruise around her eye darker, like a sooty footprint on her face, marking her as something that Cat didn't recognise.

Suddenly, Mother seemed very old.

'You won't leave us, will you?' Cat said, her voice thin as she plucked at the splintered edge of the table.

Before Mother could reply, fists beat against the door, startling them both. The kettle almost dropped out of Mother's hands.

'What on earth …' Mother hobbled to the door, and two men fell through it as she opened it.

Cat hid behind her mother's skirts and studied the men's faces. She didn't recognise them. Both had skin pinked with the warmth of too much beer, and cheeks that had not been washed clean after a day's work. Their beards were matted with clay, and their clothes were dishevelled, their shirts hanging out of their breeches, their jackets half falling off their shoulders. They gasped for breath as they stood in front of Mother, rocking back and forth on the balls of their feet.

'What is it?' Mother said.

'It's Jack,' one of the men said, running his tongue over his lower lip.

With her eyes more adjusted, Cat could see dark red smears on their necks and hands.

'What's he done?'

'A fight. Some Dudley lot.'

Mother squeezed her arms about herself, straightened her spine. 'What's happened?'

'Jack was only having a laugh, but them … they're vicious as cats those lot.'

'What's happened?'

The younger man sniffed and looked at his feet. 'They had knives. They cut him.'

Mother stilled. 'Where is he?'

'The lads'll bring him around.'

Mother nodded. 'We need water. And clean clothes. Cat, fetch Mrs Smith, she'll know of something to heal the wounds.'

'Mrs Davies,' the older man said, 'there's no point in that. He's gone.'

Silence rippled through the house. Cat didn't understand. Neither did Mother, so it seemed.

'What?'

'He's dead.'

Time stretched, then Mother's legs buckled. She crashed to the floor. The men flinched away from her, eager to get away.

'We'll bring him round,' the young one said, and then they scampered into the darkness.

Cat closed the door and stared down at her sobbing mother crumpled by her feet.

Movement caught the corner of her eye. At the top of the stairs, Helen and Lottie hugged each other as they pulled on their lips, both of them starting to cry. Michael glowered down at Cat, his eyes black and dry until he turned and retreated into the bedroom.

'It's all right,' Cat said to her sisters, to her mother, to herself, to anyone who would listen. If she said it enough times, maybe it would be true. 'It's all right.'

Mother clutched Cat's skirts, reeling Cat closer, grappling for an embrace as she wept. 'What will we do now, Cat? What will we do?'

CHAPTER 4

October 1853. Wallingham Hall.

SHE STARED at the wooden doe in the scene above her head. A crude engraving. How long until that doe was shot? Her body butchered and dismembered, her flesh stacked into roasting dishes, her head hung on a wall?

Cat closed her eyes.

There was a dull ache over her body from too long in bed. She had never lay down for so many days before, with nothing to do but stare at the flames or out of the window. She threw back the covers, swung her legs over the bed, and went to look outside.

Fields littered with towering trees and dotted with sheep stretched before her. Forests grew either side of the house, their leaves glowing red and amber and falling to carpet the ground. Sometimes, when she had rested her elbows on the windowpane before, she had seen Osborne go galloping across his land, his man close behind him, the sun making their horses' coats shimmer like spun gold. Perhaps they went hunting, for pheasants or deer; that was what his sort did for pleasure, wasn't it?

Her door opened. The housekeeper, Mrs Lewis, came in without knocking, her arms filled with clothes.

'Here you are.' She plonked the dress and petticoats on the chair by the fire. 'Washed and ironed for you.'

Whoever had taken the time and trouble to iron them would not be pleased with how Mrs Lewis had left them in such a rough pile, Cat thought. She nodded her thanks, feeling exposed in nothing but her nightgown, and waited for the woman to leave. She did not.

'Shall I send for Nelly to help get you into them?'

'No, thank you, I'll be fine.'

Mrs Lewis, an old woman, perhaps in her fifties, smirked. 'You can go back to where you came from now.'

Cat met her hard gaze. 'Is that what Mr Tomkins wants?'

'It will be.' Mrs Lewis put her hands on her hips. 'Don't get comfortable here, Miss Davies. You'll be out soon enough. He likes to do a good deed, makes him feel nice, but if you have any other ideas going on in that brain of yours, shake them out.'

'I don't have any ideas.'

Mrs Lewis took a long time to look Cat up and down. Cat held still, determined to be strong.

'I don't trust you one bit.'

Cat swallowed. 'Thank you for my clothes, Mrs Lewis. I'll tell Mr Tomkins what good care you've been taking of me.'

Mrs Lewis raised one thin, grey eyebrow, then slammed the door behind her.

A SMALL FIST pattered against her door.

'Come in.'

Nelly poked her head into the room. Her lips smeared across her face as she tried to contain her excitement. 'I've got something for you.'

She bustled into the room, her arms full of peach-coloured material. She stood before the fire, and with a flourish like any good showman, revealed the dress. The silk shimmered, and the sash around the waist glistened like a pink stream in the sunshine. Sheaves of golden corn were stitched around the circle of the skirt at calf-height. The short sleeves were puffed and pleated.

'It's one of Master's mother's gowns.' She shook her head in disbelief as she looked between the dress and Cat. 'No one's been allowed in her room for years. And then you come along, and suddenly he's making me go snooping for a dress for dinner for you!'

'He wants me to wear that?'

Nelly rounded on her. 'And what's wrong with it?'

'Nothing's wrong with it. It's too grand for me.'

Nelly dipped her head to the side and studied the dress. 'Mmh. But it's what Master wants. I'm to take your measurements and fit it for you, ready for dinner tomorrow.'

'I'm to dine with Osborne?'

'You're to dine with the master, yes.' Nelly stressed the title, and laid the dress over the armchair and found her measuring tape from her apron pocket. 'Stand in the middle. Arms up.'

Cat did as she was told, and the tape was cold through the cotton nightgown as Nelly pulled it tight around her waist.

Cat took this time to observe the maid – the girl's clear but dull skin, the wisps of mud-brown hair that escaped from under her cap and tickled her forehead, the scent of overcooked vegetables and carbolic soap that clung to her body. Nelly was still suspicious of Cat, but she was warming to her. If she could become a friend, Nelly might prove a vital ally.

'I won't know what to do,' Cat said. 'I've never eaten in a place like this before, with someone like Osborne before.'

'No, don't suppose you have.'

Cat let the insult pass. 'Would you help me?'

The girl sighed as if it was such a hassle for her, but her voice was breathy and excited when she next spoke. 'Cutlery, just start from the outside and work in. There's usually so much food you can't eat it all, so make sure you have little bits.'

Cat nodded and hoped she would remember everything as Nelly lifted the tape around Cat's breasts.

'Drink whatever is poured at any given time, you've no need to worry about what goes with what – Mr Dixon does all that.'

Nelly measured Cat's neck and her arms, then bent to do her legs.

'It'll only be you and him, and Master knows you; he won't be expecting much.'

She wound the tape up and tipped it into her pocket, then slapped her hands together.

'Think you'll cope?'

'Thank you, you've been most helpful.'

Nelly did not notice the sarcasm hidden in Cat's words. She nodded proudly.

'Good. Then I'll go and fix that dress for you.'

CAT GASPED AT HER REFLECTION. Nelly had powdered her skin clear and had curled her hair into a work of art, despite its shortness. The dress fitted beautifully, and she stroked the fine material as it cascaded over her hips.

'And these.' Nelly held out a pair of elbow-length silk gloves.

Nelly stood back to assess her work, frowning. 'That'll do, I suppose.' She lifted her eyes to Cat and cackled mischievously.

'You think he will like it?'

'I think he will like it very much.' The girl tutted – was there a hint of jealousy somewhere? 'Go on. Don't leave him waiting for you.' She shooed Cat out of the room.

'Would you show me the way?' Cat said over her shoulder before Nelly could disappear through a door which looked like part of the wall.

Nelly gestured for Cat to descend the staircase. Even the bannister was beautiful, with vines and dogs and hunting frescoes carved into the dark mahogany. Everything at Wallingham was so extravagant – she had never seen the likes of it before. At the bottom of the stairs, a cavernous room greeted her. The ceiling was thrice Cat's height and plastered in yet more ornate patterns. The walls were clad in chestnut-coloured wood, and animal's heads hung parallel to the chandeliers, their dark, soulless eyes staring across the space towards their similarly stuffed companions. A great fire burned in the left wall, the opening as wide as Cat was tall, and black ash streaked the stone neck of the chimney.

'This is the great hall,' Nelly whispered, looking around her as if she should not be here. 'This is where the big entertainments are held. Through there,' she jerked her head at the door at the far end of the hall, 'is where Master Tomkins dines. He'll be in there.' She stopped and would not take another step. 'I should be getting downstairs now.'

Cat twisted her hands together, feeling the clamminess of them inside her gloves. 'Right …' She glanced at the door, wondering if her legs would carry her that far. 'Right, thank you, Nelly.' This time, she said it without sarcasm. She really was grateful for the girl's company and did not want Nelly to leave, but to show such feelings would only be a weakness. She could not afford to be weak.

She rolled her shoulders back and inhaled. Brushing a loose strand of hair out of her eyes, she marched across the vast space.

Her hand hovered above the doorknob. Should she knock, or enter as if this was all normal to her? She glanced over her shoulder and found herself utterly alone without Nelly to ask for help. She raised her hand, knuckles ready to rap on the door, when it opened before her.

'Miss Davies.' A man with salted hair bowed to her. She vaguely recalled him as Osborne's man, Mr Dixon, a butler or a valet perhaps; Cat didn't know the correct titles. The man lifted his head, smiled warmly, and ushered her inside.

The room was a miniature version of the great hall, except for the table, which heaved with candelabras and cut glasses and crockery and polished silver. At the head of it, Osborne rose from his seat, dressed in his finest suit, his thick hair slicked to one side, his sideburns glistening with scented oil. He did not smile immediately; his eyes roamed over her figure before they came to rest on her face. Then, he beamed.

'Miss Davies, you are looking well.'

Cat bobbed into what she hoped passed for a demure curtsey. 'I am well, sir, and it is because of your kindness.'

'Come.' He gestured to the chair to his left. 'Sit. I thought you might like it here, close to the fire, so you might keep warm.'

'Thank you, Mr Tomkins.'

Dixon pushed in her chair as she sat down.

'Call me Osborne, please. I do not wish us to be so formal with each other.'

'Wine, Miss Davies?' Dixon held a decanter before her. She nodded and hoped it was the right decision. She waited until Osborne drank before she sipped from her glass.

The alcohol trickled down her throat, warming her. She rested against the back of the chair, willing herself to relax; she looked prettiest when she was relaxed, and Osborne was obviously a man who admired beautiful things.

Osborne downed his drink in one and pushed his napkin to his lips. His cheeks were a little flushed, his gaze a bit too unsteady.

'You have a beautiful house–'

'I am afraid I have–'

They talked over one another, each of them stopping abruptly to let the other one continue. They laughed awkwardly.

'After you, Miss Davies.'

'I just wanted to say what a beautiful home you have.'

'Thank you. It is over two hundred years old, you know.' He gazed at the room around him. 'Nothing but a stone hut, more or less, when my great, great–' he shook his head, 'I forget how many greats – grandfather bought it and the land. He was a merchant, a good one at that. And here it is now.'

Cat smiled, unsure of how to respond. She sipped her wine.

'I was going to say,' Osborne frowned at his empty plate, 'that I have some news. About the man who attacked you.'

The glass tingled on her lip.

Dixon and Mrs Lewis entered the room carrying silver trays of food and placed them around the table. She did not miss the stare of contempt that Mrs Lewis shot her as the housekeeper ladled out a small bowlful of soup, nor how she banged it on the table so that the liquid came perilously close to spilling on Cat's dress. Osborne did not seem to notice.

She copied how he used his spoon, waiting for him to resume his speech. 'You were saying?' she prompted when she could not bear the silence.

'Yes … Yes, the man who attacked you. Obviously, I had to get the police involved. I told them everything that happened that day, how I found him trying to kill you and that I shot him in your defence.'

Cat nodded as his gaze bore into her.

'So,' he sucked his soup off the spoon and swallowed. 'They took his body, and I thought that would be the end of it. I have since been informed that the man was wanted for murder. They've recognised his face from a description some poor fellow gave after finding a body in a house in town.'

The soup sloshed coldly in her mouth. She forced it down. 'What happened?'

'Some brawl – a robbery, they think. That swine had stabbed the fellow in the neck with a shattered bottle of whisky. I should suspect he was on the run to Liverpool when he found you and did not want to leave a witness as to his whereabouts.'

Cat nodded. The soup bowl swirled in her vision.

'Miss Davies, are you well?'

His touch roused her. She stared at his naked flesh on her gloved hand, and sickness gripped her gut.

'How foolish of me, to mention murder in front of you, bringing the whole ghastly experience up again.'

His hand disappeared. She could breathe again.

Regaining herself, she heard him dab his napkin to his lips then throw it on the table. He crouched beside her and took her hand once more, though this time the sickness stayed away.

'Miss Davies, forgive me. Would you like to rest?'

'Sorry,' she whispered, trying to focus on the darkness of his eyes. She must not be weak, she said to herself again. 'Talking about that man …'

'Forgive me, I should not have said anything.' He lowered his head and hissed some indistinguishable word.

'Dixon,' Osborne called for his man, 'I think Miss Davies needs to return to her room.'

'It is fine–'

But he insisted, and in the end, she was grateful she did not have to sit through the whole dinner, pretending – her strength had not recovered enough for that ordeal just yet.

Together, Osborne and Dixon helped Cat from her seat and led her through the hall, up the stairs, and to her room. 'Fetch Nelly, would you?' Osborne said.

Dixon vanished through the wall.

'Sorry. We were having such a nice night.'

'The fault is all mine, Miss Davies. It is me who begs your forgiveness.'

His face had grown clearer. He stood just a few inches away from her, his hand cradling her bare elbow. She felt the touch of his hot skin keenly.

'You have my forgiveness, Mr Tomkins. I am in your debt for saving my life, after all.'

She edged a little closer to him. She would not have the night – nor the dress – be a complete waste. She could not afford for him to lose interest in her, as Mrs Lewis had warned he would.

'Please, I would like it if you would call me Catherine.'

'Catherine,' he said, swilling the word around his mouth.

His face inched closer until she could feel the heat of it vibrating against hers. With each exhale, she could smell the wine on his breath, and taste it on her tongue. His grip on her elbow tightened.

'Sir. Miss.'

They broke their stare to find Nelly beside them, her chin touching her chest, her hands clutched before her waist. Osborne released Cat and stepped back.

'Miss Davies is feeling a little unwell, Nelly. See her to bed and bring her a small plate of hot supper.' He turned to Cat, a smile in his eyes. 'Goodnight, Catherine.'

CHAPTER 5

December 1850. Birmingham.

CAT BENT OVER HER TABLE, pushing the thin strip of metal along, clamping the jaws of the machine together, sliding out the circle of copper. Over and over again. All day. She didn't need to watch what she was doing anymore. She could have done the job in her sleep, and often felt like she did.

Sometimes she saw the ghosts of her sisters gliding around the shop floor, their little fingers picking up the linen. She prodded them with her stare like her mother had done to her when she saw them stop to take a breath. There was no time for air for any of them.

Outside, she squeezed their sticky hands and dragged them along on the wave of the crowd, and under the blur of the streetlight, she made sure they were all covered from the cold and the eyes of strangers. She led them through the town, through the sludge of muck and snow, cringing as the icy wetness seeped up her stockings. She had learnt the way home now, though there were still times when she thought she had got them all lost, like tonight.

She hesitated, her eyes wide as she searched for a familiar sight or smell that would tell her she was on the right path. Her sisters fidgeted, sensing her panic – she could not linger. She strode on, faking her confidence, biting a thin strip of her tongue and tasting metal once again, until she recognised the way a particular pane of glass reflected a shard of gaslight, then the familiar house with its half-rotten door hanging crookedly in the frame.

Inside their house, Helen and Lottie fixed their wet clothes close before the fire and rushed upstairs. Cat set a pot of water over the flames and dropped in the bones she had bought from the butcher yesterday. She cut the bread as she waited for the water to come to a boil, and poured small beer into their cups.

Michael flung the door open, making it bang on the wall. She glared at him as her knife sawed through the bread, but he didn't take any notice. He threw off his cap and shook his head. Dried clay and red brick dust fluttered to the ground, and more came when he drew off his coat. When he washed his hands and face it looked as if the bowl was filled with blood.

He slumped in his chair. Since Father's death, he'd lost the chubbiness of childhood. He was taller than Cat now, and thinner. His skin was more translucent than white, the blue veins on his temples as clear as if worms meandered across his skull. He had not taken to work as much as he had said he would, and now that he had no choice but to go, he resented the kindness of Father's boss, who'd offered him a job in the brickyard after Father's murder.

Cat placed his two slices of bread and dripping before him and handed him a cup of beer. He took it without thanks and chewed it in silence.

'Girls,' Cat called to her sisters, who came trotting down the stairs to eat their tea.

The water was now on a rolling boil, the white bones bobbing in the liquid. She stirred it around, breathing in the scent of beef and letting the steam thaw her face.

'I'll have some of that,' Michael said.

'It's for Mother.'

'She won't eat it all.'

'She needs it.'

'Fill me a cup.'

She faced Michael. His lips were a black line in his face. He watched her without flinching, testing her.

She clenched her jaw, marched towards him and snatched his cup from him. She filled it only to halfway and slammed it on the table before him. He raised it to his lips and slurped it slowly.

She could not stand to look at his face. She sloshed the broth into a bowl, found a spoon, lit a candle, and went upstairs.

If she had not known her mother was in bed, she would not have been able to see her. Mother had grown so thin that she barely made an impression under the blankets. The only clue that something was living in the room was the rattle of breath in clogged lungs; the sound of someone drowning.

'Ma?'

Cat set the candle on the bedside table, then eased herself onto the mattress and searched for her mother's body. The flame picked out her mother's eyes as they struggled to open.

'Eat this.'

Cat sat Mother a little more upright and began to feed her. After only a couple of mouthfuls, her mother started to cough, and the whole bed frame shook as her body convulsed. A great lump of some vile poison belched from her mother's lungs, and her mother spat it into her soiled handkerchief. As it caught the light, Cat saw the red tinge of it.

When Mother had recovered, Cat dipped the spoon into the broth again.

'Shouldn't waste your money on this for me.'

'It's to make you better.' Cat lifted the spoon to Mother's lips, and Mother winced as the hot liquid hit the rawness of her throat.

'Better to let me go.'

The spoon clinked against the bowl. 'Don't talk daft.'

Cat fed her until half of the broth was gone, until Mother closed her lips and could take no more. She placed the bowl on the bed stand then felt the heat of her mother's forehead.

'Shan't be here for long.'

'None of that. You'll be better by the new year.'

Mother's hand crawled out from under the covers to grasp Cat's. With her touch, Cat's anger and bitterness and exhaustion suddenly overwhelmed her. Her spine crumbled, and she sobbed as she held her mother's skeletal fingers.

'Eh,' Mother whispered and stroked her thumb over Cat's knuckles. 'Don't cry, love.'

'Don't leave us, Ma.'

Water glistened in her mother's eyes. 'My clever little girl. The prettiest in town.' Mother's grip tightened, and her breath groaned in her chest as she leaned forward. 'Find yourself a good husband, one who'll take care of you. Promise me?'

Cat's tears dripped onto the blankets. It seemed an impossible task, but she would not argue. She nodded, and Mother fell back into her pillows, panting for air.

'I'll take care of the girls, I swear.'

Her mother's lips quivered into a smile. 'I know.' Her eyelids fluttered like birds' wings, trying to stay open but failing.

Cat sniffed, straightened. Her mother did not need to see her like this.

'Rest now, Ma.' Cat got to her feet, pressed her lips to her mother's wet forehead, and dropped her cheek onto the familiar, crinkled hair. 'I'll bring you more broth in the morning.'

A BRIEF REST in the snowy weather, the ground crisp and hard underfoot, made the walk home not quite so intolerable. Footsteps raced along the cobbles, for it was the end of the working week, and men were rushing for public houses and women for home to get the clothes ready for service tomorrow.

Cat ushered Helen and Lottie along – they were blowing their breath in front of their faces and running through the clouds.

'Come on,' Cat said, tugging on their hands and feeling a little mean in the process.

An hour later, she would wish that she had stayed out with the girls and let them play, let them enjoy their childish games, their innocence, their last moments of happiness. An hour later, she would wish that they had run home all the way so they might have stopped what had happened.

The fire was too low in the kitchen when they got home. Cat raked through the ashes, searching for embers, and placed a chunk of coal over any that she found. She waited, crouched, her hands stinging from the cold, and watched for the flames to take.

Half of the beef broth remained in the pot, and once the fire had returned, she set the stew over the flames to warm through. She leant against the table, let the fire warm her stiff skirts, and closed her eyes. The week had taken too long to pass. She rolled her shoulders back, feeling and hearing the crunch of her spine as it straightened after days of being bent over. She had a searing pain between her eyes, and she pinched the bridge of her nose, liking the way the pressure made the blood pulse loudly in her ears, muffling all the other sounds as if she was underwater in another world.

Helen tripped over her feet and crashed onto the floor. She picked herself up, brushed the dust off her, and stared up at her big sister, unusually still at this time of night when she should have been making tea and setting the place straight for Michael's return.

'Cat?' Helen said, pulling on Cat's sleeve. 'You all right?'

With effort, Cat peeled her eyes open and forced a smile. 'Fine. Go and get your clothes ready for tomorrow, make sure they're clean.'

The girls did as they were told, clattering up the stairs, chattering between themselves. Cat never understood how they could find so much to talk about, so much to be continually upbeat about. For a moment, she resented them. If she had been Helen, then this responsibility would not have fallen on her shoulders. If she had been Lottie, she would be giggling in the snow, not worrying about cutting bread so thin that it stretched to four slices. But it did no one any good to think such thoughts.

She checked the pot. The water was not yet boiling, though tiny bubbles floated up and popped on the surface. She leant over the water, inhaled, and imagined she was sitting in a grand kitchen, where herbs and spices hung from the ceiling and perfumed the air, and a leg of beef turned on a spit, its fat collecting in a dish, ready to smear over thick slices of white bread. Her stomach moaned, and by the time the fantasy had fizzled away, the broth was bubbling.

'Cat!' Lottie's strangled voice rang through the house.

Cat raced up the stairs two at a time, her mind flashing with the worst sorts of bloody imagery. She collided with the girls at the foot of their mother's bed. Their round, white faces turned to her, their eyes watery, their mouths open.

She didn't want to look. If she didn't see, she could walk downstairs and get on with tea as if nothing had happened. If she didn't look, she could preserve the idea of her mother, alive, in her mind, just having a sleep, about to wake up at any minute.

'She won't open her eyes,' Helen said, sniffing as she clung to the leg of the bed. 'Why won't she open her eyes?'

'Go downstairs, girls.'

'What's wrong with Ma?' Lottie said. 'Why won't she wake up?'

'Downstairs!' Her voice made the room shudder. The girls ducked their heads instinctively, as if their father had shouted the instruction, then scampered away.

Still, Cat could not look at the bed. She examined the floor, and noticed, for the first time, the state of the rug, the way the scraps of fabric were squashed into each other, the colours dulled by grease and soot and dust. When was the last time she had beaten it? When was the last time Mother's bare feet had stepped onto it and shivered at the uncleanliness of it? Cat's cheeks burned. When had everything started to get too much?

'Ma?' she whispered, gaze trained on the frayed cotton of the rug, the whole thing coming loose. 'Ma?'

No reply. Not the reassuring wheeze of her chest, no crumpling of blankets. Nothing.

Cat squeezed her eyes shut. Tears spilled over her cheeks and splattered on the wooden floor. The silence was all-consuming. Deafening. She imagined the girls clinging to the banister, their ears pricked, waiting to be told what was happening, that everything was going to be fine.

Before she had time to stop herself, she forced her eyes open.

Mother's mouth gaped at an odd angle. Her skin, in the weakness of the candlelight, was grey.

Cat tiptoed towards her and touched a finger to her forehead. Cold.

She slumped on the bed and reached under the covers to grab her mother's hand. She pulled it out and rubbed it, thinking that if she could only warm her mother that she might come back to life. 'Come on, Ma.'

She dropped onto her knees beside the bed, furiously rubbing her hand up and down the white, gnarly streak of her mother's arm. She would make her mother live! She would will her mother back to life, for how could they survive without her? It was impossible.

'Don't leave me, Ma. You can't leave.'

She rubbed faster until she was scared she might tear her mother's thin skin, until the wedding ring – too large now for her mother's finger – shot off into the room. She cursed under her breath and searched for the bit of tinged gold. Where had it gone? It could not just vanish! She was on her hands and knees when a voice startled her.

'What you doing?'

Cat gawped at the dark shadow at the foot of the bed, and for a moment her heart stopped as she imagined it to be the reaper come for her mother's body, but as the figure lifted his eyes to her, she saw it was only her brother. She rested back on her heels, wiped her hair out of her face, and stared at him.

'She's dead,' he said, his voice emotionless.

Cat crawled to Mother and started rubbing her hand again. She was not going to give up on her.

'She's dead, Cat.'

'I know!' She jumped to her feet, ready to pounce at Michael, to strike at his cheeks, to make him do something other than just stare; he was as lifeless as their mother's corpse. She saved herself just in time and slammed her foot into the door, liking the distraction of the way her toe throbbed in agony.

'Don't just stand there!'

He shrugged, and red flakes of brick dust fluttered to the ground. More dust. More filth. He turned away from the bed, his face blank as he walked past her.

'One less mouth to feed.'

CHAPTER 6

October 1853. Wallingham Hall.

CAT SAT BESIDE THE FIREPLACE, gazing at the sharp blue of the sky, thinking of the day she had almost died – thinking of the cold water and the way it had filled her lungs until they had seemed to be on fire. Was that what it had felt like for her mother? Was that moment, when the fear and the pain burnt the mind to oblivion – blissful, peaceful oblivion – what it was like to die? A second of euphoria when everything ceased to matter – when all one's problems suddenly amounted to nothing.

True freedom.

What was this life she had now, after that moment in the light? A second chance, undoubtedly. She would not go back to before; she would take death over her old life. Here – Wallingham Hall, Osborne – was an opportunity. Here lay her future, if only she could be smart enough to get it.

Nelly burst into the room.

'Had no hands to knock with,' she said as a way of apology, showing Cat the bouquet of flowers in her one hand and the stack of boxes under the other arm.

'What's all this?'

'From Master Tomkins.'

'For me?'

'No, for me.' Nelly snorted and set the vase on the table by the mantelpiece. 'Of course, they're for you. Aren't they beautiful? The colours of the season. Master had them put together for you, especially.'

Cat inhaled the sweet scent of the bouquet and stroked the velvet tips of the amber roses and the waxy leaves of the green ferns.

'And these,' Nelly put the boxes on the bed – three pale pink boxes wrapped in ribbon, pretty enough as presents in their own right. 'These are your new dresses.' She opened each of the lids. One held lilac and pink striped material, the other a vibrant green with a hint of a tassel, and the final one a deep blue. 'A day dress, an evening gown, and a travelling outfit.'

Cat's belly lurched. 'Travelling outfit? Why should I need one of those?'

Nelly shrugged. 'For walking, going in the carriage, things like that. Or if you're planning on leaving soon. Are you?'

'No.' Cat crept towards the boxes and caressed the material with the back of her hand. The velvet and satin were as smooth as a cat's fur. 'Not if the master doesn't wish it.'

'Not much chance of that. He's asked if you'd take a walk with him this afternoon if you're feeling up to it?'

'Of course, I am.' She wished people would stop thinking she was an invalid. But then, perhaps it was better they considered her an invalid – maybe that was the only thing keeping her here.

'Good.' Nelly started putting the dresses in the wardrobe,

muttering to herself how grand they were. 'Ah! Almost forgot.' Her hand dived into the pocket of her apron and pulled out a piece of paper. 'From the master.'

Cat took the letter, noticing the way the corners had become dog-eared from being crumpled in Nelly's pocket. It was unsealed, the words on the page for anyone to read. She eyed Nelly. 'Have you read it?'

Nelly closed the wardrobe and a flush of scarlet spread over her cheeks. 'No.'

Nelly busied herself by straightening the bedsheets, fluffing the pillows, never meeting Cat's eyes.

'Nelly.' The sharpness in Cat's voice made Nelly stop. 'Have you read it?'

Cat waited expectantly, just as her mother used to do to her when she was little; the silence brought forth a confession sooner than a slap.

'I …' Nelly swallowed, bit her teeth together, and raised her head to look Cat in the eye defiantly. 'I can't read.'

It was Cat's turn to be embarrassed now. She felt the blood rush to her face as Nelly refused to look away. She fiddled with the letter in her hands. 'I'm so sorry. I … thought …'

'I'm not a liar.'

'No. No, of course, you aren't.'

Nelly sniffed. 'Right. Well, if that's all.' Nelly stormed towards the door.

'Wait!' She could not let the girl leave like this. 'I'd like it if you stayed with me while I read it, Nelly. Perhaps I could teach you some of the words?'

Her hand on the doorknob, her back to Cat, Nelly replied, 'I shouldn't like to know the private thoughts of the master.'

'Well … then, how about I teach you from the bible?'

'It's above me.'

'Nonsense. If I can do it, so can you.'

Nelly turned a little, softening. 'You think so?'

'Absolutely. It's not that hard, once you get the hang of it.'

Nelly raised an eyebrow doubtfully. 'If you say so.'

'Tomorrow, then?'

Nelly shrugged and opened the door. 'All right.'

The girl's pride had stopped her from sounding too enthusiastic, but Cat could tell the girl was intrigued – even excited, perhaps – and with a sigh of relief, Cat sank into her seat beside the fire.

Alone now, Cat stared at the letter. The paper was as soft as an old woman's skin between the tips of her fingers. What did it contain? A summons, perhaps? A small selection of curt words to tell her that her company had been nice but that she had outstayed her welcome – could she leave before the month was out?

She held her breath as she read the slanted, scratchy letters.

Dear Catherine,

I must apologise for my behaviour at dinner last night. It was not the appropriate time to tell you of such news, and I hope you have forgiven me for my impertinence. I do not often have visitors, least of all female visitors, and I forget your fragile natures.

I hope the flowers cheer you this morning and bring some joy to your day. I have only ever wished for your recovery and your happiness, ever since the moment I first saw you.

I should like it if we might take a walk around the grounds this afternoon, so we may speak a little more to one another and get to know each other. I should like to show you more of my home, so you may feel more comfortable in it, for I hope you shall stay for as long as you wish.

Yours,

Osborne

She met him outside the front door in her new blue cloak and bonnet. His dogs circled his legs, jumping from foot to foot, ready to be out in the open air. Against the brilliant sunshine, he cut an elegant silhouette in his black frock coat and high boots.

'Miss Davies.' He bowed to her, then scanned her outfit, checking that the cut was well-fitting, that the material was fine enough. 'You look much better.'

'Thank you, sir. And for the flowers and clothes too. You do too much.'

He laughed and shook his head. 'This way.'

He led her between an avenue of horse chestnut trees. A slight breeze trickled through the air, tickling the exposed skin of her neck. Her new, long skirt swished over the ground, now littered with spiked Conker shells and leaves which crunched underfoot. Against the azure blue of the cloudless sky, the branches of the trees reminded her of witch's fingers, the odd yellow leaf acting as the wart.

The dogs streaked ahead, playing between themselves, growls and barks of excitement erupting from them as they leapt across the grass.

'Are we going into the woods?'

'I didn't think so. Not after …'

'Thank you.' She squinted into the horizon. 'How much of this is yours?'

'Everything you can see.'

'The woods too?'

'I've twenty miles of woodland.'

Cat shook her head. Numbers meant nothing to her. Twenty miles could have been the whole of England for all she knew. 'What do you do with it all?'

He laughed. 'Enjoy it. Farm it. I've cottages rented to my labourers.'

'Hunt?'

'Deer. Game.'

'With your revolver?'

His easy footsteps stalled for a second. 'No, with my hunting rifle.'

She nodded as silence fell. In the field to their right, the sheep shuffled away from them, huddling together protectively. The dogs took little notice of the sheep, their noses stuck to the ground, their front paws kicking out their long ears.

'Tell me about yourself,' Osborne said, rousing her out of the uneasy quiet. 'Your memory is better now? You remembered my revolver.'

She glanced at his face and found him smiling. She smiled back. 'What would you like to know?'

'Where did you live? What did you do?'

'I lived in the middle of the town, in a small place. You would find it appalling.'

'I would not,' he said, without conviction.

'I worked in a button factory. It was what my ma used to do and her ma before her.'

'You said you had no family.'

'Both my parents died.'

He stopped. They had reached a gate which led into another field. 'An orphan.' He unlatched the gate and smiled sadly at her. 'Like me.'

She returned his smile, and for an instant, her hand brushed across his as she walked past him. 'I'm sorry to hear that, sir.'

She noticed his eyes drop to watch her hand as she replaced it by her side. He fixed the latch behind him, then joined her to walk on.

'And you've no other family?'

'I have sisters. Two. They don't live in town anymore. They are my most treasured things in all the world.'

He grunted, his gaze now occupied with his dogs. 'And you can read? I was worried when I sent the note that I might have done the wrong thing yet again.'

'I went to Sunday school. The vicar's wife taught us all from the bible.'

They reached a bench beside an oak tree. Osborne gestured for Cat to sit. 'You are a Godly woman, then?'

'I try to be a good Christian, sir.'

He reached for her arm. The suddenness of his eager movement made her flinch, but she did not shrug out of his grip.

'Call me Osborne.'

She nodded at his command, then felt his palm fall away from her reluctantly.

She tilted her face towards the sun and, though her eyes were closed, she knew he was gazing at her. 'I can feel God's warmth here, Osborne. Town is so harsh, the people so hard. It's difficult to feel anything but the cold and the dirt over there.'

'I should like it if you never felt the cold and the dirt again.'

The sun blinded her as she met Osborne's gaze. He drew himself towards her, his hot breath making white wisps in the space between them.

'Do you mean that?'

He nodded, and his tongue peeked out to wet his lips. He inched closer again, but she shielded herself with her bonnet.

'Please do not make promises if you will not keep them.' Too many people had devastated her before, and she could not face another.

'I am a man of my word, Catherine.'

She was about to face him. She was about to let him see the tears building in her eyes – real tears, tears of hope and longing and relief, when the gate crashed open and footsteps pounded towards them.

'Sir!' A boy, who Cat had not seen around Wallingham before, stopped a few feet away from them, his chest violently rising and falling, his cheeks as pink as pig's skin.

'What is it?' Osborne sniped, not looking at the child.

'Mr Dixon told me to tell you that there is a telegram for you.'

Osborne's breath hissed out between his lips – those lips which only seconds before had been so close to touching Cat's!

He swatted his hand at the boy who ran away immediately, his gangly legs flicking out like a colt's behind him.

'I must return.' Osborne got to his feet and offered Cat his arm. She took it, mustering all the good grace she could, trying to replace the disappointment in her face with a smile, and hoping the boy had not ruined her one and only chance.

THE GLASS HAD GROWN warm in Osborne's hand. The wine had soured as he swirled it around his mouth. The table before him was as elaborate as it had been last night (after he had told Mrs Lewis to make the room so extravagant that Catherine would be too stunned to notice his nerves), but now he looked on it as a charade, a game, a tableau of his stupidity.

Dixon hovered behind his shoulder, and Osborne could sense the words held back in the man's throat, ready to ask if he could get him anything, do anything at all, that might ease the tension that was building.

Then footsteps. Her footsteps. He was not used to them

yet; the light tap of them, the slowness, as if she placed each foot with the greatest of care. He squared his shoulders, straightened his spine, and nodded for Dixon to allow her inside.

He heard the faint murmur of her thanks, then the swish of silk satin against the door. He saw her skirts before he saw her face, the deep green fringed with delicate black lace. He studied her from the floor up. The dress suited her. Her waist was pulled in tight, one of the smallest waists he had ever seen; what wealthy women would give to get the waist of a pauper! She cradled her hands before her stomach, palms clinging together too inelegantly, showing she was not made to wear white silk. What did her hands look like beneath those gloves? He could not remember them from when he had rescued her; he had not been looking then at the finer details. They must be red and dry – working hands; ugly hands. And further up: her spine straight; her shoulders neat and low; her neck long and elegant; her hair worked into beautiful curls. Yes, from the shoulders up she passed for one of his kind.

'Good evening, Osborne.' She said it with a small smile. Such a beautiful smile, the face perfectly symmetrical. Yet, the slant of her pronunciation – the missing 'g' at the end of her words, the twang of her vowels – made the hideous truth of her town origins clear.

'Sit,' he said, the word almost sticking in his mouth. He cleared his throat, dabbed his napkin to his lips.

She took the seat to his left, and when he turned to her, he felt the heat from the fire burn his face. The light behind her made her pale hair shine like a halo. The smile which had been open before had now closed a little – her lips too hard and fixed.

'Is everything all right, Osborne?'

He gestured for Dixon to pour the wine. Her fingers

stubbed into her glass, making it teeter before she clasped it and brought it to her mouth. He watched her drink, saw the way her pink lips suckered onto the rim, the quick flash of a red tongue, the movement in her throat. He dropped his eyes to his empty plate.

'You never told me what you were doing when that man attacked you.' He glanced up quickly, quick enough to see the spark of fear flicker over her face. She set her glass on the table with precision. 'What were you doing on my land in the first place? It seems odd that two strangers would happen to bump into each other on private property.'

'I suppose I was lost.'

'Where were you going?'

She raised a hand to her head. He would not ask how she was feeling.

'You do not remember?'

'To see my sister. She works as a maid in Chester.'

He stretched his neck and felt the bones creak. He drank his wine. 'You said you worked in a button factory. Which one?'

'In the centre of town, you probably wouldn't know it.'

'Wouldn't I?' His voice was hard. The softness she had brought to him before was beginning to calcify once again. He glared into her face and saw the moisture building at the corners of her eyes. 'I know of a factory named Bronson's.'

Her lips parted, and a sheen of white ghosted over her skin. 'That was it.'

He had her! He forced himself to relax. It would all be over soon, and the pain which was beginning to bud in his chest would soon shrivel to nothing, as most of his feelings did these days.

'I sent a telegram to the police, asking if they had any information on the man who attacked you. I received a reply today.'

She raised an eyebrow, though did not speak.

'He was an Irish immigrant. He gave me a false name. His real one was Jonathan Murphy, so they've discovered. Not much information about him except where he lodged and where he worked. Where do you think that might have been?'

She looked at her hands which fidgeted in her lap. He noticed the pale blue veins on her eyelids, the dustiness of her long eyelashes as they lay against her white cheek.

'Bronson's Button Factory.'

He let the words vibrate in the room. Dixon was silent behind his screen.

'I find it an odd coincidence that two people, of similar age, who lived in the same town, who worked at the same factory, could be in the same place together all those miles away from home, and claim to be strangers to one another. Don't you?'

Her shoulders lifted, tensed.

'Would you not find that odd too, Miss Davies?'

From beneath her lashes, a tear fell. It dropped onto her skirt, marking a dark spot on the vibrant material. She raised her eyes to him, and they were like jewels of sapphire.

'It is true, I knew him.' Her voice was barely audible.

For a moment, he did not think he had heard her correctly. He had been expecting an argument, for the girl to grow savage, as those of her status always did when their true natures were revealed. He had not expected to see her crumble before him.

'John Murphy – he was the cruelest man I ever knew.' She raised a finger to her cheek, the exact place where one particularly nasty bruise had just managed to fade. 'I will tell you all, sir, if you will listen?'

He cleared his throat and took a deep breath. It would do

no harm, he supposed, to listen to whatever trite little story she could come up with.

'Dixon, leave us.' A shadow slipped from the room. 'You will tell me the truth?'

'I will, sir.' She swallowed and brushed her hand over her wet chin.

'I met John a few years ago. He seemed nice, at first.'

'He was Irish.'

Her forehead wrinkled into a frown for a moment. 'Yes. He worked as a burnisher at the factory, sir, and he offered me help when I needed it.'

'What kind of help?'

'Food. A smile.' She smiled at Osborne, the saddest of smiles … He dug his nails into his thigh to keep him still, to keep his brain sharp so he would be able to spot her lies.

'I was young, sir – young and naive, and he knew it. I thought he loved me.'

He laughed. How many times had that been given as an excuse? How many times would silly girls have to have their hearts broken before they realised that love meant nothing to young men?

'Please don't be cruel, sir! I didn't know what he was then. I had no money, no family, no friend to talk to. Ma was dead. I thought he would marry me, but he was a monster!' She wiped her nose on her hand, then hid her hand in her skirt as if embarrassed by her lack of decorum.

'He … made me do things. Things that no Christian man should ever want for his sweetheart. And when I refused, he would beat me until the world went black, and I'd wake up with cuts and scars all over me.'

Sickness gnashed inside him. Hadn't he seen what that man was capable of? He had witnessed first-hand the man's violence, the man's derangement. Suddenly, the bitterness he had felt towards Catherine ebbed. He recalled that day at the lake, the whiteness of her skin against the red gashes of her wounds – the wounds inflicted by the man she had once trusted. To be betrayed by those one loves the most must surely be the worst kind of pain.

Fumblingly, he touched her hand. She stilled, the muscles taut in her forearms, and for one dreadful moment, he thought she was scared of him. But then she threw herself at his knees, and great sobs wracked her body.

'He gambled and drank away both our wages. He made me sell my hair so he could settle his debts – said they'd string him up if not, and me with him. I knew him to be a violent man, sir, to me, but I never imagined him a murderer, I never imagined that he could do such a thing …' Her voice broke off.

Osborne pushed his napkin at her. 'Hush now, Catherine. He cannot hurt you anymore.'

'And I have you to thank for that, sir!' She raised her head. Her skin was blotchy, and her eyes were raw. He wiped her cheek.

'What happened the night he killed that man, Catherine?' If she would tell him the truth, then he might be able to understand, to forgive.

'I don't know, sir. I was at my lodgings. He used to go out, saying he'd find us money. I never asked how; I didn't want to know. I was sleeping, sir, and the next thing is my door's being rammed in, and John's there, blood all over him, looking like a madman. I only had time to pick up my bag and then he was dragging me out, saying we needed to be gone and fast. I was so tired, I didn't know what was happening. I followed him blindly for days, never sleeping. Then I asked where we were going.'

She sighed as if the exhaustion was on her again now.

'He said he was taking me to Liverpool and then we'd sail for America, start afresh.' She looked up to Osborne, horror in her face. 'I didn't want to go to America! How could I leave my home? My sisters? My mother in her grave? He hated this country, sir.'

Osborne grunted, his stomach now in a tight ball. If only he had the man before him, he would kill him all over again.

'Said there was nothing good here. Said the English were devils. And I said, in my rage, that it was him who was the devil for killing a man and that I would not go with him.'

Her tears had dried, her eyes were beginning to shine.

'I wasn't going to take it anymore. I'd never felt more proud of myself.'

He cradled her cheek and imagined her, feisty and determined. It seemed impossible now, with her here at his feet, that she could ever have had the courage to face up to someone so evil.

'That's when he came for me. I was so scared.' She rested her hot forehead against his leg and whispered, 'and then you saved me.

'I could not find the words to tell you before, sir. I was – I still am – so ashamed of everything. I will spend the rest of my life on my knees praying for forgiveness, for my own and John's sins.'

He gripped her neck and made her look at him. 'You will not pray for that man. He is rotting in hell now.'

Another tear bled down her cheek, and he gently brushed it away. Silently, he cursed his own cruelty towards her and blushed at his earlier thoughts. He peeled a glove off her hand. The skin was a little chapped but beautiful nonetheless. He brought her naked fingers to his lips and kissed them. 'Forgive me.'

'It is me–'

'My behavior just now, it was … I thought you …' He shook his head, swallowed. 'I am so sorry for what that man did to you.'

She leaned back onto her heels and sniffed. 'I will go, sir, at first light.'

He gripped her tighter. 'No.'

'I was dishonest with you–'

'I understand.'

'I did not tell you the truth.'

He pulled her close. 'You have now, and that is all that matters.'

In the quiet, he listened to her breath, as gentle as lapping waves. She soothed him. She would heal him. He could not lose her.

'Do not leave. I beg you, do not leave me.'

He kissed her wet cheeks. How could he have been so foolish? How could he have thought this girl, so innocent and small, could have been anything like that Irishman?

'You are safe here, Catherine. You will always be safe with me.'

CHAPTER 7

August 1851. Birmingham.

THE METAL BLURRED as she pushed it along the machine. Press and push, press and push. A drip of sweat fell onto her hand. No time to wipe her forehead with her handkerchief, no time to straighten up and feel the ache sigh over her body, no time to stop.

A shout above her head. Something familiar about the shape of the words … She looked up.

Across the shop floor, between the reddened faces of the women, her sisters stopped their tasks and walked together towards Mr Criton. He ushered them out of the door with a sweep of his arm, then shut it on them and turned back to face his workers. He caught Cat's gaze and raised his eyebrows. Cat dipped her head and continued cutting.

Time passed slowly. She cut circle after circle, waiting. Where were Helen and Lottie? Had they done something wrong? Had they ruined stock? In the months since Mother's passing, they'd become better workers – the dreams and the childishness had been shaken out of their innocent heads. They no longer giggled like they used to, nor whispered excitedly between themselves.

A whoosh of a door opening – she saw their moon-like faces, eyes wide, lips pursed together, chins wobbling as Mr Criton let them pass into the shop floor. They ran straight to Cat, tears bubbling over as they reached her.

'What is it? What's happened?'

'No work,' Helen said, pushing her fingers into her eyes. 'He said there's no work for us.'

'Why? What've you done?'

'Nothing,' Lottie said. 'It's not our fault. Just business.'

The metal tingled in Cat's fingers, and despite the heat, a shiver passed over her spine. 'Right. Wait outside for me. There are only a few hours left.'

'What will we do?' Helen wailed, and the women either side of them brought their heads up to stare.

'Shush!' Cat grabbed her hands and held her still. 'Go outside and wait for me on the wall. Don't go anywhere else, you understand?' They nodded. 'I'll sort it.'

She shooed them out, and the workers' eyes followed them all the way to the door.

Fear gripped her stomach. For a moment, air would not find her lungs. She stared at the shimmering metal in her hands, at the scraps that littered her lap … not even worth a button.

Her neighbour coughed, and Cat looked up. The face beside her had never been a soft one, never one keen on smiling, but there was the faintest sign of pity in the frown. 'Best get on, else he'll have you out next.'

Cat glanced at Mr Criton, such a small cog in Bronson's wheel, yet with the power to crush her. His eyes were slits as he stared back, waiting for her to make one wrong move. She ducked her head and continued to punch out the metal until the minutes and hours blended together, and Mr Criton finally called time on the day.

She flew past the women, shoving into their shoulders as they gasped and cursed at her. She ran out between the high brick walls until she was into the street. It took some minutes for her eyes to adjust to the brightness of the evening, but then she saw them, right where they should be, their heels kicking into the brickwork in boredom.

'Stop that!' Cat smacked their legs. 'You'll have nothing for your feet if you do that.'

A new wave of tears burst from Helen, and Cat wished she'd held her tongue. She pulled the girls close to her chest. 'Hush now, don't go crying.'

'There'll be no money, Cat, no food.'

'I'll sort it. There'll be other jobs, other work you can do. You're good girls. Did Mr Bronson say he'd give you references?'

'It wasn't Mr Bronson.'

'Who was it?'

They shrugged. Of course, it wouldn't have been Mr Bronson getting his hands dirty. 'Did he say you'd have a reference?'

They nodded, and Cat sighed, relieved. 'That's something, at least.'

Something brushed against her skirt, then knocked into her arm. A worker, she supposed, in too much of a hurry, though she thought they'd all passed by now. She turned to glare at him.

'Sorry,' the person mumbled, his voice low, his accent unusual. Beneath his cap, she saw the milkiness of his skin, the spots of freckles over his nose.

'It's all right,' she said, staring into his pale, blue eyes. The lashes that framed them were blonde so that they looked bigger in his face – like blue buttons in the snow.

Had he heard her and her sisters talking? Talking of poverty and interpreting the unsaid danger which hung over their conversation – the threat of the workhouse. Blood rushed to her cheeks. She would not have others knowing their desperation.

His gaze dropped to the floor, and he turned away from her. She watched him walking. He was a small man, not much taller than herself. His trousers were baggy, though the gap between his legs was wide. He walked with a rolling motion as if one leg might have been shorter than the other. He disappeared into a small crowd of men heading into the heart of town, where they would become different men to the ones who worked on the shop floor in the daytime. She hoped he was not the gossiping type when the beer took him.

Lottie's whining voice roused her, and she dragged her eyes back to her whimpering sisters.

'I don't want to go anywhere else.'

'You're big girls now; you'll go where you're needed.'

'We want to stay together.'

Cat forced a smile. 'You will. I promised, didn't I, that we'd all stick together?'

They nodded, trusting.

'Now, come on.' She pulled them off the wall. 'We'll tell Michael and see what he thinks about it all.'

'WHAT'VE THEY DONE?' Michael's hands cradled his head as he leant back in his chair, finding something on the ceiling more interesting than his snivelling sisters.

'They haven't done anything. There's no work for them.'

'Why haven't they let someone else go if that's it?'

'I don't know!' Cat dug her fingers into her hips, breathed

out slowly through her nose. There was no point letting him aggravate her; it would only make him do it more.

'You should have been taking better notice of them.'

She bit her tongue before she cursed at him. 'Instead of blaming me, can you think of anywhere that's hiring now?'

She heard the shift of his jacket against the wooden chair. A shrug. A grunt.

'Right, well, you'll go round in the morning girls.'

'Where?' Helen said. 'What if we get lost?'

Lottie's chin began to quiver again; there was nothing worse than getting lost in town.

Michael pushed out his chair and went for his cup. He filled it full with beer, leaving little for the rest of them. He drank from it deeply as he looked into the fire. 'Try the service?'

'No.' Cat shook her head. The girls frowned at her.

'Bed and board, all covered. Send their wages here.'

Cat couldn't hold back her sharp snap of laughter. 'You'd send them off to work for your beer money? My goodness, Michael, you really are our father.'

He drank again, as if he hadn't heard the insult, or had not thought it one. 'They'd have better things than here. Food in their bellies, for one.'

'And worked day and night until they're good for nothing at all.'

'What's the difference?'

'They'll be split up.'

The girls gripped her dress.

Michael shrugged, again. The girls started to cry.

Cat searched her brother's face for a sign of softness, a ghost of the child she remembered playing and chuckling with when they were little. His eyes were too dark now, the lines around them deep from so much scowling and frowning. He was an ugly boy.

'Please … I can't lose them too, Michael.'

He nodded, sniffed, then grabbed the chunk of bread on the table that Cat had yet to slice so it would stretch between the four of them. He bit into it, stuffing almost half of it onto his mouth.

He chewed it as they gawped at him, his jaw working up and down, round and round, his white cheeks stretching, and then, with effort, he swallowed. He licked his lips.

'Starve then.'

CHAPTER 8

December 1853. Wallingham Hall.

FINGERS OF SWEAT tickled the back of her neck. The fire was high behind her, too high. The wine was flowing too freely, was too easily consumed, as glass by glass was refilled. She could feel it in her stomach, swirling around the bits of partridge and pheasant and venison and beef and mutton and chestnuts and sugared fruit. She thought of her stomach like a thin strip of copper, the corset the press, clamping down on her, cutting into her, squeezing the life from her.

She pushed her napkin to her lips and inhaled, smelling clean linen, and the sharpness of the soap brought her back to reality.

To her left, the Reverend – Mr Turner – was talking about something confusing. She had not been paying attention to his words, but she smiled like the others smiled and laughed when they did so too.

Looking up, she caught the direct gaze of May Harlow.

She was a beautiful woman, some years Cat's senior but no more than thirty. She had eyes the deepest shade of brown, and her hair was just as dark and glossy, with strands of red catching in the candlelight. Her eyes were as sharp as knives, and she gazed over at Cat as if she was looking down on a mouse; it was Cat who weakly looked away first, sipping more wine as a way of distraction.

Cat had done well tonight, she reminded herself. She had learnt the etiquette of the table; she had done nothing wrong or out of place. Perhaps she had been a little quiet, speaking only when spoken to, but that was to be expected in such new company. Each time she'd glanced at Osborne she'd found him grinning at her, and a slight nod of his head would reassure her that she must stop worrying.

Suddenly, chair legs screeched across the floor, and May stood. Ruth, Mr Turner's wife, stood also. Cat hesitated as all eyes fell to her.

'Shall we withdraw?' May said, acidity dripping from every syllable.

Under the table, Osborne tapped Cat's knee – her cue to leave. She followed behind May and Ruth obediently, and wished she could stay in the safety of the dining room, in the safety of mixed company – women could be feral. Closing the door, she heard Mr Turner, Osborne, and Mr Stephen Harlow take up a suitably dull conversation about business.

In front, May led the way through the great hall as if it were her own house, her gown swishing over the flagstones, Ruth a few feet behind.

Ruth and May did not like each other either; despite their ladylike politeness, even Cat could see the way May struggled not to roll her eyes whenever Ruth spoke, and how Ruth found the tablecloth infinitely more interesting than any of May's grandiose tales.

Indeed, Ruth could be quite the shrew, so Cat had

discovered. Cat had visited the vicarage after church service twice since her arrival at Wallingham, accompanied by Osborne both times. As the men had discussed the service, Cat had felt Ruth's eyes bore into her face. Seated in the parlour, with a low fire burning in the grate and surrounded by potted plants and china ornaments and oil lamps with fringes to rival Cat's new dresses, an interrogation disguised as polite conversation had swiftly begun. On both occasions, Ruth had asked the same questions, no doubt trying to make Cat's story fold. But Cat had answered the specific questions honestly. She had described the desperate state of her previous life and the horrific way Jonathon Murphy had treated her (for that certainly was no lie), skipping only a few of the more gruesome details until Ruth's cheeks had paled – no one needed the whole truth.

But still, suspicion clouded Ruth's eyes whenever they met Cat's. She was a hard woman to win over.

Now, May led them all into the drawing room. The fire, again, was high, the room too pressing. A tea set had been placed on one of the tables, and three pretty cups and saucers were waiting for them. Each of them took their seats, keeping a fair distance from one another, and the silence stretched for several uncomfortable seconds until Mrs Lewis entered and poured the tea.

She handed the first cup to May with a smile that Cat had never seen on her face before. She gave the next to Ruth and then, only three-quarters filled, Mrs Lewis slammed the final cup and saucer on the table nearest Cat. The liquid sloshed back and forth – rather like how the contents of Cat's stomach were doing right now – and slopped over the rim of the cup.

All three women watched and waited to see how Cat would respond.

She swallowed and forced back her shoulders. 'You've spilt that.'

To her right, Ruth watched the scene blankly. Cat heard May snigger. Mrs Lewis's straight lips could not hide the glint of laughter and the flare of triumph in her eyes.

'Fetch me a clean cup.'

Mrs Lewis's smugness was replaced with anger. She did not move for a moment, only worked her jaw and held Cat's glare with one of her own, but Cat was not going to back down tonight. Tonight, she needed to prove herself.

'Now, Mrs Lewis.'

Suddenly, Mrs Lewis flounced out of the room without a nod or curtsey. When Cat looked at Ruth, the woman's face was softer; dare she say it – impressed? Cat was sure she saw a little smile brighten Ruth's face before she raised her cup to her lips.

'I must say, the house looks a treat this year. Osborne never usually goes to so much effort.' May, who was still smirking from the drama, directed her grin towards the festively decorated mantelpiece. She reached for a leaf of holly, rubbing her thumb down its smooth centre. She let go of the branch, and it sprung back into place.

'Thank you,' Cat said, though she was not sure whether it was her place to take credit for the state of the house, for she was not the mistress of it. Yet.

'Where was it you said you lived?'

'We have houses in Cheshire, Gloucestershire, and London.'

Of course, they did. Cat forced her voice to be light. 'And where will you be spending Christmas?'

'Cheshire. And you?' May said, fixing her sharp eyes on Cat once again. 'Where will you be spending Christmas, Miss Davies?'

'What a question!' Ruth said, finally joining the conversation. Her voice came out as annoyed rather than amused. Perhaps the combination of a woman like May Harlow and the lateness of the hour were getting too much to withstand. Cat did not imagine that vicars' wives were used to staying up until the small hours of the morning in such hostile company.

'Miss Davies will be here, of course. You know that.'

The bitterest of smiles, the kind that never reaches the eyes, pierced Ruth. 'Quite,' May snarled, then returned her attention to Cat as if Ruth was not worth bothering with.

'What kind of Christmas did you have last year, Miss Davies? I imagine a very different one than what you will be experiencing here.'

'Well, I attended church, of course.' She smiled at Ruth and felt a thrill ripple over her skin as Ruth returned the gesture. 'But I am afraid it was not a happy occasion. In truth, I do not wish to think of it, Mrs Harlow. I hope you will understand. I wish to think of only happy things now, and I am certainly very happy in this house.'

'I should say you are.'

'I cannot quite believe I will be celebrating here.'

'Neither can I.'

Ruth's smile dropped. She glowered at May. Did that mean Ruth was now on Cat's side? An enemy turned defender? No matter how strained the evening had been, this at least might have made the whole ordeal worthwhile.

During the long silence, Mrs Lewis returned to the room. She pushed too hard against the door so that it crashed into the wall, and as it swung open, an icy draught blew in from the corridor – almost as icy as Mrs Lewis's face.

Without a word, Mrs Lewis poured tea into Cat's new cup, though now the liquid was too dark, and as Cat took the cup into her hand, it felt only lukewarm.

'You may go, Mrs Lewis. We have no need for you anymore.'

Scowling, Mrs Lewis trudged out of the room, tugging the door behind her so that it slammed against its frame once more. Ruth tutted and shook her head. May looked somewhat forlorn to see her one ally leaving.

Cat raised her cup. 'Here's to a wonderful Christmas.'

THE TURNERS HAD INSISTED they go home, not wanting to cause a fuss, but Osborne would not allow it. Send his own vicar out into the blizzard with his good wife beside him? What kind of Christian would that make him? No, there was a perfectly decent bed upstairs for guests (several beds, in fact, Cat almost added) and so adamant was he, that the Turners did not struggle for long. Chuckling from a little too much wine and brandy, Mr Turner staggered up the steps, pushed along by his wife, as both of them looked over their shoulders to thank Osborne for his kindness.

Meanwhile, May and Cat waited at the foot of the stairs in steely silence for their men to join them. Stephen and Osborne lingered in the great hall, not quite ready to end their conversation. Finally, Osborne laughed, clapped his friend on the back, and brought his bleary eyes towards the women.

'Your husband has been humouring me with tales of London.'

May extended her delicate, gloved hand, and Stephen kissed it, then placed it in the crook of his arm. 'I do not want to know half of what my husband busies himself with in the city.'

Stephen was as handsome as Osborne and just as tall and broad. For a second, Cat imagined the two of them as boys, raking up the city streets in search of something beautiful and sinful. She imagined their charms, the way girls might have dreamt and sighed about them, the way they would have discarded everything once it had pleased them, as all young, wealthy men like them always did.

Stephen's green eyes flicked to Cat, hard, like his wife's. They stayed on her only for an instant, but the disgust in them was enough to make Cat flush.

'Goodnight, Tomkins.' Stephen shook Osborne's hand and then guided his wife up the stairs. Neither of the Harlows said another word to Cat.

Osborne slumped against the bannister, a grin spreading to his ears. His eyes were swimming, his cheeks ruddy, his hair fallen out of its hold. He unfastened his tie and tilted his head as he looked at her.

'What is it?' she said.

The Harlows' voices had faded to nothing. The air was still and quiet around them.

Osborne shook his head. 'You are a wonder to me, Catherine.'

'How so?'

He stepped closer, his feet unsteady on the floor. 'A button maker's daughter.' He laughed, but it was gentle. 'No one would ever think it of you.'

'I fear May Harlow does not take to me.'

'May is …' he shook his head and couldn't find the word. 'May is Stephen's wife.' He shrugged. 'I do not care a jot what either of them thinks, of you, of me, of anyone at all.'

His hand flopped into hers, and he pulled her up the stairs. She walked the hallway by his side, until they came to her room. They stopped by the door.

'Did you enjoy tonight?'

'Yes,' she lied.

'You know,' he lifted her curl of hair that had dropped

from its pin and twisted it around his finger, 'you are the most beautiful woman I have ever seen.'

She could not hold his gaze. She dropped her eyes to his feet, concentrating on the shininess of the leather.

'Catherine,' he breathed, and his breath was hot and tangy.

His lips brushed against her earlobe, his teeth catching on the gold earrings he had gifted her earlier that day. She tilted her head so that her neck extended in front of him, inviting his kisses. He gripped her upper arms and moved her against the wall. His leg came between hers, and a deep moan rumbled from his chest.

She placed her palms on his shoulders and gently pushed him away. 'I cannot, Osborne.'

'But, I–'

'Do not make me. That is what he used to do.'

Osborne clamped his lips together. They had whitened, and the frown had come onto his forehead as it always did at any mention of Jonathon Murphy.

'I would be a good Christian, Osborne. I have been given a new life here with you. It is like I am reborn.'

'You are,' he urged, coming closer again.

'Then let me be who God would have me be. Let me be a good woman. Do not drag me to sin.'

'I would not, you know I would not.'

She cupped his cheek and brushed her hand over his hot brow. 'I do not deserve this, Osborne. Sometimes I think it must be a dream and that I will wake and I will be back in town, back in that place with–'

'You are not dreaming.'

'I must go back eventually. I must return to it all.'

'No.' He shook his head, seemingly sober now. His eyes were bright and focused as he spoke. 'You will not go back. I promise.'

She was about to say more, but he put a finger over her lips.

'Sleep well, Catherine.'

He kissed her cheek, bowed to her, and walked down the hallway towards his wing for the night.

The following morning, only she and the Turners had been to breakfast; Osborne had been sorting business matters inside his study, and there had been no sign of the Harlows.

If slightly awkward, breakfast had cemented Cat's hopes that last night had brought her and Ruth closer together, and an easy conversation about the weather and their plans for the New Year had finally, after several cups of strong coffee, ensued.

Before noon, Osborne had found Cat and his guests in the parlour, happily chatting over cups of tea, and had suggested they go for a stroll, what with the weather being so crisp. And so, as Nelly helped her into her outdoor clothes, Cat asked what had happened to the Harlows that morning.

'They rang at eleven. Then they had their food in their room.' Nelly said it with a frown. 'Still in their nightclothes, they were, when I went in with the tray.' She shook her head in astonishment. 'Her maid's very off. Thinks herself better than all of us here.'

'I wonder where she gets it from?' Cat met Nelly's gaze in the mirror and smirked.

Downstairs, the Harlows, the Turners, and Osborne waited for her. The dogs barked impatiently, and when they saw Cat, they bounded towards her, licking her fingers before galloping out of the door.

Osborne headed the party, striding out into the grounds as the dogs raced past him.

'I fancy the woods, don't you, darling?' May said to her husband and stopped so that the whole troupe had to stop too, out of courtesy.

Osborne glanced at Cat. 'It's terribly muddy out there, May. You'll ruin your shoes.'

She swatted the air before her. 'I can buy more.' She gripped Osborne's arm and tugged him along before anyone had a chance to protest.

And so it was that May and Osborne turned left before reaching the avenue of chestnut trees, and led the way out of the field of sheep, with everyone else following diligently behind.

Cat had seen Osborne disappear this way before when he had been on his horse – when she had been watching him from her window. A moment of panic engulfed her as she saw the mass of trees spread out before her.

She should turn back. She should make some excuse of a headache or sickness, and run back to the house. Surely, no one would blame her, would they? But of course, May would be triumphant. This was a test, after all. A game. The glee at Cat's fear was evident in May's eyes as she turned back to see what was taking Cat so long.

'You look rather pale, Miss Davies. Does the air not suit you?'

All eyes turned to Cat.

Osborne extracted his arm from May's grasp. 'Perhaps we should go the other way–'

'Miss Davies is perfectly well, are you not?' Ruth left her husband's side and joined Cat. Amidst the folds of their skirts, Cat felt the woman squeeze her hand.

Cat cleared her throat. 'Yes, I am fine. Please go on.'

May's smirk fell. She reached for her husband and stomped behind Osborne into the mud.

The woods were different from how she had remembered them. The trees were now entirely bare, skeletal. The leaves had turned to sludge in the November rains, and their footsteps squelched. The ground underneath her feet was uneven, with odd rocks sticking up and making her stumble. Ruth was there all the time, striding along with ease, holding onto Cat and keeping her upright.

They came to a clearing in the trees. The view of rolling hills and hedged fields opened up before them. Small clusters of houses dotted the landscape, and faint chimney smoke was just visible in the low sunshine. The party stopped to take in the sight, quiet for a moment, enjoying the birdsong.

'Where is Birmingham in relation to here, Osborne?' May said.

'To the south. A good thirty miles away.' Osborne threw a smile at Cat who stood at the end of the line. She couldn't entirely return it.

'Will you show us the lake where it happened?'

Osborne rolled on the balls of his feet. 'I should not like to upset anyone.'

'You shan't. I'm sure Miss Davies would not mind seeing the place where you rescued her, would you, Miss Davies?'

Cat shook her head.

'Right … all right then.' Osborne flicked the brim of his hat. 'This way.'

They walked for an age. It was no wonder, Cat thought, she and John had been lost. The forest turned and twisted in on itself like a maze. When she thought the cliff edge should be on their left, she soon discovered it was on their right. She had no sense of direction amidst the trees.

Finally, they came through a dip between two mounds of earth, and then she saw the shine of sunlight on still water. It was smaller than she remembered – the lake was nothing more than a stagnant pool; a collection of rainwater running off the hillsides. The water was black, the mud vast and sucking underneath the surface. She remembered the taste of it then, the earthiness, the tang of mulch and decay on her gums.

'Are you all right?' Ruth whispered.

Cat pulled her gaze off the water and nodded.

'Tell us again, Osborne, how it happened.' May crept to the water's edge and placed her hand on the tree against which Cat had once rested.

'Well,' Osborne cleared his throat. 'It was the dogs who alerted me to the trouble. I came riding through there,' he pointed between the mounds, 'and saw two figures by the water, one of them … struggling.'

Cat closed her eyes. Hands … those hands against her throat. The way his face blurred as she stared at him through the water …

'How did he have her? Face down?' May's voice was high, thrilled.

Osborne shook his head. 'I'm not sure I can remember quite–'

'And then?'

'Well, then I pushed him off and helped Catherine out.'

'Was she breathing?'

'No, no, she wasn't.'

'The kiss of life?' May said, sniggering with her husband. Ruth tutted.

'No. I rolled her over until the water came out of her. For a while I thought I might have lost her …' Were those tears misting his eyes as he looked at Cat?

'And the man?' Stephen said abruptly, rousing Osborne from his emotions. 'Why did you shoot him?'

'Because he was trying to kill Catherine.'

'But you got her out of the water. Clearly, he didn't kill her, did he?'

Osborne laughed breathlessly. 'That was his intention. If it hadn't been for me ... And he tried to run for it. What else was I supposed to do?' His voice ended on a squeal.

'All right, Tomkins,' Stephen said, 'don't work yourself up.'

'Stop asking all these horrid questions then!' Osborne pulled off his hat, raked his fingers through his hair, then set the hat in place once again.

'A mighty good job you were here,' Mr Turner said, his voice creeping into the silence, soothing the tension. He patted Osborne on the shoulder and turned to Cat. 'What an ordeal for you, my dear.'

'What were you doing here, Miss Davies?' May said, daring to probe further.

Cat was not sure how much of the story Osborne had told his friend. 'I was lost.'

A thin line wriggled between May's eyebrows. 'An odd place to be lost when you come from Birmingham.'

May waited, but Cat could not respond.

'Osborne said you used to work in a factory, is that right?' May fingered the set of decorative buttons by her wrist. 'I wonder if it was you who made these?'

Cat ran her tongue around her dry mouth. 'Perhaps.'

'I shall know who to come to when one needs replacing.' That cold smile again. 'Did you know your attacker, Miss Davies? I heard he murdered a man in town.'

'Enough!' Osborne said. He inhaled shakily. 'We must return to the house. It is too cold to be standing out here.'

He stormed through the middle of them all, ending the interrogation. Cat looked for a smile from him, but he glared at the ground as he passed her, and the party followed him all the way home in silence.

INSIDE, Osborne did not stop to remove his coat or change

his boots. 'I'd have a word, Stephen, if you have the time? In my study.' He marched out of the hall so that Stephen had to quickly throw his coat at Dixon and trot to catch him up.

May dropped her cloak into her maid's expectant arms and strolled towards the stairs. Her heels clipped on the wood and echoed through the hall.

'Ghastly woman,' Ruth said once the sound of the shoes had disappeared. Her husband stared at her, taken aback by her honesty in front of Cat, but Ruth ignored him.

'Tea, Mrs Turner?'

'That would be lovely, my dear. And then we must leave. Walter needs to prepare for the service tonight.'

'Of course.' Cat had forgotten it was Christmas Eve. At least, she reassured herself, there was only lunch to sit through with the Harlows before they too were due to leave.

'I'll tell Mrs Lewis to get the tea, and then I'll join you in the drawing room. Please go through.'

Cat did not take the direct route to the kitchens. Instead, she crept along the corridor towards Osborne's study. She heard the heated conversation in grunts to start with until she came to the door and pressed her ear against it.

'She is making a fool of you, Tomkins!'

'It is you who is the fool, Stephen. Your wife has a tongue as sharp as a whip; she does you no credit.'

'And you? What do you plan to do with this, Miss Davies? Are you even sure that is her true name?'

'You are being ridiculous.'

'Am I? A factory girl from Birmingham, you say? Have you checked their records?'

'Yes.'

'And?'

'Everything she has told me is true. She has worked there for years, with her mother and her sisters.'

A brief lull in the conversation. Cat imagined Stephen conjuring another argument against her.

'Still. A factory worker, Tomkins!'

'Her heart is above all others.'

'Is she clean?'

'How dare you!'

The door rattled against her ear from the noise of Osborne slamming his fist into the table.

'I take it you've slept with her?'

'I have not.'

Stephen laughed waspishly.

'I would not take such advantage of her. She is a good woman.'

'My God,' Stephen's voice was now soft. 'She has you good and proper.'

'I love her, Stephen.'

'She knows your worth, I take it?'

'She does not care for money.'

'Everybody cares for money, and if they say they do not, then you know them for a liar.'

'She could take all my money.'

'Be quiet, man! Have you lost your mind completely? Just think of your father.'

'Do not dare bring my father—'

'What he would have to say about this? His son marrying a slum girl.'

'You will not mention my father!'

She jerked back, nervous even from this safe distance of Osborne's rage.

'You will leave immediately,' Osborne hissed.

'You choose her over your oldest friend?'

'Oldest, yes, but you are no true friend when you cannot see my happiness.'

'I see your happiness, Tomkins, but I fear it will shatter around you.'

Footsteps.

She dashed to the library and hid behind the doorframe just in time to see Stephen stalk out of the study. A moment later, Osborne emerged, hatless, his shoulders crumpled forward. He inhaled deeply as if exhausted, then made for the great hall.

SHE HAD SEEN THE HARLOWS' carriage roll over the drive only an hour later. She had watched from her window and had sighed in relief once they had disappeared.

'Master Tomkins would like you to wear these tonight.'

Now, she drew her attention away from the star-filled sky and found Nelly holding a chain of pearls.

'They were his mother's. He said he'd like you to have them.'

The pearls dripped around Cat's neck uncomfortably, but she kept them on, then made her way to the drawing room where Osborne waited for her. He stood beside the fire, watching the flames.

'Thank you for the gift,' she whispered.

He smiled at the sight of her. 'I knew they would shine on you.'

'Your guests left early today. I thought they meant to stay for lunch?' She perched on the edge of the silk chair opposite him, stroking her skirt smooth.

'I must apologise on their behalf. I did not mean for them to upset you.'

'Ah, I have suffered worse.'

His face was pained as he looked at her.

Somewhere in the distance, the sound of voices travelled over the air. 'What's that?'

Osborne extended his hand towards her. 'Come with me.'

He led her through the great hall and to the porch. 'Ready?' He opened the door.

She had never seen such a beautiful sight. Outside, a group of villagers had gathered. Candle lanterns lit their faces with a golden hue. Some played the pipes while the others sang the carol, *O Holy Night*.

She watched, stunned, as snow began to fall. She stepped out into the cold, palm facing the sky, and caught some flakes. She studied their perfect symmetry before they melted.

'Come inside, you'll freeze,' Osborne said, opening his arms for her.

She dived inside them and felt his chin press against her head. They watched the carollers, swaying a little to the tune, and she felt him shift beside her, then his mouth came close to her ear.

'I love you, Catherine.'

She turned her face towards him. Could she say it back? It was not love she felt, but it was close, wasn't it? It could grow if she allowed it, if she could forget …

'And I you,' she whispered.

CHAPTER 9

December 1851. Birmingham.

Two small leather cases, barely filled – a paltry amount to account for two whole life's worth of belongings – lay on the bed. Lottie's bag had Mother's shawl. Helen's bag had Mother's handkerchief. Both had a lock of each other's hair, plaited and tied and kept in the lining for safety. The only other clothes they had were the dresses on their backs; the promise of a uniform had meant they could sell everything else and take the few pennies with them, as an emergency fund.

Cat brushed their hair as they wept. She braided it and fixed it in a bun, smoothing down the flyaway strands with her spit so they would look neat and presentable.

'Hush now,' she said, stroking their heads. 'Think of the fine houses you'll be living in. And country air is nicer than town air. You'll be able to see the stars at night.'

Still, the girls cried. She sat between them and pulled them into her arms. 'You'll make lots of friends.'

'I don't want friends,' Lottie said.

'And there'll be footmen. They're the most handsome of men.'

Helen clasped her hands around Cat's waist. 'Don't make us go, Cat.'

Cat sniffed back a threatening tear. 'It's not all bad, you know. You're not that far away from each other.'

'Where is Cheshire?' Lottie said.

'Not far.'

'Will you visit me?' Helen said.

'If it's allowed.' She would make no promises. 'Now come on, you're not to be late.'

She ushered them downstairs. Their bags, though small, seemed too large against their little bodies. They gazed about the kitchen, eyes wide, not believing they would never see it again.

A rumble came from outside – wheels over uneven ground. Cat opened the door to see a cart with one short, fat horse and a mean-looking driver pulling up.

'For Ashton Hall,' he said, pinching his collar tight against his neck.

She grabbed Helen. 'Look what a nice carriage they've sent for you.'

Helen clung to her skirts. 'I won't go!'

'Stop it now. It's for the best, you know that.'

'Please.' Tears sprouted from Helen's eyes.

Cat glanced at the driver, who was fidgeting, reaching for his pocket watch. She hardened her voice. 'Enough, Helen. You are not a little girl now. Stop crying and do as you are told.'

Helen glared at her. Lottie ran for her twin and squeezed her hard.

'Come along.' Cat had to break them apart. She pulled Helen to the cart and shoved her onto the seat. 'I love you. Do Ma proud.' She turned away before she could see Helen's eyes fill with tears again.

She found Lottie waiting in the doorway, watching her sister disappear.

How could Cat do it again? How could she send another sister away to a strange place?

Lottie's lip quivered, but she rolled back her shoulders. 'I'll wait here.'

And so they stood on the threshold with the December wind slicing into their faces and waited to be torn apart.

Eyes peeped from the windows around them, trying to get a good look. Lottie would not let them see her cry. Cat took strength from her sister; when a tear fell onto her cheek, she brushed it off quickly. She kept her gaze fixed on the gutter in the centre of the road and hoped that wherever the girls ended up, they would never have to see such a gutter again.

Another pony-cart pulled up, the horse a better breed than the last one, though a little skittish; it was not accustomed to such an environment. The driver seemed kinder too, portlier, and Cat prayed that Lottie would be treated well and grow fat and healthy. She kissed her sister's forehead and guided her to the cart. Lottie's lip quivered harder.

'Goodbye, Cat,' she said, her voice cutting off here and there where it stumbled on the lump in her throat. 'I hope I'll see you soon.'

'Soon, I promise. We'll all be together again – I'll make sure of it.' Cat squeezed Lottie's small, sticky hand, trying to imprint the feel of it, the warmth of it, into her mind as her only keepsake. Then she nodded to the driver who, bless his heart, had a blanket waiting for Lottie's knees.

'She'll be right, miss.'

How she prayed for the driver to be telling the truth!

STAGGERING INSIDE, she dragged herself upstairs again. Her own case lay open on the otherwise empty bed. Mother's comb, a few bits from the kitchen that she'd chosen not to sell, some blankets from the bed – the others were in Michael's bag – lay before her.

She held the blankets to her nose, but Mother's smell was gone. Mother was not a part of the house anymore; her soul had long since risen, taking all traces of her with it.

Michael crashed into the room. He did not ask after his sisters. Ignoring Cat, he threw his shirts into his case and some of Father's old trousers which he could now wear as long as he had braces to hold them up.

Both of them finished packing in silence. Every so often, Cat glanced up at her brother to see if there was any sign of sadness in him. She found nothing in his features at all.

He closed his bag, picked it up, and began to walk out of the room. He was going to leave without even saying goodbye!

She grabbed him and embraced him. He was stiff underneath her arms, his body still as if he was holding his breath. She let go of him after only a few seconds.

'I'll miss you, Michael.' She wiped her eyes on her skirt.

He shifted his weight to his other leg. 'It's for the best.'

'I don't know if it is.'

He pinched his lips together, blew out sharply through his nose. 'Make a decision and stick to it.'

She would not argue with him on their last day together. She nodded.

'You're too much like her.'

'Who?'

'Mother.' He said it as an insult.

'And what's wrong with that? She was a good woman.'

He sighed, shook his head, and left the room. The bubble of rage inside Cat's gut suddenly burst.

'You seem to forget that our father was a violent drunk.'

He was halfway down the stairs when he turned on her. 'Only because he was driven to it.'

'How can you say that?'

'She was a useless wife.'

'She raised us, Michael.'

He laughed. 'Yes, and look how we've turned out.'

Cat grabbed hold of the bannister. She couldn't believe what she was hearing. She couldn't believe the hatred spewing from Michael's mouth, the slanderous words spilling out between his lips about their own mother, their own, dear, loving mother.

How long had Michael resented her, resented them all? There had been a time when he had been happy, she was sure of it. There had been a time when they had giggled and played together. She would never know when that had changed, but she guessed it must have been the first time Father had beaten him after he'd finished with Mother.

'I'm sorry for you, Michael.'

He marched down the stairs. 'Don't be.'

She ran after him, clutching for his coat as he opened the door. 'Will you tell me where you're staying?'

'You don't need to know.'

'Please, Michael! I could visit you?'

He stopped a few paces out of the front door. She could see his shoulders moving up and down, fast to start with, then slower. He faced her, and he was as cold as he had ever been.

'I don't want to see you again, Cat. Ever.'

SHE CLOSED HER BAG. The house loomed around her. She had always thought of it as small – the six of them had always seemed so cramped together in only two rooms. Now, with everyone gone, the place was too large.

She stepped over to Michael's bed, the same bed which Ma had died on. With the blankets gone, she could see how thin and stained the mattress was. Would the next family who came to live here sleep on it? Would they feel Mother's ghost lying beside them as they closed their eyes?

She sat on the edge of the mattress, rubbing her hand over it as she gazed around the room. Memories fluttered in her mind. She'd been born in this room. So had Michael, but she couldn't remember his birth. She remembered her sisters though, coming into the world one after the other. She remembered Mother's screams, how frightened Cat had been as she'd curled up on the top of the stairs, watching the shadows swirl hectically under the door. A woman from nearby had come to help, as well as Mrs Smith from next door. In the years which had followed, Cat had come to learn that it hadn't taken long for the twins to be born, but on that night it had felt like weeks. Cat had thought she would never see her mother alive again.

The girls had been like little worms, covered in slime and blood, wriggling in the cold. Cat had helped Mrs Smith wipe them clean, and Mrs Smith had told her how to hold them properly. She'd kissed their foreheads, grimacing at their odd smell, and had said she loved them.

'I'll get them back, Ma,' she said now, her voice too loud in the silence. 'I promise.'

Something caught her eye – something shimmering between the floorboards by her feet in the place where the rag rug used to be. She'd burnt the rug in the fire downstairs only yesterday, shuddering as fleas had jumped away from the flames. Now, she got to her knees, bringing her candle with her. In the crack of the floorboards, something smooth and gold caught the light. She touched it with her finger and felt the coolness of it.

She set the candle beside her on the floor and dug into the floorboard. The wood was beginning to rot and splinters stabbed under her nails, but she did not stop, even when blood dripped from her fingertips. With one last tug, it came free.

She held the thin, gold ring in her hand. Mother's wedding band, bent out of shape a little, the gold tarnished. It must have lodged itself in there after it had fallen off Mother's finger that time.

She took it as a sign, a reassurance. Mother was there with her.

She kissed the gold, then slipped the ring into the lining of her case and left the bedroom forever.

She did not linger downstairs – she did not think she would be able to leave if she allowed herself to wallow. So she marched straight to the door and propelled herself into the world outside. She walked away from her home and into the darkness of the night.

'Cat!' Mrs Smith hobbled out of her house, her eyes red, a handkerchief in her hand. 'You're going now?'

'Yes. And thank you for everything, Mrs Smith.'

The old woman dabbed her eyes. 'I'd have you here, but …'

In Mrs Smith's window, the old woman's daughter-in-law watched Cat with a scowl. She was a bitter woman, the bane of Mrs Smith's life, and with a voice so shrill it penetrated streets, let alone walls.

'Don't upset yourself.' Cat rubbed the woman's arm. 'I'll be fine.'

'Have you found yourself somewhere decent? You could stay with us for a few nights until you've got yourself sorted?'

'I'm going to Able Street. I have a room in a house there.'

A shadow crossed Mrs Smith's face. 'Oh, Cat. Come here with us. Come on.'

'No.' Cat could see the snarl in the daughter-in-law's face. 'No, I'll be fine there.'

'But it's–'

'It'll do me for now, just for the moment.'

Mrs Smith grabbed Cat's hand, pulled her close, and whispered into her ear, 'You come to me if there are any problems, you hear. Take no notice of her.'

Cat embraced the woman, smelling the sting of carbolic on her clothes which was as familiar to Cat as her very own face. She sniffed, bit her cheek, and forced herself to be strong.

'Goodbye.'

She turned away before another word could be said.

She knew the streets of the town now the way she imagined that her mother used to. She knew the ones to avoid, the ones where she must pull her cap around her face and stay in the shadows, the ones where she might be permitted to gawp at the public houses and the shop fronts without fear.

It was a winding path through town, and seemingly endless, but eventually the stench of the cut permeated the air. The filthy scent of the canal, and the blackness that seemed to simmer up from the water to mix with the coal smoke in the atmosphere, enveloped her – she was close.

She took the next right and delved into a narrow street. If she were to stretch her arms out, she would be able to touch the bricks, but she kept them glued to her sides – this place was alive with shadows. Indistinguishable shapes scuttled between the gutters. Doors opened and slammed shut.

Babies wailed. All sorts of sinful business took place in black corners.

She shuffled along, head down, her shoes sliding on the muck under her feet until she came to the end of the terraced houses and rapped her knuckles on the last door.

A boy, perhaps eight years of age, opened it, wearing nothing but a tattered rag over his bony frame. His hair was shaved short to his head, showing the lines of his skull.

'Miss Davies? This way.'

He stepped aside, allowing her to enter a thin corridor. The boy's candle was the only light once he shut the door behind her, and it cast shadows in the gloom. She could make out four doors on this floor. The noise of families, of children and babies mewing, of men coughing filled the silence. Cigar smoke spilt from under the nearest doorway and curled at the boy's feet as he stepped through it towards the staircase.

'Up here.'

She followed closely behind him, not wanting to be left in the darkness. Another floor, and another set of doors with the same sounds scratching from behind them. The stench of piss and shit was overwhelming as they passed by one window, and glancing outside she saw the privy below, no doubt shared by the whole house, if not the entire street. She put her hand over her nose and gratefully breathed in the lingering scent of Mrs Smith's clean clothes.

Another staircase, narrower this time, led to the attic. The roof crouched on top of them here, the eaves making her stoop. One door was to her right, and the sound of a woman's business came from behind it; grunts, giggles, moans of false pleasure. Cat blushed, but the boy took no notice. He stood in front of the door to her left.

'Rent upfront.' He held out his hand.

She reached for the purse in her bag. She counted out a

few coins, let them warm in her hands as she wondered whether she could really live in a place like this or whether she should run back to Mrs Smith.

'Staying?' The boy looked her up and down with disinterest.

She tipped the coins into his hand. He pushed the bedroom door open. From her bag, she retrieved the stump of a candle and lit it on the boy's before he ran downstairs, leaving her alone in her room.

By candlelight, she examined the state of things, then quickly wished she had not looked so hard. Animal droppings scattered the bare floorboards. Above the bed, a patch of damp stained the ceiling. The bare mattress was in a worse condition than her mother's old one, with red and yellow and brown stains. She set a blanket over it before she lost her nerve to sleep on it.

There was a washstand with one cracked bowl on it – she would have to use it as a piss pot, for Michael had taken theirs with him. A set of wonky drawers stood in one corner of the room, and she dragged them in front of her door so that no one could get in during the night.

She took her mother's ring and the rest of the blankets out of her bag and curled onto the mattress. Squeezing her eyes shut, she pulled the blankets over her head, held the ring to her face, and wept.

CHAPTER 10

May 1854. Wallingham Hall.

A shower of rice fell onto her. She laughed, exalted, threw her head back, and saw the brightness of the sky. Osborne held her hand – the left one where the diamond ring bulged over her fourth finger – and guided her down the church steps between the row of villagers who called out blessings and well wishes. Two white horses and Osborne's most elegant carriage waited for her. He helped her inside. Her white skirts caught on the latch for a moment, tugging her back, but Osborne released the material and jumped in beside her, grinning, and banged on the carriage roof.

The horses were whipped into action. Cat waved through the window, seeing the villagers pour out of the church and Mr and Mrs Turner standing in the porch, waving back at them.

Osborne grabbed her face and brought his lips to hers. His tongue flickered hard against hers.

'I am the happiest woman alive,' she said, kissing him again, opening her mouth and letting him inside.

'I wish we could go away now,' he said, his voice low. He shifted in his seat, uncomfortable and impatient.

'Soon.' She turned her face to the window, watching as Osborne's estate – their estate – engulfed them.

Wallingham Hall glimmered through the trees, and then the carriage rumbled onto the drive. Cherry and apple blossom mingled with the gravel, blown in from the orchard at the rear of the house, perfuming the air. Spring. A time for new life. She skipped like the lambs in the field towards the door. Osborne was close behind her, struggling to remain sober. He lifted her off her feet.

'What are you doing?' she said.

'For good luck.' He held her in his arms, stepped through the door, and kissed her before he set her on the ground again.

They emerged from the porch and into the great hall. Garlands of flowers draped the walls, the smell of them thick and sickly in the air. Candles burned, though the sunlight which shone through the windows rendered them useless. The grand table had been piled high with food and drink, and the cake – a white, towering masterpiece – sat as the centrepiece.

She gawped at it all. The servants, standing at one end of the room, smiled at her wonderment. She found Cook and thanked her for the cake, and the woman's cheeks blushed scarlet and wobbled as she shook her head, saying it was no trouble at all.

Osborne grabbed Cat's hand and made her sit on one of the two finely carved oak chairs. Then the servants came up, one by one, congratulating them both on their marriage. Nelly was sobbing by the time her turn came and could not get the words out.

'What a silly girl you are,' Osborne said, laughing, and Nelly laughed with him.

Only Mrs Lewis did not smile. She offered some curt congratulations to her master but said nothing to Cat.

Cat felt Osborne stiffen beside her. His lips worked, and she knew, from the months she had spent observing him, that he was angry. She felt him brace, ready to stand and admonish Mrs Lewis.

'Leave it,' Cat whispered, reining him back. 'Do not ruin our day for one bitter maid.'

Outside, the sound of laughter and footsteps crunching over gravel grew louder. 'Our guests have arrived.'

The villagers swamped the hall until the room was bursting with people.

'Should you cut the cake?' Nelly said in Cat's ear as she handed her another glass of wine.

Cat and Osborne sliced the fruitcake, fat raisins tumbling onto the stand, as the crowd cheered. Cook and some maids took the cake away to the kitchens to be sliced and packaged for the guests.

'Congratulations, Osborne,' Mr Turner said for the umpteenth time that afternoon. His white collar was slightly askew, his face pink from the sunshine and the wine. 'Your father would be so happy to see you now.'

Osborne's smile fell. 'Thank you, Walter. I wish he could have been here.'

Mr Turner patted him on the back – nothing else to be said.

'Ma'am?' Nelly again, always like Cat's shadow now. 'Should you get changed?'

Cat kissed Osborne's cheek and slipped through the gathering. On the stairs, she hesitated. The day had somehow managed to be the longest ever, and yet it had passed in the blink of an eye. And it was not over yet.

'Are you all right, ma'am?'

She smiled at Nelly. 'Wonderful.'

Her honeymoon luggage was already packed and in the carriage, and when she entered her chamber, the room seemed oddly bare.

Nelly skipped to the wardrobe and took out the dark grey travelling dress and cloak which had been specially made for this day. She sighed over the silk of the skirt and marvelled at the intricate details woven into the bodice.

Cat stood by the window and gazed at the view. A few of the villagers lingered on the driveway, heads close together as they gossiped. The dogs cavorted amongst them, playing between themselves, sliding on the gravel and sniffing for bits of dropped food.

'What do you know of Osborne's father?' Cat said, unfastening a pearl earring. These last five months, she had managed to bite her tongue whenever the question had tried to come out. Osborne's reactions regarding his father were always precarious, and Cat had not wanted to risk her position at Wallingham by probing him or the staff who might have ratted her out. But now, with her position secure and firmly rooted, she was determined to find out the truth.

'It was before my time here, ma'am,' Nelly said, suddenly serious. She came behind Cat and started taking the pins out of her dress.

'I haven't asked him, you know. He always gets so sad …' or angry, she thought but did not say. 'I would like to know so that I don't upset Osborne in the future.'

She waited, but Nelly remained silent.

'I suppose I will just have to ask him outright and see what happens.'

Nelly took the bait. 'He was killed, so I was told.'

'How?'

'Someone … shot him.'

This, she had not been expecting. What had she thought? Some terrible accident somewhere? A dreadful lingering disease slowly sucking the life from him? A sudden attack making him drop dead in his dinner?

'Who would do such a thing?'

Nelly pulled off Cat's white skirt, avoiding the question.

'Who shot him, Nelly?'

'I was told it was an Irishman.'

The satisfaction of discovering the truth was short-lived. Despite the heat of the day, a chill scratched down her spine.

'Where did he die?'

'Ireland.'

She swayed as Nelly's strong hands fixed the new skirt around her waist. Reaching for the support of the windowsill, she studied the blue sky, the clumps of white cloud building in it, and tried to think why on earth Osborne's father should have been in Ireland at all.

'Why was he over there?'

Nelly shrugged. 'Business? I don't know. As I said, it was before my time. I only heard bits from Mr Dixon and Mrs Lewis, and only when they thought no one was listening.'

'Eavesdropping, Nelly?' Cat teased to try to lighten the mood, though neither of them found her joke amusing.

'I've never heard Master Tomkins talk of it. Mrs Lewis said that Master Tomkins found the whole thing so awful that we were never to mention his father, never to ask any questions, never to speak of him at all. I've had no problem with that, of course. It's his business, his grief. I suppose we all have our different ways of dealing with such things.'

'Mmh.' But Cat was not so certain. Despite the ache in her heart, she would gladly have talked about her mother all day, if anybody had bothered to ask. No – only shame made people want to hide from the truth, and Cat knew all about that.

'Thank you for telling me, Nelly.'

Nelly smiled, and finally, the tension in the room lessened. 'Where is the honeymoon, ma'am?'

'I cannot tell you, Nelly, you know that. You may nag me all you like, but my lips are sealed until we reach the ship.'

'The ship?' Nelly jumped in the air and clapped her hands. 'We are going on a ship!'

Cat laughed with her. 'Yes, yes. But first, you are to post these for me.' Cat retrieved two sealed letters from her dressing table; one to Coventry, the other to Cheshire. 'You must be quick, or else we'll be late.'

Nelly ran from the room, too excited to ask questions. Cat had no intention of telling her that the letters were destined for her sisters, promising them a better life, just as soon as she had returned from Paris.

CHAPTER 11

January 1852. Birmingham.

A DULL THUMP of a headboard against a wall. Moans – pleasure, pain, a mixture of the two? The faint noise of babes crying, of someone stumbling around their rooms unaware of the time, the day, the year. All these sounds were her lullaby now – in the darkest hours of the night, as the sun tickled the morning, as a clock somewhere struck midday. Endless.

Her curtains, half hanging off the wall, allowed in the low, mid-morning light. Curled on her side, holding her stomach, she heard the end of the business next door, the brusque voice of a man who should have already left, the flat call from Ruby that she'll see him soon, rapid footsteps squeaking down the stairs. Then, a knock on her door.

She flinched. No one ever knocked. She raised her head off her pillow, listened, and heard someone sigh.

'It's Ruby.'

Cat sat upright. The room whirled around her and darkened at the edges. 'What do you want?'

The door handle turned. The door came open an inch before it slammed into the chest of drawers.

'Christ's sake!' A murmur. Another sigh. 'Just wanted to see if you were all right. Shan't bother again.' Footsteps retreating.

Cat stumbled to her feet, shoved the drawers to one side, and opened the door. Ruby – small, shoulders no wider than her head, corset-less. She had the wickedest of smiles – her canine tooth always managed to sparkle – and her eyes glimmered as if eternally lit by a fire. A bottle of gin, half-drunk, swung in her hand.

'Want some?'

Cat's tongue ached. She took the bottle and poured the liquid inside her, feeling the cracks of her mouth soften and sting. She stopped for air and wiped her hand across her lips.

A knife stabbed into her skull, then sawed down into her right eye. The wall came behind her. She had the sensation of falling …

'Sit down.'

She felt Ruby's hot hands push on her shoulders, and then the bed came underneath her, solid and reassuring.

Ruby took the bottle back, drank, and slumped at Cat's feet. 'We've never had a proper chat, have we?'

The room was coming back into focus now. The knife was slowly sliding out of her head. She rested against the headboard so she could observe her uninvited guest.

'I ain't heard you go out for days now.' Ruby said it as a question as her gaze lighted over her surroundings. 'When was the last time you ate something?'

The reminder of food made Cat's stomach pound. She pushed her arms into the hollow of it.

'Thought you worked at Bronson's?'

'I do.' Cat's voice cracked; she had not used it for days.

'You sick or something? You look it.'

'Less hours.'

'Oh.' It came out long, like how a woman might respond to scrap of gossip from her neighbour. 'They got you on the casual?'

Cat nodded. The gin had brought back some of her senses. There was a stench coming from somewhere. She sniffed, searching, until she realised it was her piss pot under the bed. She hadn't emptied it since … she tried to think, but it hurt to do so. She would have blushed, but her blood seemed as frozen as the ice on the window.

Ruby jumped to her feet and skipped out of Cat's room. Cat watched her become a shadow in the gloom of the corridor, then saw her bedroom door open. Daylight glowed through the smoke, and Cat could make out the rugs on Ruby's floor, the edge of a bed that took up all of the space. There was the sound of something sliding open, then Ruby's silhouette returned, and the girl was in Cat's room once again, a stained cloth bag in her hands.

'Have some of this.'

Cat pushed her fingers into the opening and felt the crust of bread. It was in her mouth, her teeth chewing through it and threatening to break, before she realised. Saliva slithered between her gums once more. She closed her eyes, feeling the bread soften over her tongue, turning to gloop. With all her effort, she swallowed, and the food bumped down her throat.

'Better?' Ruby smiled as Cat continued to eat. With only a mouthful left, Ruby snatched the crust back and ate the last bit herself. 'You ever thought of … you know? The oldest trick in the world?'

Cat pulled her feet away from Ruby's skirts. 'No.'

'I was like you, you know. Just like you. No work. No man. No food. Can't go without my food, I get nasty.'

'I would never–'

'You would never do nothing.' Ruby's eyes hardened. 'Don't think yourself better than the rest of us here, Miss Catherine. We're all getting by in our own way. And I ain't hurting anyone, the opposite, actually.'

Cat thought of the bruises, the cuts on Ruby's brows, the sores that appeared on her lips from time to time. She might not be hurting anyone, but they were hurting her.

'We could pair up, you and me.' The smile returned; the glint. 'Set ourselves up in a business, of sorts.'

'No.'

'They'd pay well for you. Clean. Pure?'

'Yes.'

Ruby threw her head back and laughed. 'You're the first virgin I've seen for years.'

'Ben,' Cat said, reminding Ruby of the boy who looked after the house.

'Even Ben.'

'If you're going to lie to me, you can get out.'

'I ain't lying to you. We're all whores eventually, Cat. Even you.'

Ruby slapped her thighs and stood. 'I'll be waiting for your knock.'

She flounced out of the room, shutting the door behind her.

Cat ran for the drawers and dragged them back into place, feeling safe once more. She returned to her sour sheets and hoped that she would sleep until she was next needed for work.

SHE PUSHED the copper strip along. The lever went down, the

metal cut. She pushed the strip up again. Lever. Cut. The familiar sounds of machinery and little feet. The dust particles filtering into her nose, drying out the crevices of her mouth, tickling her lungs. She coughed, trying to dislodge something and only making it worse. The cough continued. She felt her throat rip. The water in her eyes blinded her. There was no air to breathe.

She released the strip of metal, held her hands over her face and spluttered, feeling the flecks of blood and spittle fly onto her palms until she found her breath once more. She inhaled slowly, feeling the air snag on something. She pushed her fingers into her eyes, brushed away the wetness. She sat upright and returned to her machine.

A dozen sets of eyes stared at her. She would not look at them. She pushed the copper along…

Dark trousers came before her. She raised her eyes to find Mr Criton above her. From this angle, she could see straight up his hooked nose. His eyes seemed crossed as he glared down at her.

'You're slow, Miss Davies.'

'Sorry, sir, I had a cough.'

'Before that.' He pointed at the circles she had cut. 'Half of what you should be doing.'

She glanced at her neighbours, trying to see their work piles, but her eyes would not focus.

'Sorry, sir, I–'

'I don't want to hear an excuse, Miss Davies. Hurry up, or you'll have no hours at all.' He walked away, examining the workbenches as he went. The women doubled their speed.

The metal strip blurred before her, but there was no time to stop. She moved on, pressing and cutting, her fingers coming perilously close to catching in the vice. She would have lost a finger gladly if it meant her job would be guaranteed.

The day was long. She knew she was slowing, but as hard as she tried to hasten, her hands would not move to her command. The sky outside had darkened hours ago, and with it, she had begun to shiver. Her fingers were uncontrollable. The circles were deformed, unusable. Her neighbour watched her, and winced as Cat struggled, but offered no help.

Cat glanced at Mr Criton and found him staring at her. She forced herself to continue, wiped the cold sweat off her forehead, and bit her lip when her stomach churned in agony. She worked like that until he rang the bell, at which point she dropped over her machine, exhausted. Around her, women jumped to their feet and scurried away. Voices chattered, heavy feet plodded along the wooden boards, and bodies brushed past her.

There was no point trying to walk amidst them; she would get trampled. So, she waited for the crowd to thin. She rested her cheek on her cold, hard machine, and let her sore eyelids finally fall...

Something dug into her shoulder. She had the strange sensation of being surrounded by silence when there should have been noise and, raising her head, she realized her cheek was numb. Looking up, she saw Mr Criton's nose again, his pale lips hidden in the bush of his moustache.

'You aren't needed tomorrow, Miss Davies. Come back when you can work properly.'

'Please, sir–'

'Go home.' He walked away.

Fingers of panic raced over her spine as she realised she was all alone. The gas lights had been turned off, and darkness surrounded her. Machinery crouched in the shadows, like giant spiders, and the silence was overwhelming.

It was this unnatural fear which made her flee the shop floor, crashing into benches and tables as she ran, stumbling down the staircase until she emerged outside. Her heart beat inside her chest as fast as sparrows' wings.

Her legs shook. The ground seemed too close. She stretched out her arms and felt sharp bricks to her left. She collapsed against them, her body suddenly too heavy to lift all by herself. She worked her fingertips into the gaps of cement and dragged herself along, moving an inch at a time.

She focused on the streetlamp in the distance. If she reached it, she would be out in the openness of town. She would be free.

The light swayed and flickered in her vision, but she kept pushing on as darkness surrounded the yellow, glowing dot.

Squinting, she saw a figure standing under the light. She tried to make it out, but it was fuzzy around the edges.

She blinked. Then blinked again, the figure now starting to clarify. Strands of coarse hair stuck up from the figure's head, shining like toffee. The waist was cinched in tight. Slim ankles were visible beneath a short skirt. The face was lined and soft, like a white loaf of bread. Blue eyes shone.

Gently, a hand reached for Cat, reached for her cap. Warm fingers brushed against her cheek as her cap was pulled low, and her shawl was tightened around her neck. Velvet lips kissed her forehead.

'Ma,' Cat whispered, and let herself fall into her mother's open arms.

The ground slammed into her – something cracked somewhere, but she felt nothing of the physical pain. Her heart was breaking as she searched for her mother only to find that she had vanished; the lamplight showed only moths circling around its covered flame.

She grappled for the lamp post. The iron bit into her hands and stung the grazes on her palms. She pulled and pulled, trying to stand, but her legs buckled each time her feet found sure footing.

She slumped on the ground. In the oasis of the lamplight, the world around her was blacker than ever. Sounds clicked and ticked here and there, distant then close. She shrank away from them, fearing them to be rats or men. She held onto the streetlamp like a raft in the middle of the sea.

Death came for her. She saw it moving in the space beyond her vision. A cold death. A brutal death. A long death. She would not see the light again.

She squeezed her eyes shut and thought of Lottie and Helen, warm somewhere she hoped, perhaps beside a huge kitchen fire or eating their supper with their friends. She wished they were happy and ached at how she did not know this for a fact. She had failed her mother. She had abandoned her sisters. Who would tell them that she had died alone on the street? Who would find her body? Would anybody care at all?

Death tapped her arm. She gasped and hid her face from it. She was not ready to go yet. She would not let herself be taken.

Death gripped her elbow.

'No,' she said. She thought she had screamed it, but the sound was distant even in her own ears.

Death put her arm around its shoulder and lifted her to her feet. The ground slipped beneath her shoes, but Death caught her by the waist. It made her walk, and she opened her eyes to find herself being moved from the light into the darkness.

'Please ...'

'You'll be safe with me.' Death's voice was steady and low. Its accent was unusual.

'Where?'

'My place.'

She pushed her eyes open, suddenly alert. It was not

Death who had a tight hold of her, it was a man. She squirmed under his grip.

'Stop that!'

'Let go!'

It was all a rush of arms and hands and jackets and skirts and legs. Then bricks slammed behind her back, her hands were pinned to her sides, and a body crushed against her. Breathing hard with panic, she inhaled someone else's air and tasted their sourness on her tongue. A foreign mouth was too close to her own. She tried to pull her head back, but the wall trapped her.

'Steady now,' the mouth said.

She stilled, blinked. Another streetlight not too far away lit the face before her in monotone shades. She saw the greyness of smooth lips, a spattering of black dots on a pale cheek, the white speck of light caught in the glassiness of an eyeball. Beneath the rim of a hat, she made out the shadow of close-cropped hair.

'I won't hurt you, I promise,' the man said. 'All right?'

It was not all right, but she did not have the confidence to protest.

'What's your name?'

'Cat.'

The corner of his lips rose. 'Nice to put a name to the face. I want to help you, Cat.'

'Why?'

She felt him shrug. She waited for his eyes to roll down, the way that men's eyes always did, but he kept looking into her face. 'You seem like you need it.'

CHAPTER 12

June 1854. Wallingham Hall.

THE TENSION FROM THE LONG, jolting journey eased out of her shoulders as the carriage rolled onto the drive.

Home. Wallingham Hall.

It really was a lovely house. Purple wisteria hung onto the honey-coloured stone and draped over the doorway, the windows sparkled in the sunshine, and smoke rose from the kitchen chimney. So grand yet so cosy. And now her name would be forever etched onto its history; a factory worker amidst the names of the gentry!

Osborne grasped her hand and smiled at her as the line of servants came into view. The driver slowed the horse, then with a click, the carriage halted.

Nelly's voice boomed as the girl dismounted. Boxes! Be careful with those boxes! With glee she ordered the young lads about, buzzing between them all, her finger poking in front of their faces menacingly.

There really were so many boxes! All of them filled with new dresses, hats, shoes, lampshades, oil paintings. A whole host of pink frilly boxes and leather cases and wooden chests brimming with Paris's finest, the perfume of French shops still clinging to them.

Paris! She had never seen anywhere so beautiful. Streets of white and gold, rising into blue skies. Avenues of pink blossom. Gardens shaped like Greek statues. Golden carriages. Ballrooms and drawing rooms and parlours and hotels, every surface gilded and bursting with bouquets. The splendour at first had been overwhelming, then slightly nauseating.

'Are you happy to be home?' Osborne said, taking her hand once more and guiding her towards the door.

'Delighted.'

They reached the line of waiting servants who bowed or curtseyed to their masters, and Osborne took up conversation with them about the honeymoon. They smiled at him, eating up his words, their eyes shining as they imagined the golden city. He told them how everyone had adored his wife, had found her charming and beguiling, and the servants smiled on Cat as if they were responsible for her making. All, but one.

'Mrs Lewis, I trust there were no problems while we were away?'

'No.' Mrs Lewis said, her eyes focusing somewhere behind Cat's shoulder. 'I run a good household here.'

'Quite.' Cat turned to Osborne. 'I must see to the luggage. I shall be in my room.'

'I thought we might take some tea?'

'Later,' she kissed him on the cheek, and the servants looked away, 'once everything is sorted. I would hate anything to be ruined. Mrs Lewis, come along.'

'SIT DOWN.' Cat ushered Mrs Lewis inside.

'I'm fine standing.' Mrs Lewis crossed her hands over her chest and stood rigidly before the empty grate.

'Very well. Nelly, would you give us a moment?' Nelly, who had been studiously emptying the boxes, now bobbed a curtsey and somewhat reluctantly left Cat's bedchamber.

Cat strolled towards the window. Below, the boys were still unloading more boxes. The carriage from above was just as spectacular as on the ground, and the white horses patiently waited for a brush down and a drink.

'A grand day, isn't it?'

'Yes.'

'Everyone is so happy for our return,' she faced Mrs Lewis, 'apart from you.'

'I am happy that the master has come home.'

'But not me.'

Mrs Lewis's lips quivered as if her words were itching to come out.

'You don't like me, Mrs Lewis?'

Silence. Her chin was hard and stubborn.

Cat laughed. 'What a silly question. Why should your opinion of me matter?'

Mrs Lewis's cheeks flared red; the woman was so easy to rile. Her eyes, which had lowered, now rose to stare at Cat. 'You're right. I don't like you. I don't trust you.'

'I am Osborne's wife.'

'You have bewitched him.'

'So now I am a witch? I thought I was just a button-maker's daughter?'

Mrs Lewis stepped forward, a snarl on her lips. 'I've been at this house longer than anyone here. I've seen Master

Tomkins come into this world, I've watched him grow, I've seen him grieve. His heart is pure.'

Though he has blood on his hands, Cat thought, but she did not say it. 'I know.'

'You know exactly how much of a fool the man is. I have wished for him to find love, but with you? Never with the likes of you.'

'The likes of me?'

'There's something …' she scrutinised Cat's face. Cat stepped back. 'There's something not right about you.'

'I don't want him for his money.'

'Not only. And that's what troubles me. There's something more. There's a darkness around you.'

Cat pulled her gaze away from the woman and looked out of the glass. She held onto the windowsill for support.

'I hear you praying at night.' Mrs Lewis came behind Cat, her voice hissing over Cat's shoulder. 'I come and stand by your door. So many sins … I wonder what they are? I wonder if Master Tomkins would still love you if he knew them all.'

'Enough.' Cat turned on her, making her step back. She forced a smile to her lips. 'I love Osborne very much. He has saved me, in more ways than one, as you and he and all the world knows. I am truly honoured that he has taken me for his wife.'

For one awful moment, Cat thought Mrs Lewis might spit at her, but then she seemed to compose herself. Cat inhaled, and did not try to conceal the smugness in her voice – she had been waiting for this day for months.

'And in doing so, he has made me the lady of this house. You understand, Mrs Lewis, that for the house to run smoothly, there must be no angst between the lady and her staff.'

Mrs Lewis fidgeted, her eyebrows creased together.

'So I am sad to say that I fear your time here has come to an end.'

The uncomprehending look on Mrs Lewis's face was satisfaction for all the months Cat had endured the woman's hostility and condescension.

'How could I possibly keep you as a housekeeper after what you have just told me?'

'You wanted the truth.'

'Yes, and now I have it. Not only do you think yourself above me, but you spy on me and accuse me of sin. How could you want to work for somebody such as me?'

'I work for Master Tomkins.'

'You work for me.' Cat prowled towards her. 'You will be gone by this time next week.'

Mrs Lewis's lips opened and shut, her eyes wide in shock.

'You can't. I've been here–'

'For years, yes, I know.'

'Master Tomkins–'

'Agrees with me.'

Mrs Lewis chewed her lips; Cat thought she might be about to cry, so before that could happen, Cat opened the door and gestured for her to go. The hurt on Mrs Lewis's face transformed to rage.

'You're a witch! And a whore.'

From the doorway, Cat heard footsteps coming up the stairs; she knew them for Osborne's. 'Please control yourself, Mrs Lewis, you are humiliating yourself.'

'I will not be told how to behave by a factory girl!'

Osborne's pace grew faster, his frown deep. Cat lowered her gaze, put her hands to her eyes.

'Please, Mrs Lewis …'

'You do not fool me, Catherine Davies. You will ruin this house, and you will ruin Master Tomkins.'

Osborne ran into the room, barging past Cat and coming

face to face with the housekeeper. Mrs Lewis froze, her mouth agape, her skin whitening. She dropped into a curtsey. 'Master Tomkins.'

'Get out.'

Cat reached for his arm, sniffing back tears. 'Osborne, don't.'

'Get out, Mrs Lewis!'

'Sir, I am–'

'Gone. I will have you out of this house by nightfall.'

'Osborne no!'

'Out!'

Mrs Lewis wailed as she fled the room.

Osborne turned to Cat and pulled her into his arms. She rested her cheek against his sun-warmed jacket and cried a little longer. Osborne brushed away her tears.

'Don't let the old hag upset you, my love. You won't ever have to see her again.'

'Where will she go?'

'Damned if I know. Or care.'

'You will give her a reference, though, won't you?' Despite her contempt for the woman, Cat did not want to see her destitute. She would not wish the workhouse on anyone.

'I don't see why I should.'

'Please Osborne.'

He sighed, and his anger melted. 'I will do whatever makes you happy. And I will make sure the ungrateful woman knows it was you who persuaded me, though I would have cast her onto the streets.'

She wrapped her arms around his neck and brought his face down to hers. 'Thank you,' she whispered, her lips brushing against his ear lobe. She pushed the door shut behind them and led him towards the bed.

CAT STOOD in front of the open window, praying for a breeze. To her left, Nelly huffed as she sat on the chair, sewing. All morning, the sheen of sweat had not left the girl's brow, and she was grumpy about everything. In the field below, the sheep huddled together, unsure of the day. The air was too close, the clouds too grey and heavy. Even the flies seemed doped on laudanum, buzzing into the windowpanes and falling onto their backs. She thought she heard a rumble of thunder somewhere in the distance, but it could just have been the crunch of gravel under Mrs Lewis's boots.

Mrs Lewis threw her suitcase into the back of Osborne's black Brougham, then trudged to the carriage door and hesitated, her fingers resting on the handle. She turned towards the house and gazed at the property, and as she lifted her head to take it all in, Cat saw her face. Her eyes were wet and red. Her chin wobbled as she cried. She seemed so small and lost – like a little girl being shunned from her home.

But then she saw Cat in the window. The softness vanished. She blinked the tears away and straightened her spine. After the slightest of curtseys, she turned back to the carriage and slammed the door shut behind her. The driver whipped the horse into action. Gravel churned under the wheels until the Brougham had rounded the side of the house and disappeared.

A spot of rain hit the windowsill, splashing onto Cat's arm. The sky had morphed into a giant bruise as if God had punched it. Another drop, fat and heavy. And then the patter turned into a downpour, and the sheep in the field shuffled under the chestnut trees for protection. A white flash broke over the land, and then thunder roared. The world sounded as if it was splitting.

Mrs Lewis would not have a pleasant journey all the way to Scotland.

CHAPTER 13

January 1852. Birmingham.

IN HER DELIRIUM, she didn't recognise where she was. It was like she was a child again – the streets too dark to seem real, the shadows like demons waiting to pounce. She held onto the man's coat, feeling the greasiness of the wool under her fingertips which reminded her of Father and Michael.

He led her onwards. Hundreds of feet had churned the ice on the road into sludge, the kind that crunched under her shoes and left her stockings wet and brown. By the time he opened the door to a house, her eyes were half shut, her body so cold and numb that it did not feel as if it belonged to her.

He helped her up the set of stairs. She thought how quiet the place was and how the stairs seemed sturdier than those in her own lodgings. There was paper on the walls, curling at the edges, but still – there was paper on the walls!

He opened another door on the first floor and brought

her into his room. It was twice the size of hers. The bed was a good foot wider than her own. Two wooden chairs and a small table sat before the grate, and the man placed her on a chair as he stoked the fire and made the flames high. He pulled her closer to the heat, then set a kettle of water to boil.

'Your name?' Her skin was starting to prickle; she was thawing.

He put a loaf of bread, a hunk of cheese, and a pot of dripping on the table, along with two cracked plates and a knife.

'John.'

He sliced the bread thickly, poured himself a cup of beer, and when the water had boiled, made her some tea. She held the hot cup between her hands, feeling the stab of her blood warming in her veins.

She waited for him to eat first, then with all the dignity she could muster, she spread her slice of bread with dripping and ate.

With food now in her belly, her eyes began to droop, her jaw slackened, and her head dropped onto her chest. She woke with a start and found John watching her.

She blinked the tiredness away. 'John, who?'

'Murphy,' he said, smiling.

She didn't like to be laughed at. Her voice came out like daggers.

'From where?'

'Ireland.'

'Why are you here?'

'I'm a burnisher at Bronson's.'

She did not give herself time to consider. 'No, I meant, why are you here in Birmingham? Why did you come here?'

His smile fell. 'Hard times at home.'

She took the final bite of bread. Looking around, she noticed a cross on the mantelpiece wrapped in rosary beads.

There was a tiny framed painting of a woman beside the cross, and even from here, she could see that the artist had not been talented; the features were too large and obscure. She turned back to the table and found John scowling at her.

'I haven't seen you at Bronson's,' she said, eyeing up the rest of the loaf. Her stomach yearned for more now that it had been given a taste.

He drank from his cup and leaned back in his chair. 'You saw me a few months ago.'

'Did I?' She would not admit that she thought she recognized him – the man who had bumped into her after Helen and Lottie had lost their jobs. 'I don't remember.'

He grinned. She sipped her tea.

'A burnisher, you said?'

'That's right.'

'How long have you worked there?'

'Four years now.'

She raised her eyebrows, then shrugged. 'It's a big factory. I don't know half the people there.'

'You're a cutter.'

She swallowed, raised herself a little higher in her chair. 'Yes.'

'I've seen you.'

She breathed in deep, her mind racing, trying to work out how to play this. He was a stranger to her, an Irishman. She was alone with him in his rooms. Trapped.

She cursed herself for her stupidity.

She pushed out her chair. 'Thank you for the tea and the food, Mr Murphy.' She tried to stand.

'Sit.' He said it as if he was speaking to a dog, his hand out in front of her legs commanding her to stay down.

'I must get home.'

'Why?' He smirked, again. 'Why would you want to go back there tonight?'

'Because ...' She stood, pushing past his hand, her skin shivering when she realised he knew where she lived.

'I have food here, more tea, beer if you want some?' He held his cup to her, but she shook her head. 'It's nicer here, isn't it?'

'How do you know?'

'I've seen you on my way home.'

She strode for the door, but he leapt in front of her, blocking her way.

'Let me out.'

'Forgive me.' His breath came quickly. The smirk was lost. 'I'm sorry. I didn't mean to scare you.'

'I am not the type of girl you think I am.'

'No?'

'No,' she said, between gritted teeth, staring him down.

He dropped his gaze. 'I only want to help.'

'In return for what?'

'Nothing, I swear.' He stepped away from the door. She took the cold handle and turned it.

'Cat, there's more food and drink here. You've no need to stay, but I'll walk you home if you choose to go.'

'Why?'

He shrugged. 'Because you're exactly the type of girl I thought you were. The type who should not walk the streets of town on their own at night.'

SHE KNOCKED ON THE DOOR — three little taps; their code. John opened it with a smile. He'd cleaned himself up after his shift, set the table with bread and cheese and beer, and stoked the fire. The bed was made, the curtains drawn.

'Come in.'

She went straight to her seat beside the grate and warmed her hands over the flames. She took off her damp shoes and put them before the fire so they would dry out by the time she had to walk home again.

John cut the bread, and they ate together, talking about the news of the factory. She had only been called into work twice in the three weeks that had passed since Mr Criton had said she was not needed, and although she had worked better since then, cutting like all the other women, her hours had still not improved. But now she had John, who was happy to share his tea with her in exchange for company and a smile.

'Who is that?' she said, her mouth full, as she pointed at the painting on the mantelpiece. Over the last few weeks he had been softening, his grin not quite as calculated, throwing her titbits of information about his life in Ireland. But he had never mentioned the woman in the painting.

His eyes now glazed over. He dropped them to his plate. 'My mother.'

'Oh.' Cat nodded, a warm buzz inside her. She had thought it might have been his sweetheart.

'It's a shite painting.'

'It's not.'

'It is, and I know you think so too. The artist didn't have much to go on.'

She raised her eyebrow.

'It was my description of her.'

'Why didn't she sit for him?'

'Because she was dead two years by then,' John snapped and tore into his food, and silence filled the room. Cat wished she had not asked.

'Sorry.' John shook his head. He sighed and finally looked at the bad replica of his mother. 'I just wanted something to remember her by.'

Cat had never seen him so vulnerable. She would have taken his hand and tried to comfort him, but shyness made her keep still. 'I think it's a lovely thing to do.'

He ripped into the bread again and stuffed a handful into his mouth.

'How did she die?'

'Influenza. She was so weak from … everything going on. She hadn't the strength to fight it.'

'My ma was the same.' An image of Cat's dead mother flashed before her. She shook it away. 'What about the rest of your family? Your father? Do you have brothers or sisters?'

'Two brothers. Younger than me.'

'Where are they?'

'In Ireland.'

'Are they coming over here soon?'

'Not here. America.'

'America! Why would they want to go there?'

'Opportunities. You can be anything you want to be over there.'

'There are opportunities here.'

He sneered and swigged his beer.

'When will you see them if they go to America?'

He slammed his cup on the table and laughed. 'You ask so many questions, Cat!'

She blushed, shrunk back, but then his hand was on hers, rough and smooth at the same time. His eyes darted between her and the table, his thumb rubbing almost painfully over her skin as if he was … nervous? Surely not. Nervous was not a word she had ever associated with John.

'I heard it was bad over there?' she whispered, nervous now herself for bringing up his past again, but he did not lash out. His eyes misted slightly as he stared at the floor.

'You couldn't imagine.'

'Tell me,' she breathed. She so desperately wanted to know more about him.

He sucked his lower lip between his teeth and nibbled it

for a moment as if deciding whether to speak or not. He took a long, shuddering breath.

'Corpses in the streets ... people just lying there, right in front of you. In ditches, doorways, on the roadside. You've never seen anything like it.'

She'd heard tales of the horrors in Ireland, as well as arguments to say the whole thing was a lie. She felt the blood rush to her cheeks at how she'd thought it all a bit of a drama – every country had its problems, didn't it – what made Ireland so special? How could she have been so stupid?

'The dead were walking, that's what it looked like,' John continued. 'People were nothing more than bones. All trying to get to the docks, to the ships, and dying on the way.'

'What happened to you?'

'We were farmers.' John shrugged as if that should have been enough of an explanation. 'I thought we'd be all right at first. I got work doing the roads. Pa joined me too. But it just wasn't enough. We couldn't pay the rent, like everyone else.'

'You were evicted?'

He laughed, though there was no humour in it. 'They burnt our cottage. All of our cottages – us tenants. Made us watch.'

She grasped his hand harder and wished she could pull him into her arms. She could see him weakening, the memories threatening to make him crumble ...

'So, we moved on. Looking for work, for charity, like everyone else.'

'Your mother? When did she ...?'

'Mothers are so selfless, aren't they? She hadn't eaten for weeks.' He shook his head and brushed his fingers over his eyes. 'She died in a priest's house. He'd let us stay for a night. She never woke up.'

He dropped his head. Cat would not have known he was

crying if she had not noticed the tears which splattered against his trousers.

'I'm so sorry, John.'

He sniffed, then jerked his head up and scratched the tears off his cheeks. 'He buried her for nothing. He was a good man.'

'And then?'

'We carried on. But it was too much for Pa. The workhouse took us in, but we'd have been better on the streets. Pa didn't last a week in there.'

'He died in the workhouse?' she said, horrified.

His eyes glazed over as he remembered. 'I've been to Hell, Cat. It isn't fire and boiling pots and all that shite. It's hunger so bad you feel like nails are tearing out your guts. It's the stench of disease clawing into your nostrils and down your throat. It's babies sucking at their dead mother's breast. It's bodies piled on top of bodies in pits in the earth, rotting before they're even covered over …'

She hugged him tightly. She didn't care if it was the proper thing to do. She couldn't bear to listen to anymore, to imagine him so tortured. She held his head against her chest and pressed her lips into his short, spikey hair, wishing she could squeeze all those terrible memories out of his mind.

'I have to get them out, Cat,' he said between sobs. She knew he meant his brothers. 'I promised them when I left. I said I'd get them a new life.'

She cradled his face and made him look at her. 'You will.'

Gently, she wiped the tears off his face. His eyes were beginning to dry, and they were the palest, most beautiful shade of blue she had ever seen.

She felt something … strange. A warmth inside her. The sickness she had been feeling changed into something else – like a fluttering sensation.

His face came closer to hers, and his breath traced over

her lips. Just an inch away … she closed her eyes. His lips touched hers for a second, and then they were gone.

She opened her eyes to see him watching her, assessing her. She kissed him again, longer this time, and suddenly his hands dug into her hips. He lifted her off her feet, carried her to the bed, and lay her down. He hesitated only a moment.

CHAPTER 14

June 1854. Wallingham Hall.

OSBORNE HAD BEEN absent all morning. After midday she sought him out, finding him in his study. The curtains were shut, and the candles lit, setting the room in a sick, yellow light. His hair was unbrushed, his shirt undone and collarless, and he hunched over his desk surveying papers which splayed messily before him.

'May I come in?'

He frowned at her for a moment, as if he was struggling to place who she was, then his face relaxed. 'Please do.'

She shut the door behind her. The room smelt of ink and paper dust as if it had been shut up for too long. She drew back the curtains and allowed in the sunshine. She shoved the windows wide open, noticing how they stuck as if they had not been opened for years. The sound of bees in the wisteria around the pane filled the room.

Osborne winced at the light and glanced at the clock on the mantelpiece. 'Sorry, my love, I had no idea of the time.'

He pulled her to him, sat her on his knee, and rested his hand on her thigh.

'I do not want to disturb you if you are busy.'

He leant into her neck, nuzzling his nose against her soft flesh. 'You are a most welcome distraction.'

She kissed him and let his hand roam over her bodice.

'Are you happy?' he whispered into her ear.

'That's a silly question, Osborne. How could I not be happy? Even the new housekeeper delights me.'

Osborne laughed, then rested back in his chair and gazed at her. 'I am the happiest man on this earth.'

She swept her fingers down his cheek. He looked tired as if nightmares still lingered in his eyes.

'I cannot wait for this place to be filled with children,' she said. 'The sound of laughter in the hallways, little feet stomping, making the chandeliers sway.' She placed his palm against her stomach. 'Soon.'

His eyebrows raised, his eyes widened. She looked away.

'I didn't mean to say that … Nothing has changed for me yet.'

He sighed, then embraced her. 'We have plenty of time.'

She wriggled and giggled in his lap as his fingers traced over her skin, shifting against him until she felt him underneath her skirts. He pressed his lips against the back of her neck, his teeth grazing her skin, and she moaned.

From this angle, she saw the papers on his desk. The words were a blur for a while, all black letters, slanted – financial figures that made no sense.

'I am glad I have cheered you,' she said, facing him once more. He was flushed, ready for action, but she only kissed his forehead. He sniffed, rearranged himself, and sobered when he knew there would be no passion just yet.

'You looked so serious when I came in. Is everything all right?'

He raked his fingers through his hair and came to his papers. 'Yes.'

'There are no … problems? With the house?'

'Not at all.'

She would try a different approach. She glanced over the desk. 'I have never seen so many papers. I could never understand business as you do.'

He held her hand. 'You will never need to. You will never have to worry again.'

'I would like to help, though, if I could, if only to be someone you can share your burdens with.'

'In truth, there are no burdens.' He gestured at the papers. 'Everything is well. The land overseas is flourishing.'

She stalled. 'Overseas? I thought Wallingham was everything you owned.'

'We have over a thousand acres in Ireland.'

She swallowed, breathed in deep. She used the desk to steady herself, hoping it looked as if she was merely coming for a closer look at the papers. 'How long have you had land over there?'

He blew through his teeth. 'A hundred years and more.'

'What do you use it for?'

'Farming. Mainly beef and sheep. The land is supposed to produce good-tasting meat.'

She perched on the edge of the desk. 'What is it like over there?'

He shrugged. 'Never been.'

'You've never been to your own land?'

A hardness came onto his features, his mouth set. He folded his arms across his chest. 'Why should that matter?'

'Because …'

'Why should I visit that God-forsaken place?'

The room moved around her. The heady scent of wisteria and climbing roses suddenly seemed too sickly, as if sugar was being poured into her nose. She was clammy from the closeness of the walls.

'Are you well, Catherine?'

'I am a little light-headed.'

He came to her side and held her by the elbows. 'Perhaps you should lie down.'

'Yes. I think I will.'

He kissed her cheek then called for Nelly. The girl appeared in an instant, and he handed Cat over to her. 'Get well soon, my love.'

CHAPTER 15

June 1852. Birmingham.

THE SMELL of the town blew in through the open window. The thin curtains curled and looked pretty in the white light of morning. The house was hushed. There was nothing sweeter than a Sunday morning when the world seemed to slow and catch its breath.

Cat rested her head on John's bare chest and played with the red hairs across his skin. Looking up, she noticed the stubble on his chin, too long. He would shave tonight, ready for work in the morning. How she loved watching him shave! He was always so gentle with the razor, so particular and neat as he gazed at himself in the cracked looking glass above the washstand.

'You're staring,' he said, his lips barely moving.

'Sorry.' She snuggled into his chest again.

It could be like this, she thought. It could be like this forever, just John and Cat.

'I wish we could be married, John.' It was a whisper, a breath.

'You know I've not the money for it.'

She sighed. Lots of people, who had not a penny to put together, were married. Did he think she needed a diamond ring? A posh do somewhere? She would have been happy getting married in a hedgerow.

'You know we are married in my mind,' he said. 'I would not have anyone but you.'

'I don't need anything much, John–'

'It should be enough what we have now. Why would you want to ruin this?'

'I don't.' She gripped him tighter. 'It is enough. But I want to be a wife, John, before God. I know my wages are little, but yours are … better. We could live just as we are now but as man and wife. I could keep this place for you, and I could raise our children.'

The words lingered between them.

'I've not the money.'

'Not right now, but we could save. Your wages are triple mine.'

'I don't keep all of it.'

Half of it he sent to his brothers, he had already told her, several times.

'Why don't they just come over here for now? What's the rush with America?'

He stiffened underneath her, then raised himself. She slid away from him. 'I've told you. I'm not bringing them to this shithole.'

'Just for a while. Not forever.'

'I said no. It's my money, and I'll do what I like with it.'

'But what about us, John? What about me?' She heard

herself whining and wished she could stop herself, but lately, her passions were uncontrollable – moments of ecstasy followed by a deep, crushing sadness. She felt rages burning inside her, spewing out of her mouth when she least expected it. 'Why would they want you to live like this and be unhappy? Why can't they just come here and work themselves?'

The bed rocked, her body tipped, and suddenly John was on top of her, his hand tight around her throat. His fingers dug into her flesh until the pulse in her head felt as if it would burst through her skin.

'You will not talk about my family like that.'

She gasped for air, her lungs burning, and pulled on his arm until he broke away from her. She rolled onto her side, feeling the soreness of her throat, and gulped the air. Black dots sparked in her vision. The breeze from the window clawed against the sweat on her back, rancid and sticky.

She heard John walk across the room, the clink of a bottle against a cup, liquid pouring into a glass. She flinched when he touched her shoulder.

'Have this,' he said, gentle again, holding the glass before her.

She rolled back and pushed herself up the bed. The glass shook as she held it, the gin sloshing at the bottom of it. Hot tears pricked the corners of her eyes, but she brushed them away discreetly as John sat on the edge of the bed. The gin scorched her throat as it slid inside her.

'Sorry.' He stretched out his fingers, then clamped them between his legs. 'I shouldn't have. It's just … my family, you know?'

'I shouldn't have said anything,' she whispered. Her throat hurt too much to speak properly.

'I want a better life for them Cat. There's nothing but smog and poverty here. I want us all to be free.'

A tear ran down his cheek and dripped onto his trouser leg. She crawled over to him and wrapped her arms around him, no longer feeling her own pain.

'We need more money.'

'What can I do?' she said against his scalp.

He shook his head.

'I'm on so few hours.' She silently cursed Mr Criton for ruining her life yet again. 'Look, why don't I just move in with you here? I wouldn't have to pay for my room then. I could give that money to you.'

'No. People would say things.'

'I don't care.'

'You do.' He met her gaze. He was right, of course. No matter how much she loved him, she kept him a secret from everyone. She did not want to be known as that sort of woman.

'And I won't take it from you anyway.'

She turned his face towards her and kissed him. 'I would give you anything, John. I would give you everything I had.'

He smiled – she was forgiven for her earlier selfishness.

'I know you would.'

CHAPTER 16

June 1854. Wallingham Hall.

OSBORNE BIT INTO A STRAWBERRY. Sweetness burst onto his tongue, the pips sticking in his teeth. It reminded him of his summers as a boy. The first strawberry of the season had always been his mother's favourite. He remembered how his fingers would be stained scarlet as he and his mother filled their baskets and gobbled all of the fruit before it had time to get to the kitchens.

He smiled at his memories as he gazed at the sky outside – bright red, like the strawberry. Dusk was only just upon them, and it would be a while before the sky was black enough to see the stars. Summer was always his favourite season.

Catherine did not seem to share his jovial mood. A strawberry sat on her plate, but she made no move to eat it. She looked pale, and the skin around her eyes was darker than usual. She had been quiet too; his questions had been met with one-word replies. Perhaps her head still ached from this afternoon?

'Are you still pained, my love?'

She raised her eyes to him, and it took her a while to reply. 'A little.'

'Have you asked Cook for anything? That woman knows all about which herbs do what. Perhaps she could make you tea or something?'

'What happened in Ireland?'

The question caught him off guard. Why on earth should she be bringing up Ireland now? He dropped the green stem of the strawberry onto his plate and sipped his wine. His mouth cringed against the tannin.

'What do you mean?'

'What happened during the famine? On your lands?'

He would not think about it, not tonight, not with the sweetness of the strawberry still lingering on his tongue. He would not mar another happy memory.

'I don't know much about it.'

'So many people starved to death,' she said.

'The papers exaggerate these things, my dear.'

'Why would they?'

'To make us all feel sorry for them. To stir the country into a frenzy. To cause chaos.'

'Are you saying there never was a famine?'

He cleared his throat and smiled. He could not blame her for her ignorance. 'Let's not talk about this, eh? It's all over now, anyway.'

She nodded and picked the leaves off her strawberry. In the silence, all he heard was the ripping and tearing…

'Did your tenants die, Osborne?'

He picked up his glass. He would not think about the tenants, the Irish. Scum. 'People die all the time, Catherine.'

'Not like that.' The paleness had faded from her cheeks. Suddenly, she was ferocious. 'Did you throw them out of their homes?'

'It was their own fault. What would your landlord have done if you'd not paid the rent? You would have been thrown out too, and sooner, I dare say, than what my father allowed those tenants. He had months of nothing from them.'

'They were starving.'

He clicked his fingers, and Dixon emerged. 'Port.' Dixon disappeared behind his screen and returned with a glass of blood-red liquid.

Osborne gulped it down and gestured for another. He needed to control himself. If Catherine did not have the decorum required for the dinner table, then he must. This kind of scene would never have happened if he had married a lady, and he cursed himself for his folly whilst, at the same time, he accepted that he had chosen this type of woman – he must endure her volatile emotions.

'Catherine, I know you think you understand it, but how can you? Please trust me when I say that everything my father did was out of necessity.'

She sneered, and the sight of her face rendered so mean and ugly, mocking him, belittling him, made his fists clench.

He slammed his glass on the table. The port spilt over the side and stained the white tablecloth. 'Are you implying that my father was unfair? That he was cruel?'

She dropped her eyes to her lap, his anger weakening her resolve.

'My father was a good man, and all he got for it was ingratitude! It was them who let him down, Catherine. In the hour of need, he was over there, doing his best, trying to save his family. Those ... people couldn't see a good man when he stood before them. It was them who were cruel and unfair, Catherine. It was them who shot him!'

He found himself standing, his fists gripping the edge of the table. All of it had poured out of him, whether he had wanted it to or not. Even Catherine had whitened, scared from his outburst.

His hand shook as he smoothed his hair, regaining his composure.

'I am sorry, Osborne,' she whispered.

His legs were stiff as he tried to sit. He dragged in his chair and drank what remained of his port.

'I don't know why you try to defend them.' His voice was low again now, controlled, although it was rough after shouting. 'You could surely see their depraved nature in Jonathan Murphy?'

'Yes. Yes, you are right.'

The ugliness had vanished; now, she looked small and shamed, her head low, her eyes wet. He reached for her hand, thought how cold it was through the glove, and kissed her fingers.

'Forgive me,' she whispered. 'I won't bring it up again.'

The morning was dull and sticky. She longed to wash the night away from her, the tangled wet sheets, the sounds of gunfire and weeping and broken glass. She opened the window wide when Nelly came with her wash things, searching for a breeze but finding none.

'Feeling better this morning, ma'am?' Nelly helped soak her feet and ankles.

'Thank you, Nelly. Still a little sickly.'

'Hope you haven't caught anything, ma'am, no French cold or anything else foreign.'

She was not in the mood for talking, least of all with Nelly. She longed for her sisters, precisely as she had seen them all those years ago. To smell them, to feel the softness of their skin, to play with and plait their hair. She was alone here. She was Catherine, not Cat. Mrs Tomkins, not sister. She was a different person. Which was what she had wanted, she reminded herself, but she couldn't shake off all of her past.

Refreshed and in clean clothes, she sought out Osborne in his room. Osborne smiled when she entered, and it was as if the night before had never existed. The tension in her stomach eased as he kissed her.

'What are you doing today, my love?' he said, fastening his buttons in front of the mirror.

She shook her head. What she always did now, she supposed; sit, sew, walk the grounds with the dogs. She had never been so idle. 'I thought I might write a letter.'

'To who?'

'My sisters.'

'Ah.' He nodded and straightened the collar of his shirt.

'I thought,' she walked towards him and helped him with his waistcoat, 'they could come here?'

'We have no need for further staff.'

Speechless, she watched him in the looking glass as he fastened his waistcoat, wondering if he was jesting.

'I do not mean as staff, Osborne. I mean to live here as my sisters.'

'Oh.' He pointed to the jacket hanging on the wardrobe and Cat fetched it for him. 'I shall see if there are any cottages free.'

She stood before him and made him look at her. 'Osborne, I want them here, in this house, with me, with us, as a family. There is space for them.'

'Yes, but ... Well, we are newly married.' He held her neck between his hands. 'I do not want your sisters interrupting us when we ...'

'Why would they interrupt us?' she sniped. She wanted

nothing less than to feel his lips on her skin at this moment. 'I do not plan to have them in my room. They will have their own.'

He stepped away from her so he could see his reflection again. 'I will think about it.'

She checked herself before she argued further. She couldn't afford another row after last night. If Osborne said he would think about it, she would have to pray that he came to the right conclusion.

Strolling to his washstand, he dipped his fingers in the water, slathered them with soap, rinsed them off, dried them on a towel, then repeated the actions again. She had seen him do this before; he did it any time he planned to leave the house.

'Are you going somewhere?'

'To town.'

'Birmingham?'

He laughed. 'Yes, Birmingham. Do not fret; I am not taking you with me.'

'Why are you going there?'

'To see Mr Brent and get everything sorted out. I have been so occupied with my new wife that I have failed to get things straight.'

'What things?'

After the third time of washing his hands, he folded the towel back into place. 'For you, for the future. If anything was to happen ... What kind of a husband would I be otherwise?' He turned to her and stared at her stomach. 'What kind of a father?'

She dropped her eyes. 'I am not–'

'Not yet.'

'And what do you mean – if anything was to happen to you? You are well, aren't you?'

He kissed her cheek. 'Perfectly, but no one's future is

guaranteed. Now,' he patted her arms, 'I must hurry else I will never get there.' He marched from the room.

She trotted behind him and followed him outside. The horse and carriage were already waiting.

'How long will you be gone?'

'I shall be back in the morning.'

'A whole night!'

He chuckled and tickled her chin. 'Will you manage without me?'

She cleared her throat, nodded. 'I'll miss you.'

'And I you.' He opened the carriage door, then gasped as if a thought had suddenly just struck him. 'I could have a tour of town while I'm there. See your old parts.'

She grabbed his jacket. 'No.'

'I could go to Bronson's and tell them your good news. I would love to see their faces.'

'No!' She wished she could slap the laughter out of him. 'Please, Osborne, I beg you.'

'I would like to see your past.'

'You will not love me if you do.'

'I will always love you, Catherine.' He kissed her slowly. 'You have stolen my heart completely.'

'Promise me you will not go,' she whispered.

'Fine. I promise.'

A PINK TEA set with gilded edges sat on a silver tray on an iron table. The afternoon had brightened, and an umbrella was needed to shade the ladies as they sat in the vicarage garden surrounded by fat, scented roses. Somewhere in the house behind them, Mr Turner was reciting his service for the coming Sunday, and Ruth's maid was scrubbing and humming in the scullery.

'He does things like this sometimes,' Ruth said, holding

her cup and saucer above her chest. 'Goes off. There is nothing to worry about.'

But of course, Cat was worried. She would not be here if she weren't. She would not be trying to reassure herself that her past was indeed behind her by taking tea with the vicar's wife – to show that she was finally accepted by those who mattered in Osborne's life – if there was not something niggling at the back of her mind. Something dark and forboding.

'It's just ... Birmingham!'

'I know you have ill memories of the place.' Ruth did not need to say more.

A bumblebee floated past them, dozily, and landed on a flower head beside Cat. She watched its long tongue, as sharp and delicate as a needle, probe at the heart of the flower.

'Would you tell me some of Osborne's past? Sometimes I find him as closed as a book, and I do not want to upset him by asking about his father.'

Ruth placed her saucer on the table. 'It is a sore subject.'

Cat nodded, wincing at the memory of the argument the previous night.

Ruth smoothed her skirts and glanced over her shoulder at the window behind. 'I shouldn't talk without his–'

'Please.' Cat grabbed her hand, then dropped it quickly as she saw the shock on Ruth's face. 'I know his father was shot. I know Osborne is traumatised by it. But I feel like part of him is missing to me. Perhaps, if I understood that part, I might be a better wife to him?'

Again, Ruth checked over her shoulder, then, seeing that all was clear, leaned closer to Cat and talked in hushed tones.

'Osborne idolised his father. He was only a boy when his mother died, you see. Eight? Nine years old?' She frowned at herself. 'I forget exactly, but he was just a child.

'Theodore doted on him – too much, some said. After his

wife's death, he wrapped Osborne up in that house and never let him do a thing. He was too scared he would lose him as well. His wife, you see, died of typhus, and he was terrified that Osborne might catch something too. I suppose Osborne was all he had left of her.'

She shook her head and stared at her roses. 'Boys need to be able to grow, to go out on adventures, to get mud on their boots. It was an … odd childhood. Osborne had only his father for a friend. And Theodore … well, he had these moods sometimes. Dark moods. For months on end. Osborne would have no one but his dogs and his tutor.' She sighed. 'It was only when Osborne left for university that he met other boys like him and learnt the way of the world. But he had to come back eventually.'

She finished her drink. 'More tea?' Ruth filled their cups.

'Anyway, they fell back into their old ways together, though I understand Osborne had more of a hand in running the estate. There was even talk of finding Osborne a wife. Theodore loved children; he yearned for a grandchild to make the house happy again.'

'Was there ever anyone serious?'

'Not really. The girls adored Osborne – who wouldn't? But it was like he could only ever love one person at a time, and that was his father. After what happened … I've never known a grown man cry like that. He was angry too – no one could get near him. He shut the house for a while, locked himself alone in there for weeks. When he let everyone in again, he'd–' She stopped herself quickly and buried her nose in her cup. She drank slowly. 'I shouldn't be telling you all this.'

'Please. I would know my husband.'

Carefully, Ruth replaced her cup in its saucer. She fiddled with the china handle, flicking her nail against it until she began again.

'The doctor was called, and it was sorted. In a few months, Osborne was more himself. But so terribly sad! He blamed himself, you see, he felt he should have gone over there instead of his father. He came here once and cried on my knee,' she patted her skirts, 'and said he should have saved him.'

She glanced at Cat uneasily. 'That's why he saved you. He just wants to save people.'

Cat swallowed. 'That was why he killed Jonathon Murphy?'

Ruth's face hardened. 'How do you mean?'

'Because the man was Irish. He hates the Irish for what they did to his father.'

Ruth rolled her eyes skyward. 'Osborne shot that creature because he was trying to drown you, Catherine. That the man just so happened to be Irish was an unfortunate coincidence. Anyway, can you blame Osborne for such feelings? Wouldn't you hate the people who had killed the only person you loved?'

'Yes. I would.'

Ruth sniffed, then slapped her hands, trying to lighten the tension that had wheedled into their conversation. 'Let us not be melancholy! He has found you – or you him – whichever way around it was. You have saved each other. When Osborne loves, he loves completely, Catherine. I have never seen him so happy.'

'He has been a little cold with me at times.'

Ruth flicked her hand. 'Men. Their little moods. They say we are complicated!' She chuckled. 'Old habits are hard to change, my dear. Do not expect too much of him all at once. He is only just learning to trust again.'

CHAPTER 17

June 1854. Birmingham.

Osborne shut the door of Brent's solicitors and smiled at the ugly town. Plumes of black smoke churned into the sky, and the stench alone was enough to make one sick, but neither of these things could dampen his spirits. He simply shielded his nose with his lavender-scented handkerchief and skipped towards his carriage.

'The hotel, sir?'

'Not yet, Barclay.' He shouldn't … he had promised. But what would it hurt just to take a look? 'Take me to Bronson's button factory.'

They had to stop a few times as Barclay consulted people for directions. The whole place was a rabbit warren of streets, all looking the same with the same kinds of people scurrying from here to there. The horse was agitated in these narrow lanes – it skittered away every so often, and then halted entirely in its fright. It was not a pleasant ride, and Osborne was feeling positively nauseous by the time the carriage finally stopped, and Barclay called down to Osborne that they had arrived.

From his window, he observed the towering brick building. It was taller than his own house and was speckled with windows encased in iron bars – it looked more like a gaol than a place of work. He could hear the machines from here.

He could not imagine his Catherine in such a place. Her small, beautiful body held inside somewhere so ugly and hard. He could not even bring himself to step outside and get any closer to it – Bronson would never know what had become of one his girls. Osborne guessed that the old crone wouldn't care anyway.

He smacked the roof of the Brougham.

'Where to, sir?'

Did he want to see more of Catherine's old life? Could he bear to know the extent of her suffering? Curiosity stung him.

He recalled her terrified face, begging him to stay away from her past, crying that he would no longer love her. Did she have so little faith in him? He was not a man easily cowed – not anymore, at least. No, he would know the full extent of Catherine's previous existence. He would know exactly what he had rescued her from.

'Bailey Road,' he shouted to Barclay and settled himself in for another unpleasant journey.

BAILEY ROAD WAS SO narrow that the sides of the carriage almost touched the brickwork as it squeezed between the back-to-back houses. Either side of him, curtains twitched, and sometimes Osborne saw a ghostly face at a window, although when he double-checked, there was nothing but black beyond the glass.

He shouted for Barclay to stop and, though his heart was beating too fast, he opened his door and dismounted.

The ground beneath him was not fit to call a road. Under his Brougham, wastewater trickled in an open gutter. Desperately, he dragged out his handkerchief again and pressed it over his mouth and nose.

He should not have come. What sorts of diseases were filtering through the lining of the cotton right now? He took one last breath then sealed his mouth shut and vowed not to breathe again until he was back in the Brougham.

Quickly, he took in the houses surrounding him, somewhat absently noting how the woodwork was splintering in the doorframes, how the glass was cracking at the corners of all the windows. How should he know which had been Catherine's home? It was even more impossible to imagine her here than it had been at Bronson's. How could her sweet, pale face, so round and innocent and pure, ever have gazed out from one of these windows?

'You all right, sir?'

He turned to find an old woman standing in a doorway. Her clothes were tatty but her apron, which was fastened tight around her waist, was clean. She had rolled up her sleeves, revealing soft, sagging flesh, and her plump cheeks were pink as she smiled at him.

'Can I help you?'

His lungs were starting to ache. His cheeks would no doubt be pink now, if not turning blue. He must look most ridiculous.

He glanced at his carriage, waiting so invitingly for his return, then forced himself to inhale and speak.

'Did you know a woman called Catherine Davies?'

'Cat!' The old woman's smile grew wide, and then suspicion clouded her eyes. 'Why d'you want to know?'

He laughed, suddenly feeling foolish. 'I have married her.'

'You? You've married Cat?'

Heat flooded his face. Hearing it from this stranger's lips, it sounded even more absurd than when Stephen had shouted it at him. How had someone like him ever married someone who had originated from somewhere like this?

He nodded uneasily. 'I love her very much,' he said, finding reassurance in his own words. 'Anyway, I was in town, and she has told me so much of where she used to live that I thought I would like to see it for myself.'

The old woman lifted her apron to her eyes. 'Oh, sir, you have made me a happy woman. Such a lovely girl, she was.'

'You knew her well?'

'Knew her! I helped bring her into this world. Such a nice girl and ever so pretty. Well, all the girls were pretty, but Cat! You know all about that!' She laughed. 'Yes, they were my neighbours, lived next door. Such a pity, what happened.' She shook her head. 'Can't stand the folks who came in after. Horrible lot. Kiddies' got no manners. I hoped they'd go, tell the truth, but they've stuck for three blooming years.'

'Three years?'

She nodded. 'Hear them now? Screaming and shouting! All day and night–'

'I didn't know Catherine had been gone from here for so long.'

'Awful when she went, and Lottie and Helen being shipped off like that. I offered her a place here for a while until she'd got herself sorted, but she was headstrong, didn't take kindly to charity. You'll know that though, I bet!' She laughed and bumped him on the arm.

He stepped away. It took all his willpower not to cast his jacket into the street. He felt the woman's filth penetrating the wool as he forced himself to remain still. He would burn it later.

'Do you know where she went after she left here?'

'Able Street.' The woman shuddered, now more guarded after noting Osborne's disgust at her touch. 'I never saw her after.'

'Able Street – whereabouts is that?'

'I wouldn't go there if I were you, sir. You think this street is bad; they'll have your wallet before you've even got out of your carriage.'

He found it difficult to imagine how anywhere might have been worse than Bailey Road. Nevertheless, he managed to smile as the smell began to burn his throat. 'Thank you, Mrs …?'

'Smith.'

'Thank you, Mrs Smith, you've been most helpful.'

He found a shilling from his pocket and held it out at arm's length for her. For a moment, she hesitated, her skin blushing, but she was not quite so proud as to refuse it. She snatched it from him before diving back into her house.

'Able Street, Barclay!'

'Can't get down there, sir.'

Osborne peeked through the carriage curtain. Able Street was terrifyingly narrow; even the weak daylight could not penetrate the gap. He opened the door, boldness sweeping over him.

'Are you sure, sir?' Barclay said, peering at the street and holding the reins tight as the horse fidgeted and threw its head back.

'Wait here for me.' Osborne clutched his jacket tight, despite the heat, making sure his watch was hidden and that his wallet was safe in his pocket, and marched into Able Street.

The houses were so high that it made him dizzy to look up at them. People hung in dark doorways. Faces stared brazenly from the windows, looking him up and down, assessing him, his wealth and status and connections – was it worth the risk to rob him? He squared his shoulders, hoping false confidence would keep him safe.

He stomped forward, squelching over the muck, flinching from the vivid, lurid noises lunging at him from the open doorways. Once more, he forced the handkerchief to his nose, but the lavender was no match for the stench in the street.

Something brushed behind him, and he felt cold, damp fingers against his hand, aiming for his pocket. He jerked around, ready to fight them off, but found nothing but shadows. His skin crawled as he replayed the feeling of that putrid flesh against his, and he wished to God that there might be a clean bowl of water and some soap nearby. There wasn't.

He came to the end of the street. He had no idea what he was looking for. He hoped something might strike him as important, that he might feel the presence of Catherine somewhere, but there was nothing but the creeping sense of danger. He was alone amidst people who would club a man to death for less than a quarter of the money he had in his pocket right now.

A boy emerged from one of the houses, no more than ten years old, Osborne guessed, for the size of him. The boy eyed Osborne, then began to walk away.

'You.'

The boy stopped, turned to Osborne, and jutted his chin out as a response.

'You know of anyone called Catherine Davies?'

The boy shook his head and went to leave.

'This tall,' Osborne pointed to his chest, 'Yellow-haired. Pretty.'

'There are lots of pretty girls here, sir, if that's what you're looking for?' The boy came closer. His voice was low and scratchy – he must have been older than he looked.

'I specifically require information about Catherine Davies. I understand she used to live on this street.'

'I get confused with names, sir.' The boy waited, eyebrows raised, eyes pointed at Osborne's pocket.

Osborne found him a shilling. 'Did you know her?'

The boy nodded and waited. Osborne gave him another shilling.

'She used to have a room here,' he nodded at the house from which he had just come.

'Will you show me?' Osborne handed him two more shillings before the boy had to ask.

Osborne's shoulders were as broad as the doorway. His shadow blocked out all daylight, leaving the corridor gloomy. The smell of smoke and stale bodily fluids hit him through his handkerchief.

'This way.' The boy mounted the stairs silently, but when Osborne put his foot on the wooden slats, they screeched under his weight.

Muffled noises came from the doors off the landing. Osborne did not try to understand them. He followed the boy to another set of stairs and saw, just in time, the boy jump two steps; the boards had collapsed. He imagined the scream of someone as they had fallen through the step, legs ripping against the rotten splinters.

'This is it,' the boy said at the top of the stairs. Osborne had to incline his head so he did not hit it against the eaves.

'Which room?'

The boy jerked his head towards the door to Osborne's left. Behind the only other door on this floor, a girl's voice trilled, and metal clinked against metal. Osborne focused on the door to his left.

'Can I look inside?'

'Someone else has got it now. Shouldn't be showing you inside someone's private room.' The boy's dead eyes met his. Osborne chucked another shilling at him.

The door was not locked. Inside, a set of drawers was pushed against the far wall and topped with a piss pot. Clothes were strewn across the floor to act as rugs, an old skirt draped against the window to block out the light. A black, dripping patch of damp spread over the ceiling above the unmade bed where dirty sheets lay in a heap.

'Who is here now?'

'A girl.' The boy shrugged.

'How long was Catherine here?'

'Days turn into years. I can't remember what happened yesterday.'

Osborne gave the boy a shilling, and the boy slipped it into his pocket beside all the others.

'I still can't remember.'

The boy was frustrating him. The stench was making him queasy. He must leave – he would not find anything here. Indeed, he wished to scour this place from his mind already, especially the idea that Catherine had ever lived in it.

He turned, about to run down the stairs as fast as he could, when the door across the narrow landing opened and a man, perhaps fifty years of age, hobbled out. His wooden leg thumped along the floor and, on seeing that a gentleman had witnessed his sin, he pulled his hat down over his face and hurried down the stairs, jumping deftly over the two missing steps with ease, as if he'd had plenty of practice.

A girl loitered in the doorway. Like the boy, she seemed little more than a child for her height and size, but the way her clothes hung – revealing most of her breasts – suggested she was older. Red hair draped around her shoulders, matted and unkempt.

'All right, sir? Waiting for me?'

'He's asking about Cat,' the boy replied before Osborne had the chance.

'Cat? Why's he interested in her?'

'Did you know her?' Osborne said.

'We were neighbours.'

'Got to go.' The boy slipped past Osborne, fleeing so fast that Osborne wasn't quick enough to grab him and make him stay.

'What do you want to know about Miss Catherine?'

He couldn't look at the girl, at her unflinching stare, at her folded, scabby arms; it made him feel … odd. He stared at his feet instead. 'Her past.'

'You sure? You might not like it.'

By now, he was sure that he would not.

'I ain't standing out on this draughty landing to tell you.' She shrank into her room, leaving the door open for him.

He could leave now. He could run down the stairs, all the way through Able Street, and be in his Brougham in less than a minute. He gripped the rough bannister, feeling his stomach flip, his feet itching to get away.

With effort, he dragged himself into the girl's room.

Inside, it seemed she had disappeared. He stepped in further, looking for her, and the door shut behind him.

'Drink?'

Out of the shadows, she shoved a bottle of gin under his nose. He shook his head and watched her gulp the liquor as she sat on the edge of her bed. When she had finished drinking, she sucked the tip of the bottle and held his gaze, her red tongue rolling over the rim, menacingly.

'You seem sad, sir. May I cheer you?'

He pinched his top hat between his fingers and breathed slowly, trying to ease his nausea. With the help of the light, he could see the sore at the corner of her lips, red and angry, marking her disease.

'Were you a friend to Catherine?'

'Miss Catherine only ever had one friend. Nobody else was good enough.'

He thrust his handkerchief inside his pocket. It was useless; with the door shut, the air in the room was concentrated. He could smell the man who had just left – body odour and semen still fresh on the sheets – and all the men who had been before.

'What friend?'

'A man.' The girl grinned, mischief dancing in her eyes.

'Only a friend?'

'Can a man ever just be a friend to a woman?' She got to her feet, placed the bottle on the floor, and straightened the dirty sheets.

'Miss Catherine thought herself better than us,' she yanked the sheet into place, the sparkle and seduction suddenly gone from her eyes. 'She wasn't.'

'She is a good woman.'

The girl barked laughter, then rounded on him. 'We can all be good girls, if that is what you require, sir?' She ran her fingers over his chest and laughed again as he flinched away from her.

'Never trust a woman, sir, we're good at making things seem just as you want them to be. Who is she to you, anyway? You some kind of missionary, come to save a soul like hers? You'll find plenty of souls like that what need saving, sir, but not all want it, you see?'

'What do you mean, souls like hers?'

She met his gaze squarely. 'Like mine.'

He could not believe it, not of Catherine. 'You're lying.'

She shrugged. 'Believe what you like.'

She stepped to the window, finding a glimmer of her reflection in the grimy glass. She pushed up her breasts and ran a hand over her hair.

'I have a man coming here, any minute. He doesn't like to wait. And I need a piss. So …' She gestured at the door.

'Wait. What makes you think Catherine was … like you?'

'I haven't the time–'

'I can give you this.' Osborne held out the rest of his shillings on his palm.

She stared at them. 'You might, but this man's a regular, and I don't get the impression that you'll be returning if you don't have to. So,' she plucked the coins from his fingers, 'I'll take this from you now, and you can come back next week if you really want to know all about your little pussy Cat. If you don't change your mind in the meantime, that is. I'm quiet just after midday.'

CHAPTER 18

November 1852. Birmingham.

CAT PULLED her shawl tight around her shoulders. It was too thin for this time of year – she felt the cold and the rain as sharp as pinpricks against her chest. Her corset was looser than usual, her hair down and swishing against her back. The only warmth was from John's arm, which held her close as he dragged her towards the cut.

Their feet skidded in the mud, the path beside the water more like a bog than a walkway. John kept her upright, but it was not only the mud and the dark which was making her wobble. The half bottle of gin that John had insisted she drink had made her head feel as if it was padded with linen.

Barges lined the cut, and yells and laughter of workmen, drinking and fighting, carried over the water from somewhere nearby. Fog strangled the water, growing denser the more they walked, clutching at Cat's ankles and making her shiver.

The mist was thick enough now to shield her from the sights around her, though she could hear them; the grunts of men taking their pleasures in dark corners. John pushed her forwards, past other girls who waited and glared at her as she walked by.

'Stand here.'

To her left, there was nothing but silence and the black shadow of a low bridge. To her right, women and men and noise. Behind her, the stab of brambles and thin trees. In front, the water.

He kissed her cheek. She longed to hold his face to hers, his lips to hers, but she let him pull back.

'I'll be watching,' he whispered, adjusting her clothes, opening her shawl and exposing her to the cold.

'John, I don't know if I can.'

'Of course, you can.' He dragged a lock of hair over her shoulder and smiled. 'Remember to take them to the bridge.' Another kiss, and before she could stop him, he was gone.

She closed her eyes and inhaled. She would be sick if she did not calm herself. She dug her fingernails into her arms and focused on the pain, only on the pain, nothing else, until the world around her disappeared and there was nothing but the blissful crushing and pinching of her skin.

Footsteps. She tore her fingernails away with a gasp and watched the fog spit out a man. She dropped her gaze as he strolled towards her and stopped to look, then walked on.

She let out the breath she had been holding. Her legs shook, her head spun, and she doubled over and vomited into the cut. She felt better for it, though the gin stung just as much coming up as it had going down. She straightened herself, her head clearer, her stomach settled, and waited again.

It was not long before another man came, and this time he did not walk away.

'How much?'

She said what John had told her to say.

The man laughed, and she saw the coal smears across his cheeks, the dirtiness of his skin. It was impossible to tell whether his features were handsome, if he was old or young, if he seemed kind or not. His voice, though, was scratchy, as if he spent most of his time shouting.

'I'm clean. First time.'

He stopped laughing. He pressed cold coins into her hand, then gripped her shoulder and clutched her skirt.

'Wait,' she wriggled away from him. 'Under the bridge. I would be dry.'

He huffed but did not argue as she took his hand and led him under the bridge. His heavy breathing echoed around them. He pulled her to halt and pushed her against the stonework. It was an awkward position – her head pressed against the wall so that her neck was bent forward.

The man's hands rubbed over her body. His face came into hers, sniffing her skin. His beard scratched against her chest.

'First time?' he grunted, face buried in her bodice as he pulled up her skirts.

She grunted back at him, unable to speak. Cold wrapped its fingers around her calves and tickled her thighs. Her skirts did not take much getting up, for John had told her to wear only one petticoat over her slip – easier to deal with. How would he know, she suddenly thought? And why hadn't she asked that question at the time?

She shook her head – she would not think about John with other women, not now, when her skirt was edging up her thighs.

Blood burned her face as her arse felt the chill of the night air. She turned her head away from the man, squeezed her eyes shut, and began to recite the Lord's prayer.

'Be quiet.'

The man kicked her feet apart. She heard the ruffle of his clothes – his breeches being lowered – as he shuffled against her, until something wet and hard touched her.

She jerked backwards, but she had nowhere to go.

'Stay still,' he said, shoving her shoulder into the wall. 'Christ!'

'I haven't …'

What was the use in trying to explain? How could she tell him she hadn't done it standing before? She hadn't even thought of how it might be possible, and now, with him fumbling about, she realised that it wasn't. She would be torn in two if it continued. Panic squeezed her throat.

Then, he spun her. He gripped her hips, pulled her backside against him, and pushed her head down. Off-balance, her hands slapped into the muck on the floor, but he held her tight. His fingers clawed into thighs, and she felt his hardness come between her legs, its aim better.

She held her breath as she gazed at the dirt on her hands and waited for the rip …

Then the muck met her face. She smashed into the ground as the man's grip vanished. A foot stepped on her calf, and she cried out with the pain.

A slap of bone on stone echoed behind her. She forced herself onto her hands and knees and crawled through the dirt, pulling her skirts down as she went. A few feet away from the commotion, she caught her breath and turned to see her punter cowering below another man, their silhouettes black against the white of the fog. Something glinted and caught her eye – the shine of a knife against the punter's throat.

'Give it,' the attacker growled, holding out his other hand.

She struggled to her feet. She needed to get past the attacker to get back to John. Where was he? He should have been watching. She edged forward, hoping she could sneak past them.

She made a run for it, but the attacker was quick. He lunged for her, his palm smacking into her throat, and threw her against the bridge.

'Give it,' the attacker said again, one hand holding the knife at the punter, the other keeping her in place.

There was a rattling of coins as the punter held out his money. The attacker snatched them and kicked the man in the groin. The punter coiled inwards, groaning in agony.

'Go.' The attacker kicked the man again, urging him to his feet. The punter scrambled away and glanced back at Cat.

'Help me,' she mouthed to him, but he was soon lost in the fog.

The knife now pressed against her lips.

'Please,' she whispered, straining her head away from the masked man. 'Please, I'll do what you want.'

His body crushed against her as his hand slid from her neck, over her collarbones, and gripped her breast. She closed her eyes as the hand continued to slide down and found her purse and the coins within.

Then, hot lips kissed her, and a familiar chuckle rumbled against her ear.

Her legs buckled.

'Eh, quiet now. Hush,' John said, catching her just in time before she crashed into the floor.

'What ... Why did you ...' She pounded his chest, but she was so weak with terror that her fists made no impact. 'I didn't know it was you!'

Her anger dissolved into tears. She sobbed against his jacket, exhausted. How long the day had been! Those last few minutes had been the longest of her life. She wanted to go home, to scrub herself clean of muck and sin, to wrap herself in a soft blanket and lie on her bed until sleep allowed her to forget everything.

'Why would you …?'

'Had to look convincing, for your sake.'

She frowned at him.

'I told you I wouldn't let anybody hurt you.'

'You planned this?'

For an instant, his confidence wavered. She recalled the horror, the terror of it all. She had been so sure the knife would slit her mouth open; slit all of her open.

'How could you?'

'This is better, Cat. You don't have to fuck them. But you've got to be convincing.'

'I can't, John.'

He grabbed her face and made her look at him. Once more, his eyes shone. There was a buzz emanating from him; he was alive more than she'd ever seen him before.

'You can do this, Cat. Look.' He showed her the man's coins. 'That's over half of what you earn in a week when you're working at Bronson's.'

'It's bad money.'

'Money's money.'

'I … I'm all,' she gestured at the state of herself, hoping he would understand that however dirty she was on the outside, she felt filthier on the inside.

'We'll get you cleaned up soon.'

She sighed and rested her forehead against his. 'I just want to sleep.'

'I know.' He kissed her. 'Only a few more.'

'What?'

She backed away from him, unable to believe what he was trying to make her do. He closed the space between them until his eyeballs were only inches away from hers, hard and determined.

'You said you'd do anything to help, Cat. You said that, not me.'

'I know, but–'

'And did you get hurt? Did you really get hurt tonight?'

She shook her head.

'No, because I saved you. I'll always save you.' He kissed her again, impatiently. 'Come on.'

CHAPTER 19

June 1854. Wallingham Hall.

SHE SAW him coming from her bedroom window. Cat had been waiting, arms resting on the sill, forehead pressed to the glass, all afternoon. The sun was still fierce even now, though dinner was not far away, and it shone upon him as he dismounted his carriage. He walked towards the front door, his feet scraping over the gravel as if he did not have the energy to pick them up.

She called for Nelly to dress her; she would look her best tonight. But by the time dinner came, her stomach, cinched tight in her corset, felt too sick for food. The bannister slid beneath her gloved hand unsteadily, her shoes tapped on the wooden stairs too loudly, and she met Osborne in the dining room with a nervousness she couldn't fully comprehend. He stood to greet her, placing a cold kiss on her cheek, never quite managing to meet her gaze.

'How was your journey?' she said once the wine and the first course had been placed on the table.

'Fine, thank you.'

'Your room was comfortable last night?'

'Yes.'

Another course came and went. Cat wished the stupid fire had not been lit – why on earth did Osborne insist on a fire in the height of summer, even if it did only burn low? Her new dress, of pale white cotton trimmed with pink silk satin, which Osborne had failed to notice, clung to her hot, damp skin. She wafted her napkin before her face.

'And your meeting with Mr Brent?'

'Everything is sorted.'

She eased back and forced her hands to stop fiddling with the edge of the tablecloth. 'That is good.'

She was not a fool. Her husband had returned a different man. His gaze had not left his plate, the sweat had grown on his forehead and had not once been wiped away, his glasses of wine had been refilled more often than usual.

'Is something wrong, Osborne?'

He shook his head slightly.

She pushed out her chair, unable to bear it, and stalked to the window. 'It is that town. It does no one any good at all.'

'You are right there.'

She whirled around to face him. His lips had grown hard and flat.

'Well, I too, am feeling a little unwell. If you will excuse me, I will retire to my room for the night.' She bobbed her head, as if she was his maid, and made for the door.

In the great hall, she gulped in the cooler air. Her head felt as if it hovered a foot above her neck. She gripped the wall as she staggered for the staircase.

He did not love her anymore. That place had turned him against her, as she had warned him it would.

She was at the top of the stairs when she heard rapid footsteps below, running up towards her. She scurried down the corridor towards her chamber door, turning to see Osborne gaining on her, face furious, fists clenched by his sides. She clutched her door handle just as he grabbed her. He pushed her back against the wall.

'I have missed you,' he said, but there was no gentleness in his words. His fingers dug into the tops of her arms as he kissed her. Her head banged against the wall as his mouth drove into her, parting her lips, opening them for his tongue.

She shoved him away and wiped his spit from her mouth. He recoiled, back turned to her, as his breath blew out of him in a long hiss.

'Sorry, Osborne,' she said, forcing her words to be steady, for her voice to resemble normality. 'I am not well, my head … I would prefer to sleep tonight.'

She saw his shoulders shake before he sniggered. 'Did you say that to the other men who have known you?'

The wall came behind her again; the air punched out of her lungs.

'What do you mean?'

'Do you think me a fool? That I would not find out?'

'You promised me …' she said meekly.

'I am a grown man!' He turned to her. 'I go where I desire. Not that I can say I had any desire to be in such a rat's nest as Able Street.'

He inched closer. Cat cringed away from him, but she had nowhere to hide.

'How did you find it?'

'I will know the woman I married, whether you wish it or not – whether I wish it or not. A whore!'

She flinched. For the first time, she was aware of the size of him. Almost two heads taller than her, his shoulders broad and deep, the bones of his face cut large and angular. He could kill her with a single strike to the head.

'Please do not say such a thing.' Tears scored down her cheeks. 'I am different now. I am re-born, remember? Like we said before.'

His palm slammed into the wall beside her face. She felt the vibrations in her back.

'How do I know?'

She fell to her knees before him and grabbed his hands. 'You knew what I was before you married me.'

He tried to prise himself away, but she held him fast.

'Please, Osborne. Please believe me that I never meant you any harm, any deception. I had hoped you had taken me knowing the truth, and it will kill me if you now think me a liar.'

'Get up, Catherine,' he hissed. She remained at his feet.

'I am ashamed of my past, Osborne. Ashamed! I hoped you would never have to see it. I told you, remember? I told you that you would not love me if you went there.'

She sniffed and glanced at him. His eyes were closed, his brows knitted together painfully.

'It was John who made me do those things, Osborne. Anything for money. My soul for drinking money. And I was so stupid! But I was scared, Osborne. I was scared that if I did not go to it willingly that he would make it happen anyway, and it would be worse for me. Do you see? Do you see that I had no choice?'

His grip was beginning to soften in her hands. She kissed them, wetting them with her tears.

'I had no choice, Osborne, I swear it!'

'Stand up, Catherine.' His voice had lost its edge. Tiredness made his words gentle as he pulled her to her feet. When she rested her head against his chest, he did not push her away, so she clung to him. She clung to him, for her life depended on it.

'For years, I thought I was bound for hell. When I was in the water, when John was holding me down, I thought I was going to die, and I knew that the devil would take me. I could feel the fire, you know, before you saved me. I could feel it around my body. And then you came.' She kissed his chest. 'I did not deserve you.'

He remained tense beneath her.

'I prayed, and I still pray now, every day, for the forgiveness of my sins. Still, I am not sure if I have it. Mr Turner says that my soul is clean, but I am uncertain. If you cannot forgive me, Osborne, if you can no longer love me, then I will be lost.' A howl broke from her, and she shook with fear. She could not lose everything now when she had come so far.

Osborne lifted her face to his. His dark eyes were glassy, and there was a smear of mucus on his top lip. 'Of course, I love you, Catherine.'

'I will die if you do not. Please do not abandon me!'

Osborne pulled her closer and rocked her from side to side.

'Never.' He kissed the top of her head. 'I have been a fool. I have listened to poisoned tongues.'

She swallowed. 'Whose?'

'It does not matter now. Come on.' He opened her door, guided her inside, and sat her on the bed. He wiped her cheeks with his handkerchief.

'I am sorry for what that man did to you–'

She put her finger over his lips. 'I don't want to think about him.' She kissed Osborne's cheek and squeezed the image of John out of her mind. 'I don't want to think about him ever again.'

CHAPTER 20

March 1853. Birmingham.

A CURL of cold wind trickled through the shoddy windowpanes. The looking glass, old and greened at the edges, reflected a pale face haloed with golden hair, a strand of it tickling a perfectly straight nose as it caught in the breeze. She smoothed the hair into place with some spit, pinched the blood into her cheeks, then waited on her bed.

Her room was almost bare now. Most of her things were at John's. It had happened accidentally; one thing forgotten on the table, another left between the sheets, until shawls and combs and stockings remained in his room, turning her place into nothing but a shell. And she liked it like that. Slowly, she would migrate to John's room forever, whether he wanted it or not.

She rose from her bed and glanced outside. It was almost time – dusk had faded to blackness. Able Street was alive now more than any other time, the shadows dancing in the darkness, hiding from the gloom of the gaslights. She wrapped her shawl around her shoulders and paced the floorboards, waiting for John to arrive and lead her to the cut.

Three knocks on the door. She opened it with a smile and found John smiling too, wider than usual. She stepped forward, ready to leave, but he stopped her, checking over his shoulder before moving her inside and making her sit on the bed. He threw off her shawl, tugged her bodice loose, and pinched her cheeks hard.

'Come on!' he whispered, his breath tasting of stale beer, 'make yourself up.'

He took three giant steps around the room, stuffing old petticoats into the set of drawers and shoving old bottles under the bed as he went. He was tidying!

'What you playing at?'

He turned towards her, wild, his breath feverish, then marched from the room. She watched him go and saw the crack of light from Ruby's door across the landing. The girl would be spying; if there was one thing that could be as valuable as a fuck, it was information.

John returned in an instant, gripping a man by the shoulders – not a man, a boy. Her tallowlight barely reached him, but John pushed him inside so that she could see the length and thinness of his limbs as if childhood was struggling to hold onto him. The boy's gaze fixed on his feet.

'Who's this?'

'A friend.' John slapped the boy on the back. The boy stumbled, his cheeks flaring as he glanced up at Cat.

'Why is he here?'

A flicker of anger swept over John's face. 'Because he needs the love of a good woman, eh?'

He smiled at the boy and nudged him in the ribs. The boy nodded.

'He needs a girl with a good heart to take care of him for the night.'

Cat held onto the edge of the bed. John pushed the boy beside her, and she felt the mattress dip slightly from the boy's weight. Still, the child did not look at her.

'I'll be back in a few hours if you can last that long.' He patted the boy's thigh and laughed, winked at Cat, then skipped from the room, closing the door behind him. They listened to his footsteps trip down the stairs. The boy looked as abandoned as she felt.

In the silence, she took the time to study his face. His cheeks were smooth – never seen a razor. The light showed the fuzziness on his top lip, a few sprouting, blonde hairs on his chin. His skin was milky and clean; he was not a boy raised in this part of town.

His eyes twitched to take in his surroundings. He was stiff, uncomfortable, unused to such a state of poverty. She supposed that was the whole point – he would have a full wallet.

'What's your name?' she said, turning towards him a little.

'Matthew.'

'How d'you do, Matthew. I'm Catherine.'

'Catherine,' he breathed as if testing it on his tongue. 'That's a nice name.'

'Thank you.' She took his hand and felt the cold sweat on his palm. He tried to pull it back to him, but she kept hold of it.

'Sorry,' he said.

'What for?'

The boy shrugged.

'You've nothing to apologise for.'

'It's my ... they're all expecting ...' His gaze rose towards the window. His eyes were dark blue, the rim of them thick black. Beautiful – eyes which would break hearts someday.

'Are they waiting for you?'

He frowned. 'In a beerhouse somewhere, most likely.'

His Adam's apple bobbed up and down in his throat. She brushed her fingers over his forehead to straighten out the creases. 'A handsome man like you should not frown.'

'Sorry.'

She laughed and, for the first time, he met her gaze, and his lips tilted upwards.

'You must stop apologising,' she said.

'I …' he licked his lips. They too were pretty; full and red. 'I don't know if I can do this.'

Neither did she, in truth. She cursed John for bringing this child to her. It was one thing to rob old blokes by the cut, the ones who had hard hands and mean eyes, but to do it to an innocent like Matthew? A boy no more than fifteen or sixteen years of age – this sweet boy with a pretty face – it was just cruel.

She kissed him, trying to ease his nerves and her conscience. His lips were unresponsive for a moment, and then they moved softly against hers. When her hand came upon his knee, he gasped.

'What is wrong? Do you not think me pretty?'

'Oh, no! I mean, yes, I do, I do think you are very pretty. I think you are the prettiest girl I have ever seen.'

She smiled and pressed her forehead against his.

She would do this for John. She would do this for their future. Cynically, she told herself that at least the boy would learn never to trust so easily again.

Her hand, still on his knee, slid upwards. He squirmed.

'Hush now,' she said, her kisses moving down onto his neck. 'I will take good care of you.'

SHE STUDIED the patch of damp on the ceiling above her. It

was growing. She could feel it on her lungs, stifling her breath. The ceiling would be ruined by next winter.

Her fingers twirled the boy's lock of soft hair. She felt the gentle rush of his breath against her breasts as his head rested on her chest. He was sleeping, worn out.

Between her legs, wetness dribbled out of her. It had only been John's before, and now … now she really was what she said she never would be. How often had Ruby laid like this with a stranger on her naked flesh, watching the damp swell above her, hearing the sounds of Able Street below her? If the boy had not weighed her down, Cat would have vomited into her piss pot.

The door creaked open. John peeped his head around and smiled at what he saw. She could not look at him. She nudged the boy's shoulder until he stirred and frowned at her, dreams still in his eyes.

'Matthew, it's time to go home now.'

He rose and rubbed crusts of sleep away.

'Good night?'

Matthew jumped; he had not been aware of John. He shielded his nakedness with his hands and scurried to retrieve his clothes, which lay in heaps on the floor. Once he was dressed, he turned to Cat, a scared little boy again.

'Thank you, miss.'

'You're welcome,' she said, trying to smile for the boy so he would know he'd done well.

He stumbled towards the door and straight into John's hand. 'Ah, yes, sorry. Sorry.'

She heard the rattle of money, then the rush of metal over leather as the coins dropped into John's hand.

'Good lad.' John patted his shoulder and showed him out, watching him down the stairs.

'You should see him through the street, John. They'll eat him alive out there this time of night.'

John laughed.

'I mean it. They'll have his pocket.'

'They can have it.' John shut the door and slumped onto the bed. 'There's nothing in it.'

He showed her his full hand. She rolled away from him to find her slip.

'Don't you want to know how much?'

'No.'

'Fine.'

She grabbed one of her old petticoats and wiped the wetness off her legs, then stood in the centre of the room, her back to John. She wished he wasn't here. She wanted this time to herself. The cold air made her skin shiver, and she was sick with tiredness. She closed her eyes, and the sounds and smells disappeared. She felt the ground beneath her feet sway as if the earth was rocking her.

She longed not for John's touch, but for the taste of the medicine, bitter and sharp. She yearned to escape these thoughts that swarmed her mind and to feel nothing, absolutely nothing. She craved the black abyss.

John took her by the waist and brought her to sit on the bed beside him.

'You didn't come.' she said.

He waited before he spoke. 'No.'

'This is it, now, is it? What you want me to do.'

He coughed, sniffed. 'You're in the warm.'

To call her room in the attic warm, where the wind and the rain came through the cracks in the brickwork and windowpanes, was a stretch.

'Better money this way. Better people.'

She didn't understand why anyone, man or boy, rich or poor, would want to come here for a fuck. At least by the cut, there was an air of mystery, and the darkness made no pretence necessary, by anyone.

'He was fine, though, wasn't he, that boy? No harm done?'

She shook her head. Matthew … his body only just beginning to harden into a man. A child. Gentle. Pliable. She felt she held some part of him inside her, a pearl of him, the very last part of him that had been pure; she had stolen it from him, as John had stolen hers.

John stroked her cheek. 'You should sleep now, Cat.' He moved her under the blankets and pulled them up to her chin.

'No more tonight?'

He shook his head. 'Sleep. We need you pretty and clean.'

Her gaze wandered to the damp above her. It was blacker now, the heart of it looking as if it would fall through any moment. She couldn't take her eyes off it.

'Sleep.'

'I can't.'

'Close your eyes …'

But she couldn't. The black was growing. She felt a drip on her forehead and flinched. The water would be brown and stagnant, filled with dust and spiderwebs. It would fall on her as she slept, and it would fill her mouth. It would roll around her teeth, and she would suck it into her lungs, and only when the water had choked her would she wake, and it would be too late.

'Cat?'

There was water on her face. She wiped it off her temples, feeling the warmth of it on her hand. She jumped out of bed, ran for the drawers, and tugged the bottom one open. She flicked off the bottle's stopper and drank. She gulped it down as the water dried on her skin, and finally, her legs ceased quivering.

John snatched the bottle from her. 'What's that?' He read the label. 'Why are you taking this?'

It had done its work. Warmth tingled in her stomach as if

someone was holding hot coals against her. Her breath came easier as she slipped into bed. Her eyelids drooped as the heat trickled through her veins deliciously. She smiled at the damp above her, the blackness now fading to a grey-brown, the ceiling sturdier than before.

'Cat?'

'So I can sleep. And forget.'

John came beside her. His cold, woollen clothes pressed against her hot skin and his head rested beside hers on the pillow.

'You staying here?'

'Of course.' His lips touched her cheek, and she reached for his arm beneath the covers. She held onto it, hugging it to her, its weight anchoring her to him.

'I love you, John.'

'I know.'

CHAPTER 21

September 1854. Wallingham Hall.

Nelly's hair was like her mother's used to be; coarse, lined with ridges, short strands poking out all over the place. Cat ran her fingers through it, tugging out the knots, watching Nelly's head nod backwards as if she was on the edge of sleep.

She began to plait it like she used to do with her sisters' hair. The familiar action comforted her. She weaved the sections together, concentrating on the rhythm, the distraction, then let it spring back into its unruly mess.

She patted the girl's shoulders. Nelly stood, twisted her hair into a bun, covered it with her cap, then started to work on Cat's hair. Her fingers were as soft as falling leaves pattering over Cat's scalp.

'You seem tired, ma'am.'

'I don't sleep well.'

'Is there anything I can get you?'

The temptation was on the tip of her tongue. Say it. Beg for it. Rationed as it may have been these last months, a drop had been enough to aid sleep. Now, the bottle was empty.

'No, thank you, Nelly.' She rolled her head backwards, let the weight of it rest on the top of her spine. Nelly's fingers caressed her forehead. 'I am worried about Osborne. He has been distant.'

'Has he?' Nelly – loyal as a dog to her master.

'There's something … something growing in him. A restlessness, a guard.'

'It's almost that time of the year, ma'am.'

'What time?'

'His father. Every year around now he … well, he changes a little. I would not worry that it's you, ma'am.'

Cat sighed. 'I must go to him. After all, we women are nothing but distractions, are we not?'

'Ma'am?'

She smiled at the ignorant girl but did not try to explain. Perhaps, one day, Nelly would understand.

She found Osborne in his study, leaning back in his chair, his face to the ceiling. His eyes lowered as she entered, and he acknowledged her with the briefest of smiles. She tiptoed towards him.

'Is something wrong?' he said. Lately, his voice had flattened, the richness had faded.

'I would see to my husband. You are sad?'

He shook his head but did not meet her gaze.

'This time of the year … I understand.' She rubbed his shoulder and eased herself onto his lap. His face remained still, controlled, and unflinching.

'Might we not think of it as something else from now on? Not so much of a sad time but,' she chose her words carefully, 'as a blessing in the darkness.'

His eyebrow raised. Still, he would not look at her. 'Why?'

'Our anniversary, Osborne. Our first year of knowing each other.'

He levelled his head, frowning as if this was a new concept to him. 'Yes. Yes, I never thought of it like that.' He did not smile. 'Blessings and curses.'

She chose to ignore the stab of fear inside her and embraced him. She felt something hard in his jacket, and she trailed her fingers down to touch warm wood. She pulled out the revolver.

'Why do you carry this always?'

He shrugged. 'Protection.'

'Why would you need protection here?'

'Protection is always necessary.'

She looked at the gun in her hand. It was lighter than she had imagined it would be, and smooth in her palm – inviting. She placed it on the table, the barrel pointing away from them. 'I don't like it.'

'You'd be dead without it.'

She cleared her throat. The water … the shot, as if the bullet had blown through her ear … nothing but ringing and silence as the world turned the other way around, forever.

'Yes, you are right.' She picked it up again. 'Will you show me how it works?'

'Why?'

'Because I should be grateful for it, as you said. And I cannot be grateful for something which I don't understand.' She jumped off his lap and waited.

With a groan, he showed her the six chambers of the gun, some already filled. 'Gunpowder in there, followed by the bullets.'

'Show me.'

He opened one of the desk drawers. Amidst a sea of bullets, he pulled out a pot of gunpowder, scooped some out, and trickled it into an empty chamber. Then, he pressed a bullet into the chamber and used the ramrod to set it all in place.

'Cock the hammer and pull the trigger.' He aimed the gun at the door. She waited, readying herself for the shock of the sound, but he only set it back in its holder. He slammed the drawer full of bullets shut.

'So many dangers,' she breathed.

'Everywhere.'

'You do not trust anyone, do you?'

He looked up to her, bare, exposed. She saw the boy inside of him, the one who had been cut from his bubble so brutally, lost in a place he could not comprehend.

'How can I trust anyone, Catherine, when I do not even trust myself?'

Silence. She felt fingers of warning reaching out for her. Now was the time to tell him.

She sat on his lap once again and brushed his forehead, feeling the cold wetness of his skin.

'Are you happy, Catherine?' His breath blew against her neck.

'Of course, I am.' She held his head against her bosom, and he softened. From above, she saw his eyelids flutter, then rest. 'I am the happiest woman alive.'

The room around them was silent but for the clock. Cat counted to thirty as Osborne grew heavier, his breathing slower and deeper. 'Osborne,' she whispered into his hair, 'I am with child.'

The words stuck in the air.

'Osborne?'

She went to stroke his face, but he jerked away from her.

'You will be a father.'

He moved beneath her, and she staggered as he pushed her off him, grabbing hold of the desk for support. He strode towards the window, his shoulders violently rising and falling.

'Osborne, are you not happy?' There was a glitch in her voice as it bumped up her throat. Be calm. Breathe. But the air was having trouble squeezing down her throat. 'Osborne, please?'

Something broke in him. His spine, once so rigid, now collapsed. He turned towards Cat, his hardness replaced by a sense of sagging as if he'd been deflated. He walked towards her, his feet dragging over the carpet, and placed one dry kiss on her cheek.

'Wonderful news.' His nose twitched, like a snarl struggling to be free. She shook the idea from her mind – she was imagining things.

He returned to his chair. 'I have things to be getting on with, Catherine, if you wouldn't mind …?' He nodded at the door.

She did not wait to be told twice.

CHAPTER 22

March 1853. Birmingham.

SHE HAD BEEN SUMMONED. She rushed to Bronson's, keen to make an honest day's pay. She hadn't been required for weeks – her nights had been filled with strangers to her room. She was sore between her legs. The condom she insisted they wear now rubbed inside her. She felt raw, as if she'd been sliced open and dirt had been crumbled into the wound.

She found her old place and settled onto the hard stool like it was a soft armchair. She felt the stares from the women around her, but she did not care. She caressed her machine, ran her tender fingers over its sharp, iron ridges, and began her work.

'Miss Davies.' Mr Criton stood before her, as miserable as ever. 'Come with me.'

She followed him through the shop floor and to his small office. He did not sit, and he did not offer her a seat either.

'We are letting you go.'

He said it so casually, she did not understand his meaning. He leaned against the wall, face turned to the window in the door so that he could keep an eye on his workforce.

'I thought you wanted me to work today?'

He rubbed his fingers together. They were thin, little fingers, the type that would only be good at holding a pen.

'Bronson's do not employ women such as yourself.'

'Women such as myself?'

He sighed as if the meeting had taken up too much of his time already. 'There have been complaints about you.'

'From who?'

'That is not your concern.'

She would have pointed out that it was her concern if it was going to get her sacked, but she held her tongue.

'We are a family business, Miss Davies, with family values. We employ only good, Christian people here.' He glanced at her, staring down his nose. 'You are no longer one of those, it seems.'

She was torn between anger and despair. The cheek of it! The hypocrisy!

Who had ratted on her? How would anyone know she was a whore if they hadn't used her services? She wracked her memory, trying to imagine the faces of the men she had been with the last few weeks. One of them must work at Bronson's, that was the only explanation. Or, perhaps, one had been a husband, a son, a brother of one of the women?

Her argument was on her lips. She would beg if she had to. Bronson's was her last connection to decency, to her old life, to her mother.

'Please, Mr Criton. It is all lies.'

He sucked at his teeth, returned his attention to the shop floor. 'Our decision is final.' He opened the door and stepped back for her to leave.

'Please, sir!' She hoped the tears would help her case, but Criton was a peculiar man, undeterred and unstirred by any female emotion. She would only humiliate herself further if she continued to plead with him.

She bit her teeth together and forced herself to be calm. She would not let those hateful women see her cry. She fixed her cap on her head, took a breath, and walked.

Criton sprang before her and blocked her way. Fear gripped her; he was unpredictable. His slit of a mouth came by her ear, and she held still, afraid he would bite.

'Your mother would be ashamed of you.'

HER PURSE TREMBLED in her hand. She had not removed her coat, nor her shoes, nor her cap. She sat close to the fire which she had lit – John didn't like to burn it now unless it was absolutely necessary. Well, today it was necessary; she was chilled all the way through, stiff and shaking with it.

She remained in her seat as the daylight faded. Her saliva swam in her mouth, and she choked it down. She told herself she need not be so worried; it was her body, she would do with it what she liked. But she imagined the disappointment on John's face, and she did not know whether she would be able to hold her ground.

Hours passed. Her backside grew numb. Her bladder was full, almost to bursting, and she crossed her legs together tight. If she ventured to the privy, she would not be able to return; she would lose her nerve and run back to her own room. So, she waited until she heard him coming up the stairs ... the key in the lock ... the twisting of the door handle ...

He slunk inside, pulling his cap off his head.

'John.'

She startled him. He laughed at his fright, then saw the

fire. He frowned at it, about to remonstrate her for wasting fuel, but she held out her purse to him before he could speak.

He took it from her suspiciously and eyed the contents.

'Where did you get this?'

'I won't do it anymore, John.'

He smiled slightly, doubting her, as he poured himself a drink.

'I could do it, by the cut, when it wasn't … you know, the whole thing. But I can't have them in my room anymore, John. I can't be a–'

He slumped onto his chair and faced her squarely. He swirled the beer around his mouth, then gulped. 'I thought you'd prefer it like that. Inside. No funny business. Straight.'

She shook her head, trying to rattle out the images of all those men who had been inside her. 'I won't be a whore, John.'

He laughed, and she scowled at him.

'There should be enough money for your family now, with that added to what we've already got.'

He chucked the purse on the table. 'Why do you think that?'

'Because we've been doing this for months! Where has it all gone?'

'We have to live, don't we? Nothing in this town is free, Cat, including you.'

'Then I'll stop renting that room. I'll move in here, and we can save more.'

'Won't be enough.'

She scratched her scalp. She was getting too hot now; she was prickling all over. 'Then I'll find another job, an honest job, and you can have all my wages, every single penny.'

'That'll take too long.'

'Jesus!' She slammed her hand on the table. She knew

what he was doing; nothing she said would change his mind, nothing she offered, other than blind obedience.

'Keep doing what you're doing, and you won't have to do it for much longer.'

'Please, John, I don't want to.'

'This your conscience getting to you?' He swilled his mouth with beer again. 'You don't worry about that sort of thing when you're starving to death, when you're freezing out on the streets in winter. You'd do anything for a penny. You said you'd do anything for me.'

'I know.'

'Your promises are flimsy things, aren't they?'

She stood. She would not be insulted, after everything she had already given up for him. She raised her hand, strong, defiant, and pulled off her cap.

She was unused to the lightness of her head. She waited for the sensation of her hair falling over her back, but now the clipped ends only spiked against her neck. For once, John could not find anything to say.

'I sold it for you. I sold everything in my room. Everything I have, you see it on me now. I sold it all for you, John, for your family, so that I may once again be able to sleep soundly.'

His fingers had turned white as he gripped his cup of beer. Cat wanted to run from him; he was dangerous like this, silent and brooding, but she stayed firm.

'Please, John. I have done it for both of us. It is better this way. I cannot ... I will not have them in my room again. I will not have them inside me again. I will have no one but you.'

She saw him swallow.

'Get out.'

Her nose stung as she began to cry. 'Please understand, John. I would do anything for you but that. It makes me sick. I would go back to the cut if that is what you want?'

'Get out!'

He pounced out of his chair, teeth bared at her, fists raised. She raced for the landing and crashed into the bannister as he slammed the door and locked her out.

CHAPTER 23

September 1854. Wallingham Hall.

THERE WAS a promise he had not kept – many promises he had not kept. They plagued him that night, found him in his dreams, and taunted him. It was a restless sleep, waking in the dark, eyes wide; the thought of a child in the house, something else to fear for and protect, was too much to bear.

He pressed his face into the pillow and willed the dawn to break.

He was in his Brougham as the sun spilt onto Wallingham Hall and shouting to Barclay to make haste. He did not glance at Catherine's window; he did not need to see her to know she was watching him.

His stomach was too sick to feel the need for food, but he wished he'd got a brandy. He felt cold, inside and on the skin, the same sense of dread as all those years ago when he'd been too sick – too scared – to go to Ireland. Something was coming, something that would shatter him.

He heard the town before he saw it. The place of industry – the heartland of pretty things made for the world in a place as ugly as the devil. He felt the pounding and throbbing of machinery and people and vermin radiate through him as the buildings engulfed him. He drew the carriage curtain so he would not have to look, would not have to realise that anyone who came from these putrid streets would have seen things, done things, that he could never comprehend.

The carriage stopped. Able Street. He jumped down the steps and marched between the slum houses, determined not to look from side to side, focused only on his aim. The door to the house was open, and he did not wait for permission to enter. He ran up the stairs, dodging new holes in the floor which had not been there when he had last visited.

He strode into Ruby's room and found her naked on all fours, a man thrusting at the back of her. Ruby screamed as the man shouted at Osborne to get out, but Osborne did not move. The pair of them scrabbled to find their clothes, the man packaging himself away inside his trousers furiously.

'What in Christ's name are you playing at?' Ruby said, glaring at Osborne as she dragged her slip over herself.

The man grumbled at her, said he wouldn't pay and wouldn't be back, and they exchanged unpleasantries like cats fighting in a street until she kicked his backside and pushed him out of the room. He stumbled down the first few steps as she threw his jacket at his head.

'Piss off, then!' She returned to her room, slammed the door behind her, and grabbed a gin bottle. 'I told you – after midday.' She chewed off the stopper and spat it on the floor near Osborne's feet. 'And that was fucking weeks ago.'

'Yes.' Now, on his own in this stinking room, he felt his confidence waver. 'Yes, I know. I wasn't going to come–'

'But!' Ruby cackled. 'Thought it wouldn't bother you?' She put the bottle on the floor and dragged her leg into her lap. The soul of her foot was dirty and red as she scratched it. 'Thought you'd forget about it?'

'I made a promise to you that I would return.'

'And since when has a gentleman cared for the promises he once made to a whore? Don't try to flatter me, nor yourself. You came back because it's been on your mind, wriggling away in there.' She wiggled her finger at his face. 'I can read you all like books, if only I could read!'

'Will you tell me or not?'

She stared at his pocket, considering. 'How much?'

He fished out a shilling.

'I can make thrice that in the time it will take me to explain.'

She was playing him, he knew it. He held out a pound note, smirking as she gawped at it. She grabbed for it, but he pulled it away from her.

'Tell me first.'

Ruby climbed up the bed and propped her back against the stacked pillows. 'Will you have a seat?'

The bed was filthy and stained, and there was no chair to sit on. Osborne rolled on the balls of his feet, then decided it was best if he held his ground. This was not a sociable visit.

'Fine. She'd have men up here, in her rooms.'

'What kind of men?'

'All sorts. Nice, though, nicer than any I've ever had. But then, she'd got a prettier face. And she'd got John.'

'What do you know of him?'

'I know his name was John.' She laughed. 'Irish, from what I heard of him. Could sell a shoe to a peg leg, he could. I'd listen to him bringing them up to her, and even I'd want to fuck her by the time he'd finished describing her. Small, he was, and sneaky.'

'What happened, when ... well, with the men?'

She rolled her eyes towards the ceiling. 'What do you think happened? Don't play the fool, sir.'

'She was happy doing it?'

'Christ, no, though she bloody well should have been with the amount she was getting. I'd hear her crying sometimes when there was no one in there with her. Crying and praying.'

'Crying because …?'

'Because she was a whore! Because she was just like the rest of us. Because she loved John so much.' Ruby gulped some gin. 'Never seen a girl so stupid for a bloke. She was like a dog, pining for its master, going back after a beating.'

'John used to beat her?'

'Not in the way you think of it. At least, not what I saw. No – in here,' she tapped her head. 'I could hear her coming, you know, for all the rattling. Now, I like a drink, keeps off the cold, if you understand? But the amount she'd get through! Gin and laudanum. Enough to stop a horse.'

'Is this supposed to make me hate her?'

'It ain't supposed to make you do anything.'

Ruby jumped off the bed and picked up the piss pot. She sauntered to the window so that Osborne could see the fullness of the bowl, the stagnant yellow of old urine. She trickled the contents down the outside wall, and the foul breeze from the window caught his hot face. She brought the pot inside again, set it beside the bed, then lifted her slip and squatted. Osborne marched for the door; he would not be humiliated.

'Came back with all her hair gone one day,' she called, and Osborne halted in the doorway. 'Wouldn't tell me why. And no sign of John for days, so I was listening when he did come back.'

He heard the last trickle of Ruby's piss and the rush of her slip over her thighs. He peeked over his shoulder to find her lying on the bed once more, grinning at him.

'Shut the door, won't you? There's an awful draught.'

He stepped back inside and gently pushed the door closed, keeping one hand on the knob. 'What happened?'

'He'd bought her a wig. I saw it once when she thought she was being sneaky. Brown, it was, not like her own hair used to be. Didn't suit her.'

'Why would he buy her a wig?'

'Why, indeed?' Her eyebrows rose, she shrugged. 'Fuck-money weren't good enough? He struck me as the type where nothing was ever good enough. And why such an awful wig?'

He felt her dangling something in front of him, testing to see if he was quick enough to work it out. He shook his head.

'She'd got beautiful hair. Down to her waist and as gold as your fancy pocket watch, there. Not many folks have hair like that, do they? It's recognisable.'

His fingers twitched as he recalled the softness of Catherine's hair, the beauty of it. 'Tell me straight what you mean.'

'I was listening at the door, you see, that time he came back after all her hair was gone. I thought they must have had a row for him to have been gone for so long. I was waiting for the shouting, but he was gentle with her. He told her everything was well, that he'd got a plan for them. She said that she wouldn't do it, that she'd told him, and she wouldn't tell him again. It was the first time I'd heard her say anything against him and I thought, here it is, here comes the blow, but it didn't. He told her he'd thought of a better way.' Ruby studied Osborne. 'Laudanum.'

He didn't understand. His cheeks burned.

'She was nothing but the bait, in the end.'

'Catherine would never ... I don't believe you.'

Ruby shrugged and drank more gin. 'Don't need to. But

there were never any more punters up here with her, and she was gone in a week.'

'Gone where?'

Another shrug. 'But you don't have a regular room and rob people, do you? You move around. And someone did start robbing. And how do I know that? Because I was busier than ever. People knew me. I've been here for years, you see, they trust me. Miss Catherine did me a favour, really.'

'It could have been anyone.'

'Yes.' Ruby sighed and smiled at him. 'It could have been, you're right. This town is full of pick-pockets and poisoners. You should watch yourself, sir, in these streets.'

'I do.'

She chuckled. 'Cat could have gone anywhere, done anything, for all I know she could have married John and had an honest life. I could have misunderstood the whole thing.' She crawled to the foot of the bed where Osborne stood. 'But I don't think you'd be here if that were the case.'

He stepped away from her.

She held out her hand. 'That's all I have to tell you, sir.'

'You hated her.'

'Not hate. Didn't have enough cause to hate.'

'Then why have you told me so much?'

She snatched the note from his hands, held it up to the light, and smiled.

'Everyone has their reasons for everything, don't they? Everyone has secrets. We never really know the truth until it's too late.'

CHAPTER 24

September 1854. Wallingham Hall.

'Here now, drink this.' Ruth set the cup into Cat's trembling hands. Cat sipped it and tasted the piercing sweetness of too much sugar. 'You're worrying yourself over nothing, my dear, I'm sure.'

'Am I? He didn't say where he was going. He doesn't tell me anything at all.'

'It's just his way. He's been on his own a long time.'

The fire was burning in the parlour grate. Outside, though the sun shone, the wind was cold; October was tapping to be let in.

'He doesn't look at me like he used to.'

'Men change when they become husbands.'

'We have been married only a few months!'

Ruth sighed and stroked the side of her china cup. 'It's that time of year.'

'Yes, I know.' She breathed in deep. Don't upset the ally, she reminded herself, and drank her tea. Ruth filled her cup again and offered the sugar, but Cat declined. She pressed her handkerchief to her eyes.

'I ... I told him he is to be a father.'

A gasp of breath, then Ruth was before her, congratulating her, kissing her cheeks.

'But he was not pleased, you see. It was like I had told him the worst possible news.'

Ruth tossed a lump of coal on the fire and wiped her hand on her dark dress; there was no need for pretence and false airs in Cat's company.

'I fear he is in one of his dark moods, by what you have said. Always at this time of the year, he is worse, but the news of a child! He should be overjoyed.'

'He has used my past against me,' she whispered, glancing towards the door as if there might be listening ears on the other side of it.

'You have been forgiven, Catherine. By God and by him. He should remember his promises. He knew how you lived ...' Ruth shook her head and couldn't bring herself to finish.

'He never sees me. He is forever in that damned study! Forgive me.'

Ruth smiled and squeezed Cat's hand. 'I understand your frustration. We must learn to have only half of our husbands and lose the other half to their work.'

'But I have seen him in there; he does nothing. He stares at the ceiling as he sits in the dark. It is not ...' She would not say the word *normal*, for that would be calling her husband mad.

Ruth collapsed inwards, the chair squeaking under her weight. 'I do not want to worry you – especially not now with the child – but Osborne has done this before.' She leant closer to Cat. 'Remember I told you a doctor was called? I didn't tell you why.'

She drew a handkerchief from her skirt pocket and wiped her eyes.

'Walter found Osborne in his study that time, and he was just as you say; dull, lifeless. There was a map of Ireland that he'd shot through with bullets. And he'd … Well, he'd hurt himself, said he didn't want to live any longer.'

'Why?'

'His father's death.'

'It wasn't his fault.'

'It was supposed to be him though, you see. Osborne should have gone to Ireland. Theodore was handing all business matters to his son, preparing him for his inheritance. Osborne was meant to sort things out over there.'

'Why didn't he?'

She smiled sadly. 'Everyone knew the place was full of disease, that death was everywhere. He was too scared. He was like a little boy again.'

The warmth of the fire could not penetrate Cat. 'What happened? After Walter found him in the study?'

'Walter called for the doctor, and Osborne was taken away to rest.'

'And when he returned?'

'Recovered, so it seemed. Osborne is not a bad man, Catherine, as you know, or you would not have married him. He is a man who has been tortured with grief. Sometimes he needs help.'

'I would help him if only he would let me.'

'You already do. You are Osborne's remedy, Catherine.' Ruth drained her cup. 'He will mend, just give him time. For now, you must take care of yourself and your child.'

The candle had been blown out hours ago, and the fire was dwindling. She had left the curtains open so that the moon shone in one bright beam upon her covers, and she looked out at the splatter of stars against the black sky. Her hands rested on her stomach, on the child inside her, and she caressed the soft silk bedspread. The child was her safety.

'This will all be yours,' she whispered. What a life her baby would have! She would make sure of it.

She heard the grind of wheels outside. The weak yellow beam of the carriage's lamp reflected in the windowpane. Boots slammed into the gravel, unsteadily. The front door opened; Dixon must still be awake, waiting for his master. One of the dogs barked, and then silence fell as she imagined Osborne staggering into the heart of the house.

She finished her glass of water and brandy; it was a weak substitute, but it helped to calm her nerves. She scooted down the bed and rolled onto her side as heavy and uneven footsteps plodded along the landing, getting louder. She closed her eyes as the door swung open.

He brought the stench of town with him, and the cutting tang of too much whisky and beer and tobacco and whore's perfume. His feet dragged over the rugs, and she heard her dressing table squeak as he grabbed it to steady himself. There was a moment of quiet, and she felt the sense of eyes on her. She kept her own closed, deepened her breathing, kept her body still, as she had done so many times before.

Then the dressing-table drawers were opening and closing, too loud to ignore. Languidly, Cat raised her hand to her face, screwing her eyes against the light from the hallway through the open door. Osborne stumbled away from the dressing table and towards her bed. His attention focused on the glass on her bedside table, and he stuck his fingers inside it, then into his mouth.

'Osborne?' She made her voice soft.

'Where is it?'

'Where is what?' She held out her hand, but he would not take it.

His lips puckered as he tried to pronounce the word correctly. 'Laudanum.' He picked up the glass again and ran his tongue around the rim.

'What do you mean, Osborne?'

'The laudanum!' He punched the glass onto the table. The room shook.

She pushed herself up the bed, turning so her stomach was angled away from him. 'Osborne, you are frightening me.'

'Where is it, Catherine? And the wig.'

'What wig?'

He thumped the wall. The painting on the wall crashed to the floor, the scene of a countryside picnic splitting in two. He jerked his hand back and cradled it to his chest. The skin over his knuckles had ripped, and blood was beginning to seep into the creases of his fingers.

'Osborne?'

He looked at her again, the bleariness of alcohol and smoke just beginning to clear from his eyes to be replaced with tears. 'I loved you.'

'I know.' She took his wounded hand and kissed the torn flesh, letting the blood stain her lips as he sobbed above her. She reeled him closer until he was lying beside her, his face pressed into her neck, weeping.

'I loved you, Catherine.'

'I love you too,' she said, and he cried harder. 'We are having a baby, Osborne.' She clasped his hand over her abdomen. If only he could feel the child, feel the heartbeat! 'You will be a wonderful father, Osborne.'

She felt him shake his head.

'You will. This child will be the most loved in the world, I vow it. I will do anything for it.'

His sobs began to ebb. His arm grew heavier. Cat heard the words again, the breath of them against her ear before he succumbed to sleep, 'I loved you, Catherine.'

CHAPTER 25

October 1854. Wallingham Hall.

THE RAIN HAMMERED on the window and woke her. Water streaked the glass, distorting the grey world outside, and strong gusts of wind made the thin panes rattle.

She rang for Nelly.

'You're up early, ma'am.' Nelly brought a tray of ginger tea with her, as she had been doing these last few months. Cat poured it quickly, yearning for the bite of it to calm her nausea.

'Has he gone?'

'Would he go in this?' Nelly nodded at the weather outside.

'Has Dixon been called?'

'A few minutes ago, ma'am.'

That was all she needed. Cat slid her robe over her shoulders and ran out of her chamber, her feet thudding on the carpet. She stopped outside Osborne's chamber door and heard the muffled sound of him and Dixon inside.

She knocked. Silence.

Then Dixon opened the door with the smallest of smiles, his eyes never wholly meeting hers.

'Master Tomkins is engaged at the moment, ma'am.'

Sweet Dixon, his face reddened with the impertinence he had been commanded to give. He lingered in the doorway, and behind him, she could see Osborne reflected in the looking glass, hiding behind the door.

'Thank you, Dixon, I won't be a moment.' She pushed past him and faced her husband.

Osborne strode out of his useless hiding place and glowered at Dixon.

'What do you want?' Osborne thrust his arms through his jacket, and she glimpsed the revolver already fastened in its holder.

'There is a storm, Osborne. I don't think you should go out.'

He paced to his dresser and dragged a comb through his hair, viciously tugging out the knots. Cat had not seen him in days, ever since that night when he had searched her room. The cuts on his knuckles were black scabs now, the flesh bruised purple. He had not shaved since then, and thick stubble merged with his sideburns. The skin of his face was as grey and slick as the weather outside.

'Please, Osborne, do not go out there today. It is not safe. Think of the baby, of me, worrying for you.'

One bark of laughter. Osborne slammed the comb onto the table, then jabbed his fingers into the bowl of water and scrubbed his skin three times.

'What is wrong with you? I am with child, Osborne. You have said nothing to me about it.'

He grabbed his hat and made for the door.

Enough of this, she thought and barred his way.

'You should be happy, and you are not. Why?'

His lips worked as if he was about to answer, then he shoved her out of the way. She tripped over her feet from the force of his push and caught herself on the bed. She rounded on him, rage flaring.

'What were you doing in my room? Where had you been that day?'

He fixed his hat on his head.

'Answer me! What were you doing?' Her voice crashed off the walls.

'Looking for laudanum.'

'Why?'

'Where is it?'

'I do not have any, why would I? I have never needed it.'

Slowly, his lips raised into a smile. 'Liar.'

She tried not to show her shock.

'Whore,' he hissed.

She dropped onto the bed and held her stomach as she began to cry.

'Poisoner.'

Sickness rose up her throat, drying her tears. She swallowed it down.

'Your friend Ruby told me all about you.'

'She was never a friend to me. She is spiteful, Osborne. She is mean and bitter, and she never liked me. Can't you see that she has told you nothing but lies?'

'Why would she?'

'To hurt me.'

'She didn't think that much of you.' He prowled towards her. 'I can see her in you. I can see the filth in you. She was right; you are no different from her.'

Cat leapt to her feet and tried to shove his chest away, but she could not move him. 'I am nothing like her!'

'Vicious like her too.'

She ran for the window as he laughed at her.

Breathe, she told herself, clinging to the sill. She focused on the clouds, how they roiled and rolled in the sky, like one devastating iron mass.

Be calm, be in control. The pulse in her temples began to slow.

'What kind of man goes sneaking into brothels when their wife is pregnant?' Her voice was sharp, acid. She turned to him, holding onto her hands so they would not shake.

'I did not go with her.'

'She is riddled, you know. All that disease.' She let the word linger in the air. He flinched. 'All that disease smothering you, and now you bring it into your own home.'

'The only disease I have ever brought into this house is you.'

'You would believe a drunken, pock-marked whore over your wife? What kind of man are you?' She crept towards him. 'A man who blames everyone but himself. A man who would shirk his responsibilities. Useless. A coward!'

She did not sense the movement of his arm until his fist slammed into her face. She heard something crack somewhere near her left ear – bone on bone – as she crashed into the floor. Something else snapped, this time in her wrist. For a moment, there was nothing at all; no sound, no sight, no feeling. Then, as the light swelled in her eyes, the agony began to build.

She tried to push herself upright, but her wrist gave way. She rolled onto her side as her face throbbed, and blinked to see Osborne finish dressing himself and stride for the door. The draught from the hallway washed over her naked ankles and slithered up her legs. Then a shadow and Nelly dropped to Cat's side, whimpering and crying, telling Cat everything would be well and that she would get help.

Cat waited, alone, the cold spiralling around her and pulling on her eyelids, calling for sleep, until Nelly returned with Cook. They helped her to sit up, and Cook placed her hot, dry hands on Cat's face, looking for damage.

'Don't think anything's broken, ma'am.'

Cat cradled her sore wrist, and Nelly pointed it out to Cook. Glancing down, Cat saw for herself the crooked angle of it.

'Call for a doctor,' Nelly said.

'No.' Cat's senses were returning and, though the pain was cutting, she felt the confusion beginning to end. 'Ready a carriage, I must go to the vicarage.'

'Ma'am, it's pouring outside.'

'And Osborne is out there. Mr Turner can help him like he did last time. Please, Nelly, I am fine, I shall heal.'

'The baby, ma'am?'

The baby. She grabbed her stomach and closed her eyes, wishing she could journey into herself and check on the child within. She did not feel anything strange, there was no pain inside, and there was no change between her legs.

'He is well, Nelly, I am certain. Ready the carriage and help me dress. Now. We must be quick.'

SHE FELL out of the carriage, gripping the handle with her good hand so she did not slam into the muck. Ruth rushed out to greet her, holding out a woollen shawl which she swung over Cat's head as protection against the weather.

'What are you doing up there?' Ruth shouted over the beating rain at the driver, still in his seat at the front of the carriage. She shook her head at him – Cat knew she would have scolded the man more had the weather not been so terrible.

The gate squeaked shut behind her. The path to the

vicarage's front door was a mire of mud and decapitated flower heads as she stumbled across it, clinging to Ruth for support. It smelt of the earth, of the last dying scents of summer, of the coal smoke that spewed from the chimney.

'Walter!' Ruth kicked the door open and threw the shawl on the floor. The maid emerged. 'Get me towels and make some tea, quickly!'

The girl dipped and sprinted away. Ruth's fingers dug into Cat's arm, pulling her towards the parlour where the fire was banked high. She pushed Cat onto a seat and took a moment to catch her breath.

'What on earth are you doing out in this, Catherine?' She stopped short, her breath catching in her throat, her hands dashing to cover her open mouth. She dropped to her knees before Cat. 'What has happened?' Her fingers fluttered to Cat's face.

Cat flinched from the lightest touch. The bruise would be significant. 'Osborne.'

'Osborne did this?'

Cat quivered. She felt herself slipping, her control leaking away.

'Come here.' Ruth opened her arms and Cat fell into them. She rested against Ruth's shoulder and let the woman's warmth radiate into her. She sobbed for everything that was happening and everything that had already happened.

'The baby?' Ruth whispered.

'Well, I think.'

Ruth's shoulders eased, and she rubbed Cat's back. 'Hush now. You are safe.'

She rocked Cat back and forth until the stinging heat in Cat's eyes dried to a dull grittiness.

'Where is he?'

'I tried to stop him but he … He's out there somewhere. It's today.'

Ruth nodded, still stroking Cat's back. 'You did what you could, my dear. Wait here.'

She bustled out of the room, screeching at the maid and shouting for her husband again.

Cat watched the coals burn, orange in the black, molten and morphing. Bumps and groans sounded from further inside the house – furniture and bodies moving over old floorboards. Then Ruth returned carrying a tea tray, and Walter followed behind, holding a towel. He gawped at Cat's face.

Ruth snatched the towel from him, knelt before Cat, and began to dry her feet.

'Now, here is what is going to happen,' Ruth began. 'You are going to get yourself warm and dry and have some tea. Then Walter is going to take you back to the Hall and wait for Osborne. You are to go to your room and keep yourself calm, all right?'

Cat nodded. 'Osborne?'

'Leave him to Walter.'

'He's out there!'

'Yes, yes, I know. But he is a grown man, Catherine. A grown man who should know better,' she mumbled to herself as she wiped the muck off Cat's dress. 'He will come back when he wants. And when he does, Walter will be waiting, won't you? Now, come on, drink your tea, my dear. Walter will talk some sense into him.'

SHE STARED at the darkening clouds blindly, until she realised the grey had turned to black. Still, Osborne had not returned. She dragged her gaze to Nelly, who sat in front of the fire, picking at the hard skin on her hands.

Mr Turner was downstairs. She had left him in the library where she thought he would be happiest, and had instructed

Dixon to keep an eye on him, to make sure he was comfortable and fed and had plenty to drink.

'Can I get you anything, ma'am?' Nelly said again – the same question she had been asking all day.

Cat shook her head which made the throbbing worse. She shielded her eyes with her hands, letting her forehead rest in her palm. She felt herself falling, drifting until she stumbled and woke herself with a start.

'You should sleep, ma'am.'

'I will wait for Osborne.'

Nelly picked her hands again.

Cat listened to the grandfather clock in the hallway. Everywhere was silent; the whole house was holding its breath, waiting. Where was he? She imagined him thrown from his horse, his body crumpled at the bottom of the hillside. She envisioned his white, bloated corpse, face down in the lake in the forest. Perhaps he had ridden all the way to Birmingham and was bringing a police force back with him.

Nelly ran to the window. 'He is here, ma'am!'

Cat joined Nelly's side, and they watched as Dixon and the groom dashed to meet him. He toppled from his stallion and into their arms. The horse was just as exhausted, its coat drenched, its chest sucking in and out as its hot breath blew white clouds in the lamplight. The rain still pounded as the groom led the horse away and Dixon draped Osborne over his shoulder.

Cat marched for the door, but Nelly stopped her.

'Please, ma'am. Mr Turner says you are to stay here, for your own safety.'

'He is my husband.'

Nelly clutched her hand. 'Please, ma'am, I beg you. Stay here. If he hurt you again …' Nelly's eyes misted.

Cat's sharpness dissolved, and she embraced the girl; how nice it was to be looked after, to be cared for! She gripped onto Nelly, wishing the girl was Lottie or Helen, then returned to her seat.

'I will wait until he is with Mr Turner. Will you go and see what is happening?'

Nelly slipped from the room. She was good at being silent; Cat heard nothing of her footsteps as she went down to spy.

'They are in the library, ma'am,' Nelly said when she returned.

Cat ordered Nelly to sit and wait for her, and she would not hear another protest – she was going to listen.

She used the servant's passage for the first time. It was narrower than any corridor in the main house, its walls and floors bare and windowless, like a wormhole. She emerged just off the great hall, tiptoed towards the library door, and pressed her ear against the wood.

'Calm down, Osborne, please, you will make yourself unwell.'

'I will not! I will not be in the same house as that Irishman's whore!'

'Osborne, please–'

'I am Mr Tomkins to you, Reverend.'

Silence. She imagined Mr Turner blushing, the poor, old man so heartlessly plummeted back into his place.

'Mr Tomkins, I would remind you that you knew Catherine's past before you married her. You made your vows before God–'

'I did not know the truth! She is a trickster and a fraud.'

'I am sure Catherine is not capable of these things of which you accuse her.'

'How would you know?'

'She is a Godly woman.'

The slap of laughter.

'And if she did anything at all ... ungodly, it was because

of that man, you know that. You know what evil he was.'

'Yes, I do. And I know that she loved him for it.'

'She loves you, Osborne. She has been worried about you all day. She came out to fetch me, in this weather, when you had …'

'When I had what?' A stretch of quiet. 'When I had what, Reverend? Defended myself against her? Treated her like the animal she is?'

'Calm yourself now.' Mr Turner's voice quaked with anger. 'I will not listen to you speak like this against your wife.'

'I will divorce her.'

'On what grounds?'

'Deception.'

'She is carrying your child, Osborne.'

'Is she? Are you sure? Because I am not.'

'Are you accusing her of adultery?'

'Yes.'

'With who?'

'The Irishman!'

Her legs threatened to buckle, her weight pressed against the chill stone wall.

'That is impossible, Mr Tomkins.'

'Is it?'

'Mr Tomkins, please, sit down. I will call the doctor to see you in the morning.'

'I do not need any damned doctor! I will have her out. I will have her strung up. She will join that bastard Jonathon Murphy in hell. And you, Mr Turner, will leave my house now if you will side with her.'

'I side with no one, Mr Tomkins. But, Osborne, what you accuse her of is a physical impossibility.'

'Out! Now!'

She heard them charging for the door. She raced to the

servant's passage just as the library door crashed open. She did not wait to hear Mr Turner depart. She ran all the way up the stairs and to her room where Nelly remained seated beside the fire biting her lip and slammed the door shut. She turned the lock then took the key out of the door and held it to her chest.

'Ma'am?'

Cat dashed to the window to find Mr Turner stumbling towards the waiting carriage. He glanced up to her, squinting as the rain splashed against his face. She showed him the key, and he nodded, then ducked into the Brougham.

'Ma'am, what is happening?'

'I am in danger, Nelly.'

'What! Why?'

Footsteps pounded on the landing, then fists against the door. Nelly shrieked as the wooden frame shook and splintered, as Osborne demanded to be let inside, demanded that she leave this house immediately.

'Osborne, please, the baby.'

'Damn that bastard child!'

Cat pointed at the wardrobe. It was a weight for just the two of them to shift, and even harder with her bad wrist, but fear drove them on. She and Nelly were panting and sweating by the time they had pushed the wardrobe before the door.

They listened for more, holding their breath, their eyes wide. Osborne had seemed to wear himself out. They waited until enough time had passed for them to assume he had gone away.

Cat collapsed on the bed as Nelly cried beside her.

'What will we do, ma'am?'

Cat stared at the doe in the wooden bed canopy. 'Wait,' she said, as her eyelids drooped and the doe blurred into blackness.

CHAPTER 26

October 1854. Wallingham Hall.

'MA'AM?' Nelly nudged her awake.

She found herself still dressed in yesterday's clothes. The curtains remained open, but outside the storm had passed. Dead, sodden leaves stuck to the window, but beyond, the sky was a pale blue laced with thin white clouds.

'Should we …?' Nelly gestured at the wardrobe.

It was harder to move the bulky thing this morning, without fear making them strong. The feet of it pushed up the rugs and scraped the floorboards, but they managed to drag it a few feet away from the door so they could get out of the room. A couple of the boys could move it back to its proper place later.

The landing was surprisingly busy, the servants in a rush, stopping and curtseying to her quickly before moving on. They were scurrying in and out of Osborne's room, arms piled with towels and hot water jugs and bowls of food.

Nelly was close behind Cat as she made her way to Osborne's chamber. She peeked through the door to find Dixon pacing at the foot of the bed, instructing the servants where to place the towels, to take away the chamber pot again, to refill the bedpan.

Within the bed, Osborne lay shaking. His skin was flamed red and drowned in sweat, but he clutched his covers close to his chin as his teeth chattered.

'What is going on?'

'Master Tomkins has fallen ill, ma'am, during the night.'

She stepped towards her husband. His eyelids were thin and wet and jerked as he dreamt. She touched his forehead gently, so not to wake him, and gasped at the heat of him.

'Close the curtains,' she said, taking charge. 'Stoke the fire. Dixon, you have done well, my husband is gravely ill. We must call for a doctor.'

'He forbade it, ma'am. When he was awake, he said he would not have a doctor in his house.'

'Then he is a fool.' She caught herself and smiled tightly at Dixon's shocked face. 'I will nurse him as best I can, but I fear this is beyond me. Have Cook prepare some more broth.' She busied herself with a wet cloth, wringing it out and perching by Osborne's side to wipe his forehead clean. 'I trust you will send word to Mr Turner to say what has happened?'

'Yes, ma'am.' Dixon bowed and departed.

Nelly lingered in the far corner of the room, watching. Cat could see the terror in the girl's face as she looked at Osborne as if she thought he could rise and kill them all at any moment.

'Nelly, sort his clothes, would you?'

She nodded at the heap of sodden clothes which steamed before the fire. In his rush to care for Osborne, Dixon must have forgotten to have them taken away. Nelly picked them up with her fingertips as if Osborne's sickness – or madness – might be catching.

'Hurry now. I would not have them pollute the air.'

The girl did as she was told and disappeared. Only Cat remained in the room.

'What have you done, Osborne?' She laid the back of her hand across his trembling cheek.

She should not nurse him like this. She was no healer. And what if he died? What if he died the day after he had told her to leave, after he had said he would divorce her – after she had watched over him, fed him, cared for him?

She should not be alone with him. She rang the bell, summoning whoever was available, and saw the revolver lying on the dressing table. One of the maids arrived and waited in the doorway. Cat ushered her inside, despite the reluctance of the girl, and told her to keep an eye on Osborne.

'I will not have this in the room.' She took the revolver and left the room.

The revolver weighed heavily in her hand. She held it awkwardly; away from her side, the end pointing at the floor. Her arm was stiff, afraid any sudden movement might make the thing go off. She hurried to the study.

Being in Osborne's private world without him was strange. It was like she was a child, wandering into forbidden territory. She held her breath, imagining a hand may strike out and grab her.

She tiptoed to the desk and perched on the leather chair. It was soft underneath her; the leather stretched over the years by Osborne and his father's weight. She surveyed the room from this vantage point, and her eyes rested on the papers on the desk. A letter of correspondence from a Mr Griffin caught her attention.

Mr Tomkins,

I write to inform you that your orders have been seen to. The last of the cottages have been evacuated, and I have found several farmers eager to take on the larger proportions of land. They shall begin the tenancy by the end of the month under the rent system we agreed.

Yours sincerely,
Mr G. Griffin

She shoved the paper away from her in disgust.

A few minutes later, she returned to Osborne's chamber and replaced the gun where she had found it.

CAT STROKED Osborne's head as Nelly came into the room with a tray of broth. 'Osborne? Osborne, can you hear me?'

He grunted as his head jerked from side to side.

'Osborne.' Cat shook his shoulders as the two servants watched in silence. After another gentle nudge, his eyes opened. They were red around the rims, sore and dry, unseeing for a moment until recognition clouded his face.

'You must eat something, my love.' Cat held the bowl before him.

Osborne dashed it from her hands, and the scalding liquid seeped through her dress. She leapt away, pulling her skirts off her legs.

'Don't come near me,' Osborne said, his voice rough and low.

'Osborne, I am trying to care for you.'

'What was in it? What have you put into it? *Poisoner!*'

Cat fled from the room, followed swiftly by the servants.

'Get Dixon. He is the only one Osborne trusts.' The maid ran through the servant's doorway. 'Nelly, you must call for the doctor.'

'Master Tomkins said—'

'I know what he said, but does he look like a man in his right mind to you? Without a doctor he will die, and I will not have that on my conscience. Fetch the doctor at once.'

Inside her own chamber, with the door locked once again, Cat found the bottle behind her bed. She unplugged the stopper and sniffed one last time, then threw it into the grate. The glass smashed and fell into the flames.

Next, she threw in the wig and shoved all the windows in her room as far open as they would go. As the fire roared and the cold wind whipped her back, she watched the glass and the horsehair burn, until the final bits of her past had disintegrated.

THE CHILL WOULD NOT CEASE. The piles of blankets crushed him, but still, Osborne could feel no warmth. His damned teeth would not stop chattering; his muscles in his jaw were beginning to ache and spasm. And all he saw, when he dragged his eyes open, was Dixon staring at him.

Then, his stomach convulsed, and he arched over the bed. Dixon was swift with the bowl, and a trail of clear gloop spilled from Osborne's mouth, scratching his throat as it came up. He collapsed onto his pillows, cringing at the gush of cold air against his back. His mouth gaped open, searching for breath, and Dixon was beside him, wiping a damp cloth over his face.

Something caught his attention, something by the door. Knocking? Dixon left his side to answer it, and a man entered. He could not make out his features, nor his words until he came closer, then, a face not much older than his own, appeared.

Blonde haired and handsome. Stephen.

His friend had returned to him. How could he have ever

let him go for that whore? Tears slid across his temples as his friend sat beside him.

'You came,' Osborne said, struggling to lift his arm out of the covers to touch his friend.

'How are you, Mr Tomkins?'

'Do you forgive me, Stephen? I should never have–'

'Mr Tomkins, my name is Norton.'

Osborne frowned at the figure beside him, the stranger, not at all like Stephen – he could see now.

'I am a doctor.'

Osborne scuffled backwards, but he was too weak to get far. 'Get out of my house.'

'Please, Mr Tomkins, I am here to help.'

'She sent you.'

'Dixon, your man here, sent for me.'

'No!'

'Mr Tomkins, you have an extreme fever. You are very ill, sir, and I will try to help you.'

'You will take me away.'

'I shall not take you anywhere. You are to stay in this bed until you have recovered, I will not have you moved.' The doctor turned his face to Dixon. 'Keep the room warm and clean. Clean clothes and sheets daily. Plain food, little and often.'

'He won't eat,' Dixon said.

The doctor turned to Osborne again. 'You must eat, Mr Tomkins, to keep your strength up.'

'She has poisoned me.'

'Who has poisoned you?'

'My wife.'

Hovering above him, Dixon and Norton looked at each other uncertainly.

'She is trying to kill me. She is a whore, a trickster. She has been feeding me poison.'

'What kind of poison?'

'Laudanum.'

'You do not show the signs of taking laudanum, sir. You have a fever, most likely brought about by being outside all day in the storm.'

'Why can you not see? It is her!' His arm sprang free of the covers and gripped the doctor's hand. 'You must tell the police.'

The doctor pulled his hand away as he stood. 'I will do all I can, sir, I promise you, but for now, my priority is to ensure your recovery. You must rest and calm yourself.'

'How can I be calm when she remains in this house?'

'Mr Tomkins, I promise you she will not come near you.'

'You will tell them?'

Sensing the vague motion of Norton's head moving up and down, Osborne slumped onto his pillows, exhausted.

'Thank you.' He closed his eyes, finally able to rest.

CAT CREPT AWAY from the door and waited down the landing. Doctor Norton emerged from the room, sagging, different from the spritely man she had seen hop down from his cab and make his way to the door less than an hour ago. He pulled out a patterned handkerchief from his pocket and wiped his hands on it.

'Doctor?'

She waited for him to approach. There was mistrust in his face as he regarded her.

'How is my husband?'

'The fever is bad.'

'Will he recover?'

'I will do my best for him. You are to keep your distance.'

She nodded and retrieved her silk handkerchief to dab her eyes. 'He hates me.' Her voice broke. 'I don't know how it has happened. He will not let me near him. What have I done?'

Doctor Norton cleared his throat. 'He accuses you of–'

'I have only ever loved him. He saved me, Doctor. He saved me from the most terrible man, and now he thinks I wish to kill him. Why? Why would I want to do such a thing? I am carrying his child.'

The doctor stepped forward, surprised. 'Mrs Tomkins, I did now know you were expecting. I would urge you to calm yourself for the sake of the child.'

'How can I?' She sobbed and turned away from him, and his hand came to her face.

'What is this?' He touched the edge of her bruise.

'It is nothing.'

'Mrs Tomkins?'

'He was so angry with me.' She held out her hand. Her wrist still throbbed, and it had swollen and bruised. 'Can you help with this, Doctor? I would sit down if that is all right with you?'

He followed her to her chamber. She sat on one of the chairs and rested her feet on the stool as the doctor fastened a sling around her arm.

'You must rest it and let it heal. I will send a surgeon to see if the bone needs resetting.'

'Tell me, Doctor,' she gestured for him to sit beside her, 'what it is my husband accuses me of.'

He took the seat. Cat noticed the way he sat, his legs wide, his clean, soft hands resting on his knees. He glanced at the fire, then to her, then back at the flames.

'I do not wish to upset you, Mrs Tomkins.'

'Please.' She reached for his hand, then pulled away quickly. 'He accused me of poisoning him earlier today. I only tried to feed him. I have not even been into the kitchens since his illness, I swear. I am only trying to help him, that is why I sent for you.'

'I know.'

'You will help him, Doctor? You will help him in all the ways that you can?' She stared at him, willing him to understand. 'He needs rest, Doctor. Did you help him before?'

He shook his head. 'My father.'

'So, your father understands him. Good.' She dabbed her eyes again. 'Please, let him be a father, Doctor. Let him be able to love his child. I do not care if he despises me forever, but let him love his child!'

It was Doctor Norton who reached for her this time. She let him hold her hand, softly, as though he were an old friend, as he promised that he would do whatever he could.

CHAPTER 27

October 1854. Wallingham Hall.

DIXON HELPED OSBORNE DRESS. His clothes felt alien as they slithered onto his skin, too hard, too constricting, compared to his nightclothes. They made him stand up straight, and his muscles trembled as he did so.

He coughed – a hacking cough, like usual. He spat into the bowl, then rinsed his mouth. The water shook as he held it to his lips, and he had to sit down on the bed to stop the room from moving around him.

'Sir, are you well enough for dinner?'

He pointed at the revolver on the cabinet, and Dixon fixed it around Osborne's waist. He saw Dixon's frown, felt the man's unease, but Osborne would not be in this house without protection when she still lived in it.

He was panting by the time he had made it down the stairs. The chill of the house pressed against his wet forehead, and he shivered; he had become used to the fire and the bedpan in his room. He wiped the cold sweat away and held onto the bannister as he collected himself. His breath came too short nowadays as if he could never get a proper lungful of air, and it made his insides flutter with panic until he told himself to stop being so foolish.

He forced his spine straight, struck out with his cane, and stalked to the dining room.

Catherine sat at the far end of the table. She rose when he entered, and for a moment he thought she might run to him, embrace him, kiss him, but his stare made her remain where she was. Dixon helped him into his chair, then poured the wine.

'You look better, Osborne,' she said.

He noticed how she tried to smile, but the warmth did not spread to her eyes.

She was a beauty. Even with the faded bruise and her arm in a sling, he could see how he had been so easily bewitched. No one would have ever known, as she sat at his grand table, wearing beautiful clothes he had bought, her golden hair perfectly styled by the maid he paid for, that she was a street rat.

He could hear Dixon behind the screen, readying dishes.

'Leave us.'

Silence.

The fire was beginning to warm him. The more he relaxed, the more she stiffened.

'I will divorce you.'

'Osborne, I am–'

'Carrying my child, yes, you said.' He swirled his glass, and the red wine whirled high towards the rim.

'Why do you not believe me?'

He set the glass on the table and watched the liquid settle before he allowed himself to answer. He would not waste his energy getting angry.

'You have done nothing but lie to me, Catherine, ever since the day I met you. You are a whore.'

'Was. I was a whore, and I am not proud of it. You knew that from the start.'

'Perhaps, though I tried to deny it to myself. But I certainly did not know you for a poisoner. You were no victim of that Irish scum, were you? You were his accomplice.'

She pursed her lips. Her face, even when hard and bitter, was still beautiful.

'Gutter rat,' he whispered and smiled as she blushed. 'I will not forgive you, and neither will God.'

He saw the pale blue veins across her eyelids as she stared at her lap, then, the dimpling of her cheeks as she smiled back at him. The tiniest peal of laughter fluttered out of her, like the ringing of a distant bell.

'You find this amusing?' He spat his words at her. He would strike that smile off her face if she were not so far away.

'I could have loved you, Osborne. I could have made you happy.'

'Never.'

'I would have forgotten him, for you, eventually. If you'd have kept your promises. But you lie like all men lie. You think you scare me, Osborne, but you are a mouse.' She laid her gloved hand against the bruise he had given her. 'This is nothing. The men I have known would tear you limb from limb if you ventured where I have been.'

'So, you accept it?' He would not acknowledge her insult. 'You accept my accusations?'

She inclined her head, the smile smaller now but sharper. 'Nearly.'

'What do you protest against?'

She pulled her lips between her teeth. She was teasing him, dangling bait before him.

'Tell me, Catherine!'

Another peal of laughter.

'Tell me!' He did not use his cane as he flew towards her. She was too slow to move out of his way. He had her by the throat in seconds, hauled her from her seat, and threw her against the wall. 'What do you not accept?'

'Irish scum,' she said, her breath hot against his face as he pinned her against the wooden panelling.

He held her still, his grip tightening around her throat, his fingers meeting his thumb at the back of her neck.

'You think yourself different from John and you are; you are worse.'

Her cheeks were burning. He tightened his grip around her neck until she was struggling to speak.

'Why did you save me? Because you couldn't save your father, could you? You were too weak. A coward. You sent him to his death – a death which he deserved.'

He growled as he lifted her off the floor. Her feet jabbed at his legs, her free arm battered his chest, and her face turned from red to purple, bloating …

There was knocking on the front door of the house. He heard Dixon permit the men to enter, their voices deep and terse, the words indistinguishable from this side of the wall.

He dropped Catherine. She crashed to the floor at his feet, her skirts puffing around her. Her breath sounded scratchy as she sucked it in, and her eyes shimmered with tears as she glared up at him, rubbing her throat.

He steadied himself on a dining chair, smoothed his hair into place, then hobbled for his cane.

'The police are here for you, Catherine. They know everything about you. I will divorce you on the grounds of adultery. Your unsavoury nature will go against you. You will be charged with conspiracy and theft.'

'There are no witnesses.'

'Ruby.'

Catherine snorted.

'Laugh, Catherine, while you have the chance. I will throw every charge against you that I can.'

A cough bubbled up his throat. He pounded on his chest, tasted the mucus on his tongue, and spat it into the fire. He must calm himself – he would not let her ruin him like this.

'If the law does not hang you, I will find another way to have it done. Perhaps one of those men, the ones you said would tear me apart, would be happier to tear you apart instead?'

He marched towards her and pulled her up by her hair. She screamed in agony as he kicked open the dining room door and threw her out into the great hall where the men were waiting for her.

SHE FELL INTO THE ROOM. The flagstones cut against her knees, and she caught herself with her good hand, feeling something else shudder in that wrist too. She dragged her eyes upwards to find Norton in front of her. Beside him were two men, taller and broader than Osborne.

'Take her,' Osborne said from somewhere behind.

Norton offered her his arm.

'Get her out of my house.'

She spluttered as she stood, her sobs choking up her sore throat. She put her hand to her neck and winced. Norton held her by the elbow and moved her hand to see the red rash of finger marks on her skin.

'I said, get her out!' Osborne's voice bellowed.

At the far end of the hall, the door creaked open, and Nelly's pale face peeked between the gap.

'Stay there,' Cat said, and the sound was rusty. Nelly did as she was told.

'Norton! Take her away. Why are you waiting?'

Doctor Norton pulled his eyes away from Cat's throat and stepped between her and Osborne. The men stepped forward too.

'Mr Tomkins, will you please come with me?'

She peeped over Norton's shoulder. Osborne leant on his cane and looked as if he might topple over with the shock. The blood seeped from his skin as confusion morphed to understanding.

'You need rest, Mr Tomkins,' Norton continued, edging closer like he was nearing a wild animal. 'You need to get better for the baby.'

'I am not the father of that whore's child! Get away from me.' Osborne flicked his cane at them, jabbing the air with it so Norton would stay back.

'Mr Tomkins, calm yourself. You are still unwell; you must not exert yourself.'

'She is a liar!' He was raging now, shaking with anger. His eyes were wide, terrified, crazed as he scowled at her. 'She is a whore, a poisoner!'

'Osborne.' She sobbed harder and rubbed her drenched face with her gloved hand. 'Osborne, please, you must rest. Please.' She touched her stomach.

'No!' Osborne yelled, breaking with tears. 'No! It is not mine.'

'I swear to you, on my sisters' lives, the baby is yours.'

'Your lips have never spoken the truth!'

She hardened. 'I would not lie about this. The child is yours, whether you like it or not.'

They glowered at each other. Osborne panted, sweated,

staggered against the wall. Norton nodded at the two men, and they advanced on Osborne.

Osborne dropped the cane and pulled out his revolver. 'Stay away from me.'

The men halted and glanced at Norton.

'Put it down, Osborne,' Norton said, his voice slow and controlled.

'Osborne, my love, please do not do this.'

'You are false, Miss Davies. You have always been false. God will curse you and your child.'

She stepped towards Osborne. The doctor tried to pull her back, but she slipped away, gesturing for him to stay where he was, to trust her. She saw Nelly at that moment, crying in the doorway, mouthing at her to keep away from Osborne. Cat turned her back on the girl and crept into the gaping space of the great hall.

Her audience watched and held their breath. The gun pointed at her heart.

'You will not hurt me, Osborne.'

'Stay away. Stay there!' He shook his gun at her. She felt the men behind her step forward, eager to pull her back to safety. She stopped them with her hand.

'Give me the gun, my love.'

'Do not call me that!'

'I love you, Osborne.'

He shook his head, and mucus flew from the tip of his nose. He was weakening, his arms were drooping with exhaustion, the gun lowering so the tip pointed at her stomach. He raked in a breath and, in that instant, he was a little boy again. A little boy who would grow into a cruel man, like her brother had, like all the men she had ever known had. She would not be their victim anymore.

'You are my saviour.'

His eyes met hers, and she smiled just for him.

He tensed, raised the gun, and aimed for her face.

She froze. She closed her eyes. She held her breath.

The trigger clicked.

Silence.

The trigger clicked again. And again. And again and again.

Osborne screamed at his weapon, at how it had failed him in his time of need, and while he was yelling at it, the two men balled into him.

Norton caught Cat as her legs gave way.

'Catherine?' His lips were close to her ear, and she felt his sweet breath catch the wisps of her hair. 'Catherine, you are safe.'

Real tears burst from her eyes. She clung to him, letting everything flow out of her, the fear, the anger, the shame.

'Catherine, you are safe now.'

How many times had a man told her that before? All of them had lied to her.

She glanced at Osborne through the open door. The men were barrelling him into a carriage and the horse, unused to such a commotion, fidgeted and whinnied as it waited. She heard Osborne scream, his profanities aimed at her, and she shied away from the scene.

'What will happen to him?'

'He is going to a good place. He will get the rest that he needs.'

'When will he come back?'

Norton cleared his throat and scratched his nose. 'I cannot say. When he is recovered, and these delusions have ceased.'

She dropped her head onto his shoulder and shuddered. 'He will send me away. I will have no home to go to.'

'He cannot do that, Catherine. He made vows to you,

promises, assurances, before ... Those cannot be changed now his mind is unsound.'

She wiped her tears away. 'My child?'

'Will be safe.'

That was all she had ever wanted. And hadn't she told Osborne – hadn't she warned him – that she would do anything for her baby?

'Catherine.' Norton licked his lips and put an awkward hand on her arm. 'If you ever need anything, anything at all, you must call for me.'

'Will I be able to visit Osborne?'

'That is not advised.'

She nodded. Good. She wished to never see him again. 'Then, perhaps you could call for tea sometime and tell me of his progress?'

Norton smiled such a handsome, sweet smile. He reminded her of Matthew, the boy who's purity she had stolen on a cold night in Able Street, a lifetime ago. 'I would like that.'

CHAPTER 28

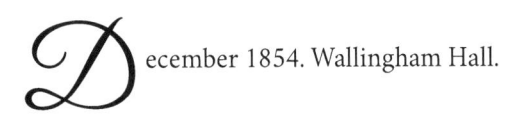

*D*ecember 1854. Wallingham Hall.

SHE STROLLED THROUGH THE HOUSE. It smelt of Christmas; bows of holly and ivy and bay lined the bannister, the mantelpieces, the door frames. The fires crackled with forest wood. Cloved oranges hung on red ribbons beside ornate glass baubles on the tree which reached to the ceiling in the great hall. All was quiet. Peaceful.

She patted the dogs' heads as they sat before the fire, warming themselves after Dixon had taken them for their walk around the estate. They nuzzled into her legs and licked her hands, then lay down and closed their eyes, contented.

She climbed the stairs, growing a little short of breath, though the child was still a few months from birth. She had been so tired ever since Osborne had been taken away, sleeping for hours, catching up on all the sleep she had been deprived of during those long, wakeful nights in previous years.

She entered Osborne's mother's room. Two months ago, she had never stepped through the doorway; now she came whenever she pleased. It was a grander room than her own. The bed was bigger, softer, though she had never had the nerve to sleep on it. A portrait of the woman hung on the main wall, observing; Cat could never look into the eyes of it. Whenever Cat entered, she came only for one thing: the jewels.

The dressing table drawers were full of them. A locked chest beside the fire held an even larger hoard. Gold chains lined with emeralds, rubies, gemstones. Threads of pearls and fat diamonds. Rings which dwarfed Cat's fingers. Earrings so heavy that earlobes must surely have ached under the strain.

She had stared at it all, initially, dumbstruck, unable to move or think. She had tested it out on herself, but the sight of her reflection had made her sick — so much wealth. Fury had taken hold. She had thrown the jewels across the room in her rage, taking delight in how they had smashed against the walls, but the plaster had come off the worst. She had burnt herself out and had crumpled on the floor amidst the treasure until she had come to think of a better use for it.

Now, she took out a handful of tangled gold chains and piled them in her arms. She left the room to return to her own chamber where Nelly was waiting for her, eyes cast to the floor. Cat spread it over the bed.

'Take your pick.'

Nelly had been reluctant the first time, keenly aware of the bribe, but she had not refused. Now, she chose a fine gold chain, small and delicate, with one tear-drop pearl attached to it. She slipped it into her pocket; perhaps she would wear this one rather than sell it. Maybe she was thinking of wearing it on her wedding day, for she had started courting one of the grooms with Cat's permission.

Cat piled the remaining jewels into the cotton bag. Nelly would take this to town today, to the jeweller who Cat had told her to go to, for he was a decent man who gave fair deals. Nelly would stay a night at an inn on the outskirts of Birmingham, and Cat wouldn't ask whether or not she and the groom had taken separate rooms for the night. In the morning, Nelly and the groom would return, as formal as ever, and Nelly would hand over the bag of money and not ask any further questions.

'Any news of Master Tomkins?' Nelly said as Cat tied the bag tight.

'I am waiting on Doctor Norton for the latest information.'

'I hate to think of him there, in one of those madhouses.'

'Doctor Norton assures me he is well cared for.'

Nelly nodded and did not press further. Her hand wriggled in her pocket as she played with the necklace.

'And how are you today, ma'am? How is the baby?'

Cat beamed at her rounded stomach. The sickness of the first months had ended, and now she was radiant. 'Strong.'

Nelly jumped up, excited for the arrival of a baby in such a quiet household. 'May I?'

Cat nodded, and Nelly placed her hand on Cat's stomach. They waited, then a kick. They giggled together.

'I have a message I want you to deliver to Brent's solicitors while you're in town.' Cat retrieved the letter from her dressing table. She had sealed it now that Nelly could read – she did not want the girl to know its contents; how she had commanded Brent to write to Osborne's Irish estate and inform Mr Griffin that the new, wealthy farmers would have to find themselves different land. If Mr Griffin wanted to keep his job, he was to allow the previous tenants back into their cottages with the promise of lower rents.

Nelly stuffed the paper into her pocket.

'Hurry.' Cat ushered Nelly out of the room. 'You must be out of town before nightfall, remember.' She would not have her maid – her confidante – in that wretched place as darkness descended.

CHAPTER 29

October 1853. Birmingham.

THE NIGHT WAS blacker than usual. There was a mist hanging in the air, choking the light from the moon, the streetlamps, the windowsills. It crept over her skin, making her shiver, making the hairs on her arms stand rigid.

The muck on the street was deep, but this was a better part of town. The door of the address that John had given her was smart, unsplintered, painted, and some plants grew either side of the frame, though they were beginning to wither as autumn took hold. Through the bay window, she could see the fire burning in the parlour, the chairs soft and inviting, and empty.

The door was unlocked, as John always made sure it was. She slipped through the hallway and headed straight for the stairs; she had to look as if she knew exactly where she was going. The house was quiet, the rooms on the first floor seemingly unoccupied. A gentle clearing of her throat and the door at the rear of the house opened. She slid inside.

'Anyone see you?' John said, his head poking into the landing, checking it was clear.

'No.' She placed her bag on the bed and unwrapped her cloak.

The room was small but elegant. A fire burned in the grate, and there was a four-poster bed with clean sheets and plump pillows. A set of drawers sat in front of a window which overlooked the backyard and the privy directly below. Beside the door was a mahogany wardrobe which shone like treacle in the candlelight.

She closed the curtains then opened her bag and removed the bottles and the two glasses. She set it all on the drawers and poured herself a whisky. She took the stopper out of the laudanum and began to pour it into the other glass.

'Not too much tonight. He might notice.'

She stopped, then topped the rest of the glass up with whisky. She plugged the laudanum and put it in her bag again.

John locked the door and paced before the fire, wringing his hands; he was always excited on these nights. Cat sipped her drink and scratched at her scalp through the wig.

'What time's he due?'

John checked his pocket watch – a trinket acquired some weeks ago from another unsuspecting victim once he had fallen asleep.

'Not long now.'

Cat fiddled with herself; pushed up her breasts, pinched her cheeks, bit her lip until John marched towards her.

'Not tonight.' He pulled off her wig.

It was a relief, at first. The horsehair was itchy and hot, but it was protection. Her own hair reached just to her shoulders, unbrushed and tangled. John ran his fingers through it, trying to neaten it, tugging out the knots and making her wince.

'Take this off.' He pulled off her shawl, loosened her corset, pushed her breasts down.

'What you doing?'

He stood back to assess her.

'And your shoes and stockings.'

She did as she was told. 'John?'

'Say you're fourteen tonight.'

She laughed. 'And who will believe that?'

'It's not a stretch.' He nodded as he looked her up and down.

'Who is he then?' she said, sitting on the bed and taking another gulp of whisky. It seemed she would need it tonight.

'An officer.'

She stood up. 'You know they're bad, John. I don't like them sort. They're too rough.'

He jumped to her, his hands smoothing over her cold, upper arms. 'Eh, quiet now, you'll be fine. Last one tonight, remember? Last time.'

'Forever?'

'Forever, I promise.' His thumb brushed against her cheek, rough against smooth.

She rested her head against his chest. How she wished it could just be the two of them tonight, in this little room, locked inside together. She could feel tears niggling at her as they embraced and listened to each other's breathing, so she bit the inside of her cheek to stop herself.

One last time … And after tonight, John would send the money they had saved to his family. And then, it would only be a matter of time before John asked her to marry him. And then, when they'd got themselves sorted, Lottie and Helen could come to live with them in their house.

She kissed him. 'I love you, John.'

He patted her back, then prised her away from him to check his watch.

'He'll be here any minute.' He made his way to the wardrobe and settled himself inside.

'You won't let him hurt me, will you?'

He pulled his coat over himself, so it didn't get stuck in the wardrobe door. It would be an uncomfortable time for him in that cramped space, but he never seemed to mind if he got a wallet full of cash at the end of the night.

''Course I won't. Remember to lock the door.' He gestured at her to shut him inside.

She strolled back to the bed and rolled her glass in her hand until it had taken her heat. She sipped the warm liquid, letting it bite at her nausea – she hated army types. Ruby used to get a lot of them, especially the deformed ones. Bitter, most of them, too keen to take their pain and rage out on the women they were fucking. She'd heard Ruby's cries often enough, her body hitting against the walls, the floor. Cat had only ever had one army bloke take her by the cut, and John had stepped in before the man's fist had thrashed into her face. Perhaps an officer would be different; a better class, a better man.

She did not have long to ponder as there was a quiet knock on the door. She set her glass next to the other on the drawers. There was only the slightest variation in the shades of the liquid as they sat side by side; a man with sex on his mind would never notice.

She unlocked the door and peeked through the gap. She met a face, meaty, bearded, smirking, and allowed it to enter.

She watched him come through. He was a good head taller than her. He wore regular clothes, no uniform. He removed his hat to reveal waxed hair combed into place, his beard oiled and tidy, though the skin of his face was somewhat piggish; bloated and pink.

He faced her as she locked the door behind him.

'Name?'

'Sophie.'

He grunted, a smile showing his set of good, sharp teeth, as his gaze studied every inch of her.

'Age?'

'Fourteen, sir.'

He nodded, threw off his coat, and sat on the bottom of the bed. He patted his knee. She obliged, and he grabbed her thighs to pull her closer. His fingers gripped the tips of her hair as he raised an eyebrow.

'Sold it for the money, sir.'

'Pity.' He pulled her head close, rubbed the tips over his cheek, and said into her ear, 'you'll do anything for the money, then?'

'Yes, sir.' Her head held fast, she felt his other hand slide up her thigh and over her corset, his fingers plucking off the ties of her bodice. 'Drink, sir?'

He shoved her off him and laughed as she stumbled on the floor.

Her cheeks stung. 'Would you like a whisky, sir?'

'Take your clothes off.'

Her hands wrapped around herself as he chuckled again. The room was too bright to be naked in, his stare too intense. When she did not move, he clawed at her until her skirts hung off her.

Officers, so it seemed, were no different after all.

'Take them off.' He returned to his place on the bed and resumed his position as watcher as she rolled her skirts away and dropped her bodice on the floor until she was in nothing but her slip.

'Everything.'

This was not how it was supposed to go. The others had taken the whisky the minute they had entered. They hadn't been bothered about nakedness as she'd laid them on the bed and crawled on top of them, satiating them with her words, her hands, until the laudanum had started to do its job.

The officer slapped his hands together, making her jump. She did as she was told, half-heartedly trying to cover herself with her arms as the slip fell to her feet. He ogled her for another minute, frowning, then smiled.

'Now, I'll have that drink.'

She crept to the drawers, handed him his glass, then took her own and downed it.

'Come here.' She turned to find him rubbing his trousers and, reluctantly, she crawled onto his lap. He nuzzled into her neck, his teeth grazing her shoulder as he gripped her breast.

The glass was still in his other hand. He rolled it over his lips as his fingers trailed from her breast, down her stomach, and came between her legs. He studied her face as his fingers pushed against her, bit his lip as she gasped, and then, finally – she sighed with relief – he drank.

She held eye contact with him as he gulped the liquor, his fingers circling and pressing against her, and she moaned for him. His hardness was against her thigh now; he would not be long.

He threw her off him and onto the bed. She forced herself to lie still, open, exposed, as he got to his feet and grappled with his breeches.

One last time …

He was unsteady, but she did not know if that was the alcohol, the laudanum, or lust.

'Turn over,' he said, sucking at his lips, sneering, frowning; confused.

She rolled onto her front, trying not to notice his growing unease, trying to ignore the sense of dread that was growing inside her. She heard him slowing and glanced back at him. He had stopped, his breeches half-open, his tongue poking out between his teeth.

She raised her backside off the bed, hoping to distract him. 'This what you want, sir?'

He turned towards the drawers, picked up his glass, and sniffed it.

'More whisky, sir?'

'The taste …' He licked the inside of the glass.

'I'm sorry it's so cheap, sir. Not the kind of quality a man like yourself is used to, I'm sure.'

His tongue traced his teeth. His lips pursed, and Cat saw his jaw working. His eyes were black slits as he glared at her. 'It's you, isn't it?'

She rolled onto her side and pulled her knees up to her chest. 'What is, sir?'

'What did you put in my drink?'

'Nothing, sir.' She edged up the bed away from him as he stalked towards her.

'You would trick me.'

'No, sir.'

'You would rob me.'

'I wouldn't, sir! Please, you can go if you like.'

The officer nodded, turned for the door. She held her breath, praying that he would leave, that John would stay in the wardrobe, that in a few minutes, this would all be over forever.

His hand hovered above the doorknob. He chuckled, low and quiet. His fingers slipped off the handle and found the key.

'Why would I leave now?'

He took the key from the lock and dangled it before him. Stretching onto his tiptoes, he slid the key onto the top of the wardrobe where Cat couldn't reach it. He pulled his leather money bag out of his pocket and hurled it at her. She dodged it just in time, and it slammed against the wall behind her.

'You can take it all at the end if you're still alive.'

He lunged at her. She shrieked and dived off the bed. She was on her knees, crawling as fast as she could, as he grabbed her by the hair. She struggled against him, beating at his arms to no avail. The bed was behind her. She squirmed, wriggled onto her side as she felt clumps of hair tear from her head, then his knee thrust into her stomach. Her breath rushed out of her mouth, the pain eye-watering.

Suddenly, she was reeling through the air, and she slammed into the wall. Whimpering, she slid to the floor, her vision blurring, trying to make out the shape of the officer towering above her and holding onto himself inside his breeches.

She saw the black blur of his boot too late; it crashed into her stomach again. She slumped forward, willing it all to be over, when his fingers dug into her skin. He ripped her from the floor and hauled her around the room. She struck out her arms as she tumbled into the furnishings and heard the smash of one of the glasses as she hit it.

She had no idea where she was. The sheets were all around her suddenly; the room swirled so that she didn't know which way was up. The heat from the fire burned the top of her head, and as her eyes focused, she realised she was at the foot of the bed. The officer straddled her, and she wished that she had remained blinded, for then she would not have seen the smirk on his face, and so she would not have felt such terror as he waited a moment, collected himself, then raised his fist and punched her in the face.

The blow stunned her. Her ears rang, and the world around her was silenced. Her head lolled off the edge of the bed. Upside down, she saw the fire raging, the golden light catching on shards of broken glass on the rug.

Something was fiddling with her, down there. Her legs were shoved apart as her arms flailed over the back of the bed, flimsy from shock. His hand crushed into her chest as he thrust inside her. She felt herself rip and heard the involuntary scream from her throat as he continued to pummel into her, shoving her further off the bed until her fingertips grazed over the glass.

The pain suddenly made her keener. The ringing in her ears stopped as she gripped a long, sharp shard. She held it tight, and it cut into her palm. She breathed in deep, readied herself, then hurled her arm over her head and slashed his face.

His hand came off her chest. He fell back, sliding out of her as he clutched his face. She slithered from under him and landed on the floor, the shards of glass pricking into her legs. She gasped for breath as she watched him hold onto his face, the blood oozing between his fingers. He was panting, grunting; he was coming round. She did not have long, but where could she go? The door was locked.

She jumped to her feet as he rallied himself, then grabbed the whisky bottle. She smashed the end of it on the side of the drawers. Whisky and glass rained onto her feet. She turned, the bottle stretched out before her, as he charged at her.

She aimed well. The glass lodged into his neck, stopping him in an instant. He frowned, unsure, then flung his fists at her. She took more blows until he wore himself out. He staggered backwards and thudded into the foot of the bed, falling to the floor, surprised, tiring – the laudanum was beginning to take effect.

He stared up at her, suddenly childlike, as blood pulsed out around the bottle in his throat.

Cat slumped against the wall and stared at the officer. Blood seeped down his front, and his eyes blinked as if they could not focus. She peeled her gaze from him and looked down on herself. Red dots freckled her flesh where the glass had spiked against her skin. Her hands were bloodied and trembling, and try as she might, she could not still them. There was a throbbing inside her skull, her abdomen, between her legs. Her knees shook, unable to hold her for much longer.

In the silence, the wardrobe door squeaked open. John stared at the scene before him, white-faced and wide-eyed. He lurched out of the wardrobe, keeping his distance from the officer who gazed stupidly at him.

'What have you done?' he whispered.

She stumbled towards him and fell against him, her body quivering as she sobbed.

'What have you done?' he repeated and pushed her away.

'What have I done? He was going to kill me, John!'

John kneeled in front of the man. 'He needs help.'

She couldn't believe what she was hearing. She grasped the mantelpiece as John pushed against the wound, trying to slow the bleed.

'What are you doing?'

'He's dying, Cat.'

She strode across the room, her naked feet crunching over the broken glass; she felt nothing. She shoved John out of her way, gripped the neck of the bottle, and wrenched it out of the officer's neck. The blood flooded out of the man now. She stepped back as it raced towards her toes.

'Shit!' John said, straining against the wall, panicked.

Cat watched until the officer's red breath stopped bubbling in his mouth, until he did not move. She turned for her clothes and wiped the blood and glass off herself with her slip. She chucked the soiled rag on the fire, then dressed – her hands were surprisingly steady as she laced her shoes.

She grabbed her wig from her bag and arranged it on her head. She found the money bag at the side of the bed, full of shillings and notes, and tipped the contents inside her own case; she was alive, after all.

A knock at the door made them freeze.

'Everything all right in there?' A woman's voice, old, frail, scared.

John stared up at Cat, horrified.

'We need to go,' Cat whispered and helped him to his feet. She gestured to the window. The privy roof was not a long drop – she only prayed it was strong enough to hold her weight.

John helped her out first, holding onto her arms as her legs dangled in the air, then let her go. She landed with a thump. The roof was precarious, but it held her. She jumped down into the yard, wincing as her ankle gave way.

'Come on,' she called to John, who she could see was hesitating, glancing back at the officer. He disappeared from the window.

She waited, assessing her escape route through the back gate, wondering if she should run now, without John, but then she heard him scrambling out of the window. He dropped beside her in an instant.

'What were you doing?'

'Covering him,' he gestured to his trousers. 'Shouldn't just be left all out like that.'

She grabbed his hand and dragged him out of the yard, despising his sentimentality for the man who had just ravaged her. They emerged into a narrow street, and she pulled him into the shadows.

'What will we do?' How long did they have before the old lady raised the alarm?

He rubbed his hand over his face, trying to concentrate.

'Did you meet with the landlord?' she said.

He nodded.

'He knows your face?'

He nodded again.

She cursed, and wiped her hands on the brick wall, hoping to scratch off the dead man's blood.

'I'll be hanged,' John said.

'Don't say such things.'

He glared at her, and she shrank away from him. 'We need to go,' he said, suddenly determined.

He lugged her through town. She remained silent as they followed the path along the cut, curling away from strangers, hiding their faces.

'The money, John, at home! Your things?'

'Too late.'

He walked fast and never looked back at her. His hand was cold in hers, and hard. The ground underfoot was slippery and uneven, but he caught her when she tripped and didn't let her slow for an instant. She kept her eyes on his back and didn't chance a look at the strange streets and alleyways they passed. She followed him blindly, as the drizzle ebbed away, and the clouds broke up in the sky to reveal a full moon which lit their path out of Birmingham.

CHAPTER 30

October 1853. Birmingham.

TWO DAYS HAD PASSED since that night. The whole thing already seemed like years ago. Had she really killed a man? Had she really been beaten and raped? It all seemed dreamlike now, a bad nightmare. Surely, they could turn back, head home, and get back to their normal lives?

But John pressed on.

She had not slept for ... hours? Days? John had pulled her forward, stopping only when the sun was at its peak. They had hidden inside dead trees, empty cowsheds; anywhere they could find which was quiet and warm.

At night, they never stopped. John needed the stars to guide him northwards, and so they had walked as shadows under the moonlight, through back gardens and deserted village streets, setting dogs barking and geese honking. They traipsed across crop fields and amidst flocks of ghostly sheep, their bellies moaning for food, their mouths stinging for a drink, their feet aching for rest.

At least the rain had washed them clean the first day. There was no trace of the dead man's blood on either of them now, and Cat's cuts had been swilled with the rainwater so dirt had not infected them. The pain in her head had been replaced with an ache in her hips, and it was getting harder to lift her feet. She tripped many times; at first, John helped her up, but now he let her stagger.

Last night had been icy, but good for star spotting. John had tugged her into a forest, where the thinning canopy had not hindered his view of the North Star. Now, only the moon remained in the pale blue sky where the sun was beginning to rise. John slowed once again, uncertain of where to walk without his astrological guide.

They followed some sort of path through the trees. To their right, the hillside fell away. Through the tips of the branches, they could see the valley below, the cluster of villages, the patchwork of fields. Birmingham was a long way away; the air was clean here, and the sun fell in bright, straight beams upon the green grass. She inhaled, drinking it in, feeling her lungs expand unlike they had ever done before.

'John.' She stopped and held out her hand for him. He came closer but did not touch her.

'What is it?'

'Look. It's beautiful, isn't it?'

He grunted and continued to walk. He led them away from the cliff edge and further into the woods. Thick tree roots contorted the ground, hidden under layers of amber leaves, waiting to trip her up. They startled game birds, which in turn, surprised them as they flew away, shrieking. Squirrels ran along the branches, blackbirds rustled in the undergrowth, and spiders weaved their silken threads around holly leaves. So much life! She had never seen anything like it before. She slowed, watching the world around her, and her fatigue took control.

It was like dirt was under her eyelids as she blinked. Her feet dragged, stumbled. Tears pricked at her, making a lump in her throat that she tried to swallow, but could not.

What had she become? A whore, a thief, a poisoner, a murderess. Out here, it was heavenly; the landscape around her served as a reminder of the hell to which she was destined. Above, in the calm, clear skies, her mother looked down on her – what did she think of Cat now?

'I'm sorry,' she whispered, leaning against a tree trunk, swiping the tears off her cheeks.

'Come on!' John shouted from ten feet away.

She tried to push herself forward, but she fell to her knees. She heard him puffing as he strode towards her, gripped her under the arms, and yanked her to her feet.

'I need sleep.'

'No time.' He pulled her along behind him, and she closed her eyes and let herself be led as she thought about all the promises she had made and broken.

When she opened her eyes again, she cried out with relief. Water. So much of it. Her tongue ached for it, and she dived from John's grip towards the edge of the pool. She was on her knees at the water's edge when John gripped the collar of her dress and pulled her back.

'It's stagnant.'

'Don't care.' She lunged for it again, and again he shoved her away. She had no strength to fight him this time and stayed where he had pushed her, staring up at him. Her tears fell once more, and she let them trickle into her dry mouth.

Laudanum! She had the bottle in her bag … just a small sip of it would quench her thirst. She opened her case.

'None of that. You'll be asleep, and I can't carry you.'

She slammed it inside her bag again and yelled in anger. John stood before her, arms crossed over his chest, his lips thin and straight. He looked dreadful. His cheeks had hollowed. His eyes had shrunk into his skull. He was angry and bitter and exhausted, like her.

'Where we going?' she said. How had she not asked before? She had followed him without question; her mind blurred from the trauma and fatigue and agony. How bizarre that they were so far from home, that she had let herself be taken away so easily.

'Liverpool.'

Liverpool? Such a long way! Another town, dirty, drunken, infested.

'Why?'

John sighed. His fingers pinched the bridge of his nose. He took off his cap and rubbed his head, and his cropped hair bristled under his hand. 'To get the boat.'

'The boat?' Why would they need a boat? She imagined a tiny sailing boat made of sticks and paper, the like of which her brother used to make when he was little to take to the cut and let it float amidst the barges.

'The boat to America.'

She could not understand anything today. She shook her head, trying to clear it, but still, she could not comprehend.

'We're going to America, Cat.'

She smiled at such an absurd notion, and her dry lips split and bled. She tasted the fresh, metallic zing on her tongue.

'We're not.'

'We are.' John slumped onto the ground beside her and brought his foot over his knee. The sole of his shoe was caked in mud and dead leaves, and he removed the flick-knife from his sock and started to slice off the dirt.

'Why?'

'Because we can't stay here, can we? They find that dead man and they'll come looking for me.'

'They won't find you.'

'That's right. They won't find me in America.'

She watched him jab at his shoes, muck flicking in all directions.

'I don't want to go to America,' she said.

'I told you, it's a new world out there.'

'You'll marry me out there?'

He sighed again, angrier than before. 'I haven't the money. We'll need to save for my family again, seeing as we had to leave it all behind.'

She focused on the meaning hidden in his words. He couldn't think that …? He wouldn't make her …? After he'd promised the officer would be the last one?

'I won't go, John.'

He slammed the knife together and dropped it beside him. 'You will, and if you don't, I'll go straight to the police in Liverpool and tell them what you did to that man. It's America or the noose.'

She stared at him, open-mouthed. 'I can't leave my sisters.'

'They're better off without you.'

She felt as if she'd been kicked in the stomach again. John rolled his eyes skywards.

'You're a mess, Cat. Jesus! You're a murderer!' He sprang at her. 'What did I tell you? Pretend. It's all pretend.'

'He was going to kill me, John.'

'He wasn't. If you'd done it better … but no. You made him suspect.'

'I tried, John. I can't do it.'

'You have to, so get used to it. We're all liars, Cat, every single person in this world is a liar. You too. You have to make sure your lies work.'

Her tears dripped off her nose as she lowered her chin to her chest. 'I can't.'

'Then, you'll die.'

She cried into her arms, resting her head on her knees. She couldn't take the cruelty, the truth of his words. She wept, and he did not comfort her.

She sobbed as she thought of that night, the pain and the terror. How did it all go so wrong? Why had she insisted on the man drinking the laudanum? He was a smart man; she knew that as soon as he came through the door. He was dangerous. If she'd just laid back, taken it, taken the money he'd given rather than try to rob him, he would still be alive and she would not be here, miles away from her home, about to be taken even further away to a foreign land.

Her tears slowed as the images played out in her mind. The sparkle of the cut glass ... the pink of his flesh ... the closed wardrobe ...

'Why didn't you save me?'

She lifted her eyes from her skirts. John gazed at the water, silent.

'John?'

She saw his jaw press together.

'Why didn't you stop him?'

He remained still. A ball of sickness fluttered up her throat.

'My hair ... you didn't want me to wear the wig – no disguise. And less laudanum than usual. Why?'

Finally, his gaze dropped to his lap. He sniffed but did not answer. He didn't need to. God! How had she been so foolish? So blind? All this time ... years of doing his bidding because she loved him. How she had loved him!

'You never had any intention of saving me, did you?'

His silence was her confirmation. She rushed a hand to her mouth, trying to stop the vomit but she couldn't. The emptiness of her stomach slid out of her as thin, clear drool and trickled into the leaves.

'I gave you everything,' she whispered, wiping her mouth. She thought of the first time they'd met, the first time they'd made love, John's promises of safety. She had believed him entirely. All the times she'd said she loved him. All the times she'd said she'd do anything for him – how he had preyed on that! All the times he'd promised to take care of her ...

We're all liars.

'Was any of it the truth?'

Nothing.

It felt as if God was squeezing her lungs.

'Your family?'

'I'd never lie about them.' His voice made her flinch.

'Only me, then. You only lied about me. You never loved me.'

He faced her. Hard. Brutal. 'I haven't loved anybody for years.'

She stared at him as he got to his feet and brushed the leaves off his trousers. There was nothing in his face, no sadness, no regret. It was as if nothing had changed between them.

If only! If only she could forget the last few minutes of their conversation. If only she could keep believing he was the man who she thought he had been. If only she could trick herself into thinking he loved her.

But she couldn't.

'Come on,' he said, 'we need to keep moving.'

'I'm not going.'

'Come on!'

She grabbed the knife by his feet, flicked the blade open, and crawled away from him. 'I'm not going with you, John.'

'Give me my knife.' He held his hand out.

'Get away from me.'

'You have to come.'

'You'll use me for a whore again, but I won't do it!' Her voice echoed through the trees. 'You have ruined me, John!' She could not stop the screams now. 'You have taken everything I was and ruined it!'

'You killed him, Cat,' he said softly. 'You ruined yourself.'

She charged at him, knife outstretched, aiming for his face. She would silence him. She would cut the lies out of his mouth so she would never hear them again. She would cut his heart out and tear it apart so that he would know her pain. She would beat and slash and pound him the way the officer had done to her until he was begging for forgiveness, until he was sorry.

His arm slammed into hers, sending the blade flying out of her grip before she could get to him. In an instant, he had fistfuls of her skirt and was dragging her towards the pool. She kicked and thrashed against him, yelling at him, but his face was blank and cold as he pushed her under the water.

The shock of it made her gasp. Water filled her mouth. She choked on it, beating on John's chest, pulling on his arms that held her under. The ripples blurred his face. Bubbles of her breath broke against the surface. The noise of the water, the splashing, her racing heartbeat, her burning lungs, were all-consuming.

She was weakening. When her mother smiled down on her, she stopped fighting. Why would she wish to live anyway? What kind of life would there be without her mother, without her sisters, without John? She let him push her down further until the light ebbed and the water swelled in her chest.

THE WEIGHT LIFTED. She felt herself floating upwards. Death

cradled her, and wrapped its darkness around her once again
…

She heaved the water out of her lungs. She felt it come out of her, warmer than when it had gone in. She sucked at the air, choking it inside of her, unable to get enough of it as leaves brushed against her lips.

There was solid ground underneath her. She opened her eyes, squinted at the brightness, and saw two dark figures in the distance. Dragging herself away from the commotion, she found her bag and hugged it close; she must not lose her mother's ring. She pulled herself towards a tree trunk and rested against it, gulping air as if it might again be stolen from her at any moment. Her vision cleared. She saw John scowling at her, a fresh cut bleeding over his eye. He was wild now, suddenly alive, fighting for survival, and his survival meant her death.

Another man, taller than John, broad and dark-haired, looked at her. He was the only thing between herself and John.

'Help me,' she begged, but her throat was unable to make a sound.

John pounced towards her. She braced herself, brought her knees up so she was in a ball, and waited for his attack. It never came.

Numbly, she listened to John denying all knowledge of her as cold water dripped off her head and dribbled down her bodice. She would have sobbed, had she had the energy, as she watched the man she had loved say she was a stranger to him.

Then, silence.

John's horrified face.

The calm as the stranger raised the gun.

'Scum.'

CHAPTER 31

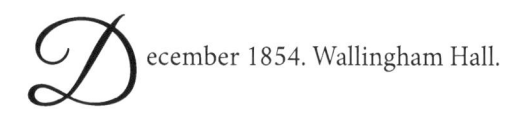

December 1854. Wallingham Hall.

INSIDE THE STUDY, alone, Cat wrapped a small wad of notes into a parcel, bound it tightly, and sealed it with wax. Another instalment to be sent to Birmingham, Able Street, but it would not be long until she could stop buying Ruby's silence; the girl's disease had come back stronger. Cat had seen its marks on her welting skin and in the crumbling of her nose when Cat had personally delivered the first package.

She fixed the parcel and rang for Nelly.

'Send this in tonight's post.' It would be a welcome New Year's gift.

'Your guests are here now, ma'am.'

Cat stood and let Nelly straighten out her scarlet satin dress.

'You look beautiful, ma'am, all ready for Christmas.'

Cat kissed her maid on the cheek and ushered her from

the room, asking her to tell her guests she'd be with them shortly.

She took a moment in the silence of the small space. She liked it here nowadays; no longer was it Osborne's domain. She had fresh flowers in here now, framed portraits, beds for the dogs – it even felt cosier and homelier than the rest of the house. The ticking clock on the mantelpiece relaxed her. Studying the finances and writing letters occupied her otherwise idle hands and did not let her mind drift. The study had become her haven.

But now, she would have to become the hostess, would have to entertain and delight – would have to pretend.

Her gloves lay on the desktop. She slipped them over her naked fingers. Her diamond wedding ring waited to be worn, begged to be admired. She took it in her hand, felt the weight of it, then dropped it into the drawer with the bullets.

She coaxed her mother's gold band over her finger instead. It was so thin it would barely be noticed, but Cat would know it was there. She held it to her heart then rolled her shoulders back, raised her head, and smiled as she glided out of the study, locking it behind her, and made her way to the drawing room.

Her guests rose when she entered.

'Sorry to keep you waiting.'

'Not at all,' Ruth said, as Mr Turner kissed Cat's hand. 'We've all been enthralled by your sisters' stories.'

Lottie and Helen, both now taller than Cat, drifted to their sister to kiss her cheek. They too wore new scarlet dresses, and the three of them, with their golden hair, their beautiful faces, and graceful bodies, could have been mistaken for triplets.

'They are treasures to you,' Ruth said to Cat, embracing her.

'They are.' Cat beamed at her sisters. They had quickly

grown accustomed to life at Wallingham Hall. Most astonishingly, they had remained pure after all this time apart. Cat would never let them know what she had done to get them here.

'Mrs Tomkins.' Doctor Norton, dressed in an elegant dinner suit, bowed to her. She offered him her hand and a warm, tearful smile.

'I am overjoyed you accepted my offer, Mr Norton.'

'It is my pleasure.'

She inched closer to him, lowered her voice. 'How is my husband?'

The smile dropped from his lips. 'He remains unwell, Mrs Tomkins.'

'His delusions persist?'

Doctor Norton nodded. 'His lungs seem to be failing him too, but I do not wish to upset you on Christmas Eve.'

'Please, Doctor, I must know the full extent of his illness.'

Doctor Norton scratched his nose, a habit, Cat had observed, he performed every time he was uncomfortable. 'He suffers from suspected pneumonia. He is in the infirmary ward.'

'What can I do?' She grasped Norton's hand.

'Nothing, Mrs Tomkins. He is in the best place.'

She sighed and hoped it sounded melancholic rather than irritated. She would have preferred Osborne to have been suffering, to have been isolated in one of those sweating padded cells.

Bringing Norton's hand close against her bodice, Cat whispered, 'I am sure the Lord is watching over him.'

She felt Norton tense as his fingers grazed her stomach. She dropped her gaze when his cheeks flushed, and slipped out of his grasp as her sisters' chatter and far-off singing floated on the air.

'Carollers!' Ruth said, hopping up from her seat and

taking hold of Lottie and Helen's hands, pulling them to the front door.

Cat and Norton followed them out to stand in the porch and watch the Christmas scene. It was the same song as last year, the same snow falling, the flakes shimmering in the light of the candle lanterns, but how things had changed! Her heart had been so raw; now, it felt like a lump of rock inside her chest. Only the sight of her sisters' joy and the stirring inside her womb made her smile.

Norton brushed closer to her. In the darkness, she turned her face towards him. The space around them was intimate; the candlelight did not reach between them. She could hear his breath louder than the carollers and smell his scent of orange blossom and soap.

'This time last year, Osborne told me he loved me for the first time,' she whispered.

Norton stepped closer, his leg amidst her skirts, using the lack of space in the porch as an excuse. She cupped her rounded stomach.

'At least I shall have a part of him in his son.' Her voice broke on the last word.

'Please, Mrs Tomkins, I would not see you upset. Please do not cry.'

In the shadows, Norton held her arm, shooting nervous glances towards Mr Turner in case the vicar might see the improper conduct between them. She was glad to see his nervousness, his covetousness. She had him. And she knew, by the innocence in his eyes, that he would do anything for her. Anything at all.

THE END

AFTERWORD

Thank you for taking the time to read *The Button Maker*. I hope you will consider leaving a review online as it truly helps authors to get their work into the hands of those who will love it.

If you would like to hear more about my work and get a **FREE** standalone novella, *The Butcher's Wife* – which is part of the *Convenient Women* collection – then please join my mailing list by visiting my website:

www.delphinewoods.com

The fourth novel in the *Convenient Women* collection, *The Little Wife*, is released December 2019.

ACKNOWLEDGMENTS

Once again, thank you for reading!

I would also like to thank my family for being so supportive and encouraging me to follow my dreams. Thank you to my mother for always being there with constructive criticism and for being the first to read my work. Thank you to my father for all his technical support. Thank you to my fiance for believing in me completely.

My passion for this book was rekindled following a writing retreat. So, I would like to thank Arvon, and the fabulous tutors and peers who I found on the historical fiction course during one week in November in 2018.

Finally, a big thanks to the online Indie community, who share their knowledge and expertise and continue to fill our world with wonderful new books.

ABOUT THE AUTHOR

Delphine Woods graduated with a First from The Open University in 2016, where she studied for an Open Degree, specialising in Creative Writing.

After a busy couple of years writing her collection of Victorian mystery-thrillers, she released her debut novella, *The Butcher's Wife,* in July 2019. *The Button Maker* is the third full-length novel in the *Convenient Women* collection. These books are set in Victorian England and have been inspired by nursery rhymes.

She lives with her fiance in Shropshire where she writes in her spare room, her dog by her feet to keep her warm. You can keep up to date with her news and get in touch with her via her website, newsletter, and social media platforms.

www.delphinewoods.com

ALSO BY DELPHINE WOODS

The Butcher's Wife: Convenient Women Collection Novella

A proposition of murder. A chance for freedom. But at what price?

Wolverhampton, 1862, and Nettie's husband is drunk. Again. With rent unpaid, food scarce, and money-lenders on the prowl, professional slaughterer, Russell Taylor, offers to help. But what does his devilish plan involve, and who is watching from the shadows?

As she fights for survival, Nettie must discover the real cost of life, death, truth, and lies.

The Butcher's Wife is a Victorian gothic thriller novella, part of the *Convenient Women* collection, and is available exclusively to the Delphine Woods Reader's List. It is inspired by the nursery rhyme, *Pop! Goes the Weasel,* and contains mature themes.

The Cradle Breaker: Convenient Women Collection Book One

A familiar face. A guilty secret. Vengeance is coming.

Luella Blyth's life has never been the same since the death of her father ten years ago. She can still remember his long walk to the gallows, her mother's screams, her own heart shattering as she watched him hang for a murder he did not commit. All she wants now is revenge, and for that she needs Bonnie.

On a sweltering summer afternoon in 1865, Bonnie Hearn is being watched. The girl staring into her window is somehow familiar ... the girl she had hoped she would never see again.

After blackmailing Bonnie, the two begin on Luella's quest to avenge her family, but as Bonnie struggles to keep her secrets and Luella battles to reveal them, who will survive this game of deception?

The Cradle Breaker is a standalone Victorian gothic mystery-thriller novel, book one of the *Convenient Women* collection, and is available on Amazon. It is inspired by the nursery rhyme, *Rock-a-bye Baby*, and contains mature themes.

The Promise Keeper: Convenient Women Collection Book Two

A game of deception. A house of secrets. A matter of life and death.

On a bleak January afternoon in 1869, Liz Oliver is escaping her past and travelling to a new life, one of luxury and idleness in the grandest house she has ever seen. Yet, forced to live with her brother's new, spoilt wife in a mansion on Devon's Jurassic coastline, this is not the life Liz had dreamed about.

Liz must bide her time until her brother's plans unfold, but as the weeks turn into months tensions build, and as the isolation becomes unbearable, no one can be trusted.

Amidst a stifling atmosphere of paranoia and resentment, Liz's past finally catches up with her. Will she be able to outrun it one last time?

The Promise Keeper is a standalone Victorian mystery-thriller, the second book in the *Convenient Women* collection. This book is inspired by the nursery rhyme, *The Wise Old Owl*, and contains mature themes.

The Little Wife: Convenient Women Collection Book Four

After Beatrice Brown's husband is summoned to Scotland to fulfil an old duty, Beatrice must come to terms with her new life at Dhuloch Castle.

Isolated and starved of affection by her troubled husband, Beatrice finds comfort in the castle's mistress, the recently widowed Clementine Montgomery.

Embarking on a passionate affair with Clementine, Beatrice soon learns of Dhuloch's terrible past and why her husband fled its confines ten years ago.

But something dark still lurks inside Dhuloch's walls.

Will Beatrice discover the truth before the castle claims another victim?

The Little Wife is a standalone Victorian mystery-thriller, the fourth book in the *Convenient Women* collection. This book is inspired by the rhyme, *The Little Hen*, and contains mature themes.

Printed in Great Britain
by Amazon